FAKE DATE

FAKE DATE

MONICA MURPHY

Cover design: Hang Le
byhangle.com

Editor: Mackenzie Walton
Proofreader: Holly Malgieri

ALSO BY MONICA MURPHY

One Week Girlfriend Series

One Week Girlfriend

Second Chance Boyfriend

Three Broken Promises

Drew + Fable Forever

Four Years Later

Five Days Until You

Standalone YA Titles

Daring The Bad Boy

Saving It

Pretty Dead Girls

FAKE DATE

ONE

SARAH

SOMETIMES I MARVEL at the path my job choices have sent me down. For instance, I'm currently wrist-deep in lace and silk, facing a naked mannequin whose bare boobs are at eye level, so I can't avoid them.

And I also can't help but think that she has way better boobs than me.

Welcome to Bliss, where we sell fantasy.

We actually sell lingerie. Bras, panties, nightgowns, sleep sets, you know. Pretty, frilly stuff. Very expensive, high-end lingerie you don't find at Victoria's Secret—though I have no problem with Victoria's Secret.

Please don't tell my boss that.

What Bliss doesn't sell are sex toys. Marlo—my boss and the owner—finds them, ahem, distasteful. Though she does sell beautiful feather ticklers and silk eye masks, though she claims they're for sleeping.

The customers I've sold them to? They're definitely not using them to sleep.

I've worked here almost two years. I started out in the stockroom, opening boxes and preparing items for the floor, i.e. taking them out of their packaging and putting them on hangers. A totally thankless job, though I worked hard at it because I needed the money. Marlo noticed my hard work and promoted me to a part-time sales associate within two months of me starting.

Now I work full time, and I even have benefits. I also have seniority over most of the staff, which means I can pretty much pick my hours and the days I work.

What I can't pick, though, are my clients. I'm a personal shopper for some. One in particular who's coming in this morning. In fact, *he* should be here soon.

Yes, I said he. Insert massive eyeroll here.

"Sarah." The gentle whisper voice knocks me from my wayward thoughts, and I finish folding the Belgian lace-trimmed, virginal white negligee before turning to face my coworker, Bethany. I smile at her and she offers me a sympathetic smile in return, because I know why she's talking to me, and she knows I know why too.

She also knows how much I hate these appointments. How they—*he*—drives me crazy. "Mr. Gaines is here to see you," Bethany says with the slightest grimace.

I keep the smile pasted on my face because I never let it slip. Not when Mr. Jared Gaines is in the building. Taking a deep breath, I tuck my hair behind my ears as I stride toward the front of the store, hoping my vibrant red lipstick isn't smudged. Praying my ankle doesn't wobble as I walk in these new, extraordinarily high-heeled shoes. I wore the shoes for Mr. Gaines today because supposedly he likes me better when I'm taller (pretty much a direct—and odd—quote from a past interaction). He's early too, of course. Otherwise I would've gone to the mirror and made sure I looked the part.

What part, might you ask? Why, dutiful lingerie shop girl, of course.

Here's one of Mr. Jared Gaines's quirks—he likes to keep me on edge. He told me exactly that the last time he came into Bliss, to buy a black silk camisole and tap pants set for his latest mistress. He wants to keep me guessing, he said. Predictable is boring.

Well. He's anything but boring, what with all the lingerie he buys. I'm guessing that means he has a long list of countless women he's been with. And that brings me to another thing I don't like about Jared Gaines. He has way too many mistresses. Well, he calls them lovers, dates, girlfriends, whatever, but *I* call them mistresses, which annoys him.

I do whatever I can to annoy him, but I can't be *too* annoying. There's a fine line I walk when I'm dealing with him. And he knows it.

The bastard.

All the girls who work at Bliss Lingerie in downtown Carmel-by-the-Sea know Jared Gaines. They all lust for him too, because he's gorgeous and young and rich and successful. He's a billionaire with a house on 17 Mile Drive that has a bazillion bedrooms, yet he's the only one who lives there. Oh, he has a quaint little cabin (insert sarcasm) in Tahoe, too. Where he goes skiing or snowboarding during the winter, I'm not sure which. Sailing in the summer, because of course he has a boat. I'm sure it's massive. The biggest, baddest boat on the entire lake, because that's the kind of man he is.

I've wondered more than once if he has a small penis. That's why he buys all the toys—to make up for what he's lacking.

I recently discovered he owns enough cars to take a

different one out for a drive every day of the week, maybe more. How do I know all of this? There are countless articles about him on the internet. Google his name. You'll find out the scoop.

Well. Maybe not *all* the scoop. You see, there's one little secret not that many people know about Jared Gaines.

He's kind of a dick.

Harsh words and all that, but it's the truth. I bet he'd own up to it. In fact, I'm sure he's really proud that he's considered a dick. Yes, he's gorgeous and young and rich and successful, with all his money and houses and cars. And that's great and all, but he's also rude and demanding and cold and discerningly quiet. I don't like quiet.

I don't *trust* quiet.

Don't trust men with too many "girlfriends" either.

"Ah, Miss Harrison. You're looking extra lovely today," Jared Gaines says when he sees me heading toward him. He's leaning against the cash desk, his arm propped on the counter's edge, and he stands up straight as I approach, his appraising gaze raking over me, making my entire body go warm.

I remind myself the way his compliments and how he looks at me mean nothing. He's a man whore who thinks he can have any woman he wants just by looking at them. Most of the time I think he looks at me in a certain way and says those sorts of things just to get under my skin.

And it works.

I come to a stop directly in front of him, my pleasant smile so wide I can feel the corners of my mouth start to tremble. It's difficult to maintain the façade when I just want to hurl insults at him and kick him out of the store. But I'd get fired on the spot for doing that, so I keep my instincts in check. "Mr. Gaines. You're—early." I say that last word with a hint of disdain, hoping he notices.

Of course he notices. The man doesn't miss a thing. "Better early than late, don't you think?" A single dark brow lifts, and I tell myself an eyebrow can't be sexy.

But damn it, his is. Everything about Jared is sexy. His glossy dark brown hair, those equally dark brown eyes, the square jaw and full lips and amazing body that I've only ever seen clad in an expensive suit. I bet he looks equally gorgeous in worn jeans and a casual button-down shirt. Shorts and a T-shirt.

Or hmmm, maybe nothing at all.

You dislike this man. He represents everything you hate. He's a player, a user. You mean nothing to him, and he means nothing to you. Don't forget that.

I clear my throat, somehow keeping my smile in place. My mental arguments never seem to work when I'm around Jared Gaines. "I've set aside a few exceptional items I think you might like for Miss…"

I let my voice drift, like I can't remember the woman's name, but that's the truth. I don't remember her name, because he never gives me a name. He shops for a bevy of anonymous women. Women he buys lingerie for at least once a month, sometimes twice.

Seriously. Who *does* that?

Irritation fills his dark gaze, and I swear he practically growls. "Perfect. Show me," he snaps.

There are no pretenses, no real pleasantries between us beyond the occasional compliment he offers just to get under my skin. He doesn't have time for that sort of nonsense—another little something he told me once, after I tried to make small talk while showing him a variety of skimpy G-strings for yet another long-gone mistress. I'd fumbled around with the delicate, lacy things as I spread them across the marble countertop, hardly able to look at him as I rambled on about the comfort and practicality of thongs.

My boss Marlo gave me a long lecture after he left without making a purchase. Something he *never* did. She informed me we don't sell practicality and comfort.

We sell fantasy, remember?

That particular incident occurred approximately six months ago. For some reason, even after my bumbling attempt at selling him practical thong underwear, he keeps requesting my assistance, which honestly makes no sense. Most of the time he looks at me like I disgust him. It takes everything within me not to sneer back at him like he disgusts me as well.

Though he doesn't. Disgust me. Not at all. God, it's so annoying how *disgustingly* attractive he is. And he knows it. When he's at the store, I never see a hair out of place. His suits are immaculate. His shirts wrinkle-free. And his ties are always perfectly knotted and straight.

I'd love to yank that expensive tie out of place. Haul him closer to me by pulling on that tie, press a lingering kiss on his warm, strong neck and leave a red lipstick smear on his skin.

I bet he'd hate that.

"Miss Harrison?" His deep voice knocks me from my illicit thoughts, and I realize I've come to a complete stop, fantasizing about him. Yes, *fantasizing* about him. What's wrong with me? If he could read my mind...

"Sorry." I shake my head and shoot him an apologetic smile, our gazes meeting, but he looks away quickly, like maybe he can't stand the sight of me?

Asshole.

"Follow me," I tell him, my voice sharp, my heels clicking loudly on the hardwood floor. Mr. Gaines falls into step behind me as I escort him to one of our small, private showing rooms in the back of the store. I can sense he's following close, can smell his expensive cologne, hear him tapping on his phone before he shoves it into his pocket.

I'm hyper-aware of his nearness, and I hate it. Hate myself more for being so aware. He doesn't even notice me. Though I don't care.

Really, I don't.

"I don't have all day," Gaines complains, and I send him an irritated glare over my shoulder before I stop and open the door to the private showing room. He follows in after me, practically at my heels, and I step out of his way before he mows me over. I shut the door with a soft click and take a deep, cleansing breath before turning to face him. He's already sitting at the small table in the center of the room, his gaze going to mine as I approach. I pause mid-step, taken aback by the unfamiliar gleam in his eyes.

An almost...*hungry* gleam.

No. No, no, no. He barely tolerates me. I despise him. Yes, he's attractive, but he's also annoying and rude and the most insensitive man I've ever encountered in my life. Who has that many mistresses? Who spends thousands of dollars on lingerie? He doesn't even have a steady girlfriend. The man clearly has a problem.

A non-commitment problem. As in, he can't commit. As in, he doesn't want to.

"Did you bring the items I requested?" he asks as I settle into the chair across from him and cross my legs.

Leaning forward, I tap the sleek black box sitting on the table in between us. He sent a text to Marlo the night before with specific requests for today's appointment. So. Weird.

"Yes, I did." I smile, but he frowns in return. Like he can't trust me to get it right.

"Sheer? Lacy? Bright and colorful?" His words are clipped, and he shoves his jacket sleeve away from his wrist to check his Rolex. Like he's already wasted enough time on me and needs to leave.

Annoyance fills me. He's the one who made the appointment, yet he acts like it's a big waste of his time. The moment he exits the store, I'm telling Marlo I don't want to deal with him any longer. He can find another Bliss associate and terrorize her instead.

"Miss Harrison?" he asks when I don't answer him.

Whoops. Caught lingering in my head again. My mother always said I was too much of a dreamer.

"All of those things, yes." I rest my hand on top of the box, letting the anticipation hang in the air for a moment. I'd never admit it to him, but every one of these items I chose for his perusal, I would wear. In fact, I might be wearing one of the items at this very moment.

But that's my little secret.

"Go on then. Show me what you've got." His dark gaze meets mine, full of irritation, and I press my lips together to keep back the retort that threatens.

I'd give anything to stand and drop my skirt. Let him see the panties I'm wearing. That would really show him what I've got now, wouldn't it?

Instead, I take the lid off the box and carefully push away the pale pink tissue, then pull out a delicate coral-colored, sheer bra trimmed in mint green lace. I move the box aside and lay the bra across the table, my fingers skimming along the lace. "Sheer and bright, just as you requested."

He reaches out, his fingers brushing against mine, and I

jerk my hand away like he burned me. My hand, my entire arm, tingles from the seemingly innocent touch, and I keep my gaze averted so he won't see how much he affected me.

So...odd.

And unexpected.

Totally unexpected.

"Is it bright enough?" He's holding the bra in his big hands, stretching it out carefully, his expression impassive, like he's closing a deal versus considering unmentionables for the special—ha ha—lady in his life.

"I think it's very bright," I say after a quiet moment. My voice rings in the otherwise silent room, and I bring my fist up to my mouth, coughing as lightly as I can. "The colors are fun, like a '90s vibe—"

"So you're saying it's not modern enough." He toys with the bra strap, twisting it around his index finger much like he twists everything I say. I watch, distracted by his hand. His fingers are long, his palm broad. I imagine him touching me, tracing my skin with his fingers, cupping my—

"It's modern." My gaze flies to his. He's smiling, a knowing glint in his gaze, like he actually could read my mind. *God.* "Yet with a vintage feel. Both cute and sexy. Fun, even. Does your *mistress* not like vintage items?"

"I don't have a mistress," he growls, dropping the bra like it's a dead animal. The sneer on his face tells me he's displeased. I'm guessing he believes I overstepped my boundaries? Who knows? "Do you have something else to show me?"

Sighing loudly, I pull a sheer pair of panties out of the box. They're trimmed in vibrant pink lace, little red cherries randomly stitched across the black fabric. The backside is practically non-existent, with a heart-shaped cutout that would expose pretty much—everything. I planned on showing these to him last, but his attitude is making me impulsive.

Most likely a mistake on my part, but screw it. The man drives me nuts.

"What are these?" His gaze flares with interest as I hand him the panties. He holds them up, then flips them around, smiling faintly when he notices the backside. "Very cheeky."

Oh. Did he just make a joke? I didn't know he had it in him. "Extremely."

"The cherries are a nice touch," he adds.

I nod, blatantly studying him since he's not paying attention to me. "I like them."

"The underwear or the cherries?" He's still not looking in my direction, giving me ample time to drink in his handsome features. He is almost annoyingly good looking.

"Both."

Jared lifts his gaze to mine, his dark eyes practically smoldering. I remain fixed in my chair, my breath catching in my throat the longer we stare at each other. What is happening right now? What are we doing?

He drops the panties onto the table and spreads them out, his gaze remaining on the underwear as he asks, "What size do you wear, Miss Harrison?"

Um.

Say what?

"What size are these panties?" Right. Must've misheard him.

"They're an extra small," I tell him, trying my best to keep my voice even. I feel jumpy. Anxious. His nearness sets me on edge. I can smell him. I swear his body heat is radiating toward me, making me warm. Like, I can feel sweat forming along my hairline. Is it suddenly hot in here?

"And what size do you wear?" His gaze meets mine across the table, unwavering. "Miss Harrison."

Oh shit. It's *definitely* hot in here.

I swallow hard. No way should I answer. He's crossed a line. A line I shouldn't cross with him because he's a client, and a rude one at that.

Yet it's like I can't help myself.

"I'm a small," I confess, wondering why he's asking.

He clears his throat, his gaze dropping to my breasts for the briefest moment before he asks, "What size bra do you wear?"

Well. This conversation just got weird.

"Um..." Oh, this is awkward. Isn't it? I should hate him. I hate everything he represents. He's the last man on earth I would ever be interested in.

So why are my breaths coming faster? And why do I suddenly feel lightheaded?

"The woman I'm buying this for—she's similar in size to you," he further explains, leaning back in his chair. He studies me with disinterest, like he's discussing the weather, and I try to compose myself. We're talking business. And our business happens to focus on lingerie. No big deal.

Right?

"I'm a thirty-four C," I tell him, sitting up straight and squaring my shoulders. I can't let this man unnerve me like this. No other client does this to me.

Of course, no other client of mine is remotely like Mr. Gaines.

"Really." His gaze is on my chest again, and I'm tempted to unbutton the black silk shirt I'm wearing and let him see for himself. "Do these panties have a matching bra?" He dangles the cherry panties from his index finger, the scrap of fabric swinging to and fro.

Hearing him say *panties* in that melting, deep voice of his is making other things melt. Like me. Between my thighs. I clench them together, ignoring the sudden ache I feel there. It's been too long since I've had a boyfriend. That's my problem, I swear. "Yes, they come in a matched set."

"I'll take it." He rises to his feet, and I stand along with him, noting how tall he is, even with my heels on. Though, I'm a shrimp, so everyone is taller than me. "I'll meet you at the register."

He exits the room without another word and I watch him go, taking a deep, shuddery breath when he's gone. I remind myself it's no big deal. Jared Gaines asked for my bra and panty size. He claims his new side piece—oh my God, I sound just like my brother—is about the same size as me. No problem. Nothing strange about our conversation. I'm here to help him. That's it.

That. Is. It.

TWO

JARED

I WAIT for Sarah at the register, keeping my eyes on my phone so I won't have to make small talk with the other associates who work at Bliss. They're all perfectly nice women, if a bit...obvious.

Understatement. They're totally obvious. The last one who assisted me kept her composure for two visits. Until the third time we met, when she scrawled her name and number across the back of my receipt along with a message:

Call me ANYTIME.

She also drew a generous set of breasts beneath her name.

Pass.

I've been a regular customer at Bliss for over two years. There have been plenty of sales associates I've worked with. Every single one of them beautiful. Every single one of them flirted with me, some more than others. The number and the boob drawing were the most recent and overt one.

But there was that other one. The one who shall never be named. The one who I got fired for her inappropriate behavior. The one who actually showed me her tits in one of the private rooms. The one who also tried to dry hump my leg while shoving her bare breasts in my face.

Talk about a total disaster. Marlo, the owner of Bliss, was embarrassed. So was the one who shall never be named, and Marlo fired her on the spot despite the crying and the carrying on. I remained as impassive as possible as it all unfolded, though deep down I'd been thrown. Don't get me wrong, I appreciate a beautiful woman, and I love a beautiful set of tits, too. But a crazy woman who strips while on the job and tries to dry hump me?

That's a whole different story.

I changed after that happened. *Do not engage* became my mantra. It was best. If you smiled, if you were friendly, if you said something even remotely interesting, the women thought I was flirting with them. So I became cold. Quiet.

And then I met Sarah.

Beautiful, sweet, smart-mouthed Sarah. With the long, dark hair and the flashing blue eyes and the bee-stung lips. More than once I've imagined those lips wrapped tight around my...well, you know what I'm talking about. And I've never had a dirty thought about *any* of the girls who work at Bliss.

Not until Sarah.

From the moment I first laid eyes on her, I wanted her, which is ridiculous. I've bought more lingerie these last few months than I have in the past two years I've shopped at Bliss. I'm not currently fucking anyone, yet I'm purchasing a bra and panty set that will set me back approximately five hundred dollars.

Worse? The only woman I imagine wearing the sweetly sexy cherry bra and panty set is Sarah.

What the hell is wrong with me?

"Will this be on your black card today, Mr. Gaines?"

I glance up from my phone to find another associate standing behind the counter with an expectant smile on her face. Her name is Bethany, and she's worked at Bliss for over a year, I believe. She's always pleasant toward me when I see her.

But she doesn't interest me like Sarah does.

"Sarah will be handling this," I say, my voice gruff, my attention once more on my phone. My inbox has exploded in the past fifteen minutes—shit always goes down when I ignore my phone—and my text message notifications sound like they're going haywire.

"Oh, I'm sorry Mr. Gaines. But she's currently busy assisting someone else." When I lift my head once again, Bethany offers me a slow, seductive smile. I scowl at her in return. "But I'd be more than happy to help ring up your purchase."

"Where are the items I want to buy?" And where the hell is Sarah? Who is she helping now? How dare she assist someone else?

The smile disappears from Bethany's face. "I thought you brought them with you."

I shake my head, irritated. "No. Sarah always boxes them up for me and brings them to the register."

"I'll go find her and get the items for you—" Bethany starts, but I interrupt her with another shake of my head.

"I'll go find her," I say tightly, pushing away from the counter. I stride through the tiny lingerie store, thankful it's empty, searching for a glimpse of Sarah's dark head and those big blue eyes. But she's nowhere to be found. I have no idea what other clients she could be helping when *I'm* the only one she should be dealing with, considering I have an appointment. I slam open the door of the private room we just occupied only to find it...

Empty.

Where did she go?

"Mr. Gaines." I turn to find Marlo standing in front of me, elegant as ever in severe black, her expression serene. She's holding a thin box in front of her. "Sarah boxed up your items for you."

I'm frowning so hard it hurts my damn face. "Where is she?"

"She had an—emergency." Marlo's bright pink lips turn up in the faintest smile. "She sends her regrets that she wasn't able to finish your transaction."

Such a businesslike way of putting it. I'd like to finish a transaction with Sarah—preferably with both of us naked, the pretty lingerie I'm about to buy torn to shreds and lying on my bedroom floor.

But then I remember her word choice. An emergency.

That doesn't sound good.

"Is she all right?" Worry hits me like a punch to the gut, surprising me.

Marlo's eyes widen the slightest bit. I think I've shocked her with my question. I'm not one to show concern for anyone. "She's fine," she reassures me. "It's a personal matter, but everyone's okay."

A personal matter. And everyone's fine—who, exactly, is everyone? A boyfriend? A—holy shit—*husband*? No. She's too young to be married, though I don't know her exact age, but she looks young. Innocent, with those big, blinking blue eyes. Feisty and sweet, with a mouth I want to ravish and a body I want to explore...

No. That would be a mistake. I can't be interested in her. And I'm guessing there's no husband, not that it's any of my business. She doesn't wear a ring. I know nothing about Sarah's personal life, and despite my wanting to know what's going on, Marlo won't reveal a damn thing to me. She's discreet. That's why I come here.

I take the box from her. "Thank you."

"Bethany can ring you up." Marlo leads me toward the register, where Bethany waits for me with that same seductive smile. She needs to give it up. I'm not interested. "I hope you have a nice day, Mr. Gaines."

"Thank you, Marlo, I hope the same for you."

Bethany takes care of my purchase, trying to make idle chitchat, but I don't respond. I'm staring at my phone trying to concentrate on my texts, yet I can't help but think of Sarah. My mind is filled with endless possibilities. What could've driven her out of here so quickly? What's wrong? Where is she? Does she need help?

"Do you want your items gift wrapped?" Bethany asks, her phony sweet voice knocking me from my thoughts.

"Please," I tell her, still staring at my phone.

"Would you like to include a personal note?" Bethany is clearly fishing for information.

"No." An idea hits me and I glance up, watching as Bethany tears off a sheet of shimmery pale pink wrapping paper and starts to wrap the box. "I was wondering if you could do me a favor."

She folds the paper around the box, then grabs a roll of tape. "What exactly do you need, Mr. Gaines?" Her every word drips with sexual innuendo. Subtleness isn't Bethany's strong suit.

"I'm—worried about Sarah." Bethany meets my gaze, her mouth dropping open. I'm guessing I shocked her. I'm shocking myself as well. "I want to send her something to cheer her up."

Bethany's brows rise so high they're practically in her hairline. "Really?"

I nod.

"I'm sure she's fine," Bethany says.

"I would still like to send her a little something."

"Such as?"

I want to tell her that's none of her damn business, but I don't. Instead, I ignore her question. "Could you give me her address please?"

Bethany looks around, like she's making sure Marlo isn't nearby. "I'm afraid giving out the address of a fellow employee isn't allowed."

"But I've been a loyal customer for so long. You can trust me." I put on my most charming smile, and I see the interest flare in Bethany's eyes. "I've worked very closely with Sarah these last few months, and I want to send her a— token of my appreciation." My words ring false. But it's like Bethany doesn't even notice. "To let her know I'm thinking of her during this troubled time."

Jesus, where do I come up with this stuff?

Bethany frowns, focusing on wrapping the present, her movements efficient as she folds and tapes the paper into submission, then wraps a strip of gauzy white ribbon around the box. "I really shouldn't."

I remain quiet, hoping my silence breaks her.

While I sign the sales receipt, Bethany shakes open a shiny black Bliss shopping bag and stuffs the wrapped box inside, then hands it over to me. "You promise you won't tell Sarah how you got her address?"

Triumph seizes hold of me, and I try my best to remain neutral as I take the bag from her. "I promise," I say solemnly.

With a sigh and a roll of her eyes, Bethany taps a few keys on the nearby computer and then grabs a pink Post-it pad and a pen, scrawling a few words on the paper before tearing it off and handing it to me. "You never got this from me."

I take the Post-it note from her and slip it into my jacket pocket. "Got what?" I ask innocently.

"Perfect answer." She smiles with seeming relief. "Thank you. Have a wonderful day, Mr. Gaines."

"You too, Bethany. Thank you." I exit the store and head to where I parked my car, ignoring the many people who fill the sidewalk. It's a gorgeous, sunny day, the area is crowded with tourists and locals, but I have zero time to appreciate the weather.

I'm a man on a mission, with a gift to deliver.

THREE

SARAH

IT WASN'T A LIE. I did have an emergency. The second Mr. Gaines left the private room, Marlo entered, holding my phone out toward me.

"Your phone's been blowing up for the past five minutes." It was funny, hearing Marlo use the term "blowing up". She's such an elegant, proper woman who doesn't use much slang. At least, she doesn't around me,

I take my phone from her and check it. Three hangups and five texts from my little sister Andie.

Sarah

Sarah call me please. I'm freaking out.

SARAH! I NEED YOU!

OMG pick up ur phone I need you rn!!

SARAHHHHHHHHH

Ugh. She's so annoying.

"Do you want Bethany to take care of Mr. Gaines?" Marlo asks as I skim through the text messages from my overly dramatic sister.

"If you don't mind?" I send her an apologetic look. She knows how it is with my family. They're a little—fine, a lot—needy. "I should call Andie back."

Marlo smiles. "Not a problem. And if you have to leave early, I completely understand. Family emergencies happen."

"Thank you for being so understanding," I tell Marlo before I head outside. I really hope I don't have to leave early thanks to Andie. I need the hours. Meaning, I need the money.

I step outside and call my sister.

"Sarah! Please come pick me up from school. I can't take it here anymore." This is how Andie greets me. She doesn't even bother saying hello.

Have I mentioned my sister is a sixteen-year-old drama queen?

Have I also mentioned that it's just me, my sister, and my brother who live together? Our parents died four years ago in a terrible car accident. We only have each other, and since I'm the oldest and the most responsible, I take care of both of them.

Well, Brent can pretty much fend for himself. He's twenty-one, has a full-time job, and loves to hang with his bros when he's not working. Andie, on the other hand? She's a sophomore in high school. Almost finished with the school year, since it's late May, so she's basically a junior. According to her.

"I'm working, Andie," I tell her, glancing around to make sure no one's around before I launch into my big sister lecture. I feel like I keep doing this lately. "I know you have no clue what that's like, having to actually work for a living, but I just can't leave to come get you because you have a serious case of cramps."

Andie actually whimpers, which means I called it. "But I'm out of tampons."

Ugh. I do not want to have this conversation right now. "Call Brent. He's still at home. I bet he'll bring you some." My brother would be so pissed if he knew I said that.

"Please. He'd tell me to take two Midol and call him in the morning."

That sounds exactly like him.

"Doesn't one of your friends have a tampon stash somewhere?" I can't believe she called me away from the sexy, wretched Mr. Gaines to complain about cramps and a tampon shortage. "I have to get back to work."

"So you're not gonna come get me?" she whines.

"No, I'm not. Bye." I end the call, heading for the door that leads back into the building when I catch a glimpse of a familiar someone out of the corner of my eye.

I go completely still, turning just my head to see who it is.

Jared Gaines, walking down the sidewalk.

Without thought I follow after him, keeping my distance so he won't notice me. A black Bliss shopping bag dangles from his fingers, and his stride is hurried, like he has somewhere to be and he's running late.

Typical.

I pick up the pace, my gaze dropping to his backside. He's wearing a jacket so I can't really see his ass, but I'm sure it's nice. Firm.

Actually, I'm sure it's perfect because I'd bet a million dollars that he thinks his body is a temple and treats it that way too. I bet he works out in his private gym every single day and carefully watches what he eats. He looks like one of *those,* you know what I mean?

I bet he doesn't indulge in much of...anything. Well, maybe sex, but even that he does in a cool, concise manner. He never keeps a woman around for any length of time. I mean, why bother? That would just disrupt his schedule.

I assume he works, he exercises, he eats right, he works some more, and then he gets four hours of sleep before he's up and back at it again. The same thing, day by day. Boring, boring, boring.

Not my type at *all.*

Though if I'm being real with myself, I'm not quite sure what my type is...

Mr. Gaines glances at his wrist, and I swear I can hear him growl with irritation. Or maybe I just imagined the sound since I've heard him growl more than once during our interactions. The sun glints off his dark hair and more than one woman turns her head as he walks past them.

He doesn't even notice.

I stop when he stops. He pulls a keyless remote from his pocket and presses it, the blinding white Tesla parked at the curb beeping as the doors unlock. He opens the passenger side door and tosses the bag inside, then shuts the door, rounding the car before he slips into the driver's seat. He starts the car and lets it idle, most likely checking his phone.

While I check him out.

Breathing deeply, I press my lips together, knowing I need to head back to Bliss. I'm sure Marlo is wondering where I am, and Bethany is probably floating on a cloud since she got to ring up Mr. Gaines instead of me. I remain rooted in place though, unable to move, caught up in watching the most infuriatingly gorgeous man I've ever met do something as mundane as check his phone while he sits in his car. I should be bored out of my mind.

But I'm not. I could watch him all day.

Ugh. I hate myself so much right now.

He suddenly lifts his head, his forehead creased in confusion. Like he can feel me watching him.

And maybe he can. His gaze finds mine immediately and I freeze. A single word keeps running through my head over and over again.

Caught.

Caught. Caught. Caught.

Yet I can't move.

We stare at each other, people passing by on the sidewalk cutting off my view for a moment but then he's there again. Still sitting in his expensive car, still watching me, though that single, sexy eyebrow is raised, like he's asking me a silent question. What does he want? He parts his lips, mouthing the words...

Come here.

I shake my head. No way. I know if I walk over there, he'll most likely insult me because I bailed out on him mid-appointment. He might even yell at me, though he's never yelled before. In the past, he's barked out a few orders like a drill sergeant, but I'm used to that. Sometimes he says the *worst* things.

Like the absolute worst.

But it's as if my feet have a mind of their own because despite my reluctance, I'm heading toward his car, coming to a stop by the passenger side. The window slides down and he's leaning over the console, his expression unreadable.

"Why didn't you finish our transaction, Miss Harrison?" he asks, his voice cold. So incredibly cold I almost shiver.

"Family emergency," I say weakly, wincing when I see

how his eyes narrow in disgust. Clearly he doesn't believe me. Whatever. "My sister needed me. She's, uh, sixteen, and very dramatic."

Damn it, why am I trying to explain to him what happened? He probably thinks I'm making up an excuse. Sometimes, I wish I could kick myself.

"Really." His voice is flat, his gaze full of irritation. "You have a sister."

I nod, suddenly too nervous to say anything more.

"With an emergency."

I nod again, wondering where he's going with this.

Sighing, he looks away, seemingly watching people as they pass by on the sidewalk. He's certainly not paying attention to me. "I have a younger sister. I know what that's like."

I blink at him in surprise. Are we...are we actually relating to each other on a human level? I didn't know that was possible.

"I suppose the two of you are close?" He's watching me again, his gaze direct, and I shift from one foot to the other, wondering if I should answer him.

It feels almost *too* personal sharing information with him, out on the street like this. Like we're just two people having a conversation versus the client and employee relationship we normally experience.

"Very close," I admit, my voice soft. I'm tempted to tell him about my parents and how we lost them, but I clamp my lips together before the words fall out of me.

No point in spilling my secrets to this man. He doesn't care.

"That's—nice." He looks away, staring straight ahead, and I get the sense he's uncomfortable. Perhaps I'm the one who's stepped over the line, bringing my personal life into our professional relationship. "Though you should've completed our transaction. The customer always comes first."

And just like that, he's done a complete one-eighty.

"But—"

He cuts me off. "Goodbye, Miss Harrison." The passenger-side window slides up and I step away from the car, startled when he pulls away from the curb and merges into traffic.

I watch until his expensive car disappears before I head back to Bliss, telling myself what just happened between me and Mr. Gaines was nothing.

Absolutely nothing.

FOUR

I WORK ALL DAY, then on my way home I stop at the grocery store to pick up a few things, get gas for my crappy little Mazda and finally make it to the house around six. I open the door to find Andie lounging on the scratchy plaid couch, noting her bored expression as she watches the world news on TV.

Normally, she doesn't even watch TV, especially the news.

Andie catches sight of me and leaps from the couch, her expression going from bored to excited in approximately five seconds.

"You got a package," she says, looking like she might start bouncing up and down at any moment.

"Awesome," I say wearily as I kick the door shut behind me and head for the kitchen. I drop the bags on the counter and pull out the half-gallon of milk, placing it in the refrigerator. "It's probably from Amazon." The three of us are always ordering stuff from Amazon.

"It's definitely not from Amazon." She enters the

kitchen holding a narrow brown box. "There's not even a return address."

"What? Give me that." I shut the fridge door and grab the box out of her hands, staring at the address label with a frown. Andie's right. There's no return address. There's no FedEx or UPS information on the label either. It's almost like someone hired a courier service and had this package hand delivered to me.

Odd.

"Open it!" Andie squeals.

"I need to put the groceries away first," I tell her as I set the box on the counter. My stomach bubbles with nerves and I look away from the box. Something tells me I should be wary of opening it. Not that I think it's filled with anything dangerous—that's a bit extreme. But whatever is in there, I might not like it. Or I might not like who it's from?

My intuition is going haywire right now.

"I'll put the groceries away." Andie hip checks me, so I move out of her way and immediately dive into the giant reusable bag. "Did you pick up tampons?"

"Yes," I say with a sigh. I'm tired. My feet hurt. I kick off the heels and blow out a ragged breath, twisting one foot around and flexing my toes before doing the same with the other foot. Those shoes pinched like a mother.

"Open the package," Andie urges again as she moves about the tiny kitchen and puts everything away. I'm grateful she's helping me. Usually she's locked away in her room and I have to put everything away.

After grabbing a pair of scissors from the knife block next to the stove, I cut the tape away, popping open the lid to see a smaller box nestled inside. It's covered in shimmering pink wrapping paper and topped with a white gauzy bow. I'd recognize that wrapping paper anywhere.

It's from Bliss.

My heart in my throat, I slowly untie the bow and remove it. Then I flip the box on its side and run my finger under the tape, undoing the wrapping paper as neatly as possible. Andie's watching me out of the corner of her eye, impatience written all over her face, and when I pull the paper completely off and start folding it, that's when she loses it.

"Oh my God, just open the damn box!"

Sending her an irritated look, I pull the lid off the box, staring at the carefully folded pale pink tissue inside. Did Marlo send me something? On occasion, she'll give the associates a gift, but she's never sent one home before. With a frown, I peel back the tissue, a gasp escaping when I see what's waiting for me within.

The cherry bra and matching panties set that a certain Mr. Jared Gaines purchased earlier.

What. The. Hell?

"Oh, that is super cute." Andie leans over my shoulder to peek at what's inside the box. "Did your boss send that to you?"

"Uh..." I scramble for words as my little sister scoops the panties up and holds them in front of her. Now she's the one who's frowning. "Wait a minute, these panties are one-sided."

I snatch the panties out of her hands, my cheeks on fire. "It's a cutout. On the butt."

"And your *boss* sent these to you?" Andie shakes her head in disbelief. "That is freaking weird."

"Marlo didn't send them." I toss the panties back into the box, shove the lid back on and push it away from me. "I don't know who they're from." *Lie.* I glance around the kitchen, looking for something to put away, eager for a distraction, but for once, Andie already took care of everything.

"Sarah." My gaze meets Andie's. The knowing look on her face is obvious. My teenaged sister is way too perceptive for her own good. "Then who is that set from? And why is he sending you cherry lingerie? Does he want to pop yours?"

Andie starts to laugh at her joke.

I start to fume.

"You shouldn't assume it's from a 'he'. And for your information, my cherry was popped a few years ago." I grab the box and clutch it to my chest, fighting embarrassment at the semi-crude way I just said that. "Not that it's any of your business." Please, we've had more sex talks this last year than I ever got in my teen years. My sister is *fully* informed, unlike me at her age. "And I have no idea who this is from."

I head toward my bedroom, ignoring Andie's laughter, how she calls out, "Yeah, right! Be real with me, Sarah! You have a secret admirer? Some pervert regular who's always at Bliss? Tell me!"

The bedroom door slams, cutting off the rest of her scarily accurate words, and I toss the box on my crappy double bed, staring at it with disdain. Like there's a snake coiled inside, ready to strike and kill me dead.

Yeah. Now I'm the one feeling dramatic. Yet I can't help it.

Why in the world would he send me that set of lingerie? The set he bought for one of his many mistresses? Is he trying to imply that he...that he wants...me...to be...one of his...

Mistresses?

My blood starts to boil and I take a deep breath,

reminding myself I need to calm down. I collapse on the bed and open the box once again, pulling the bra out, then the panties. I lay them out on top of my comforter, running my fingers along the hand-embroidered cherries, pressing my lips together.

It's such a beautiful set. One I would willingly wear. Could he sense that I liked the lingerie? I pretty much like everything I show him, so I doubt it. We had some flirtatious moments though. I saw interest in his eyes more than once. The questions he asked me. The conversation we had by his car...

I still don't understand though.

Why, why, *why* did he send me this? I pull the tissue out, my heart leaping in my chest when I hear the distinct sound of a card hitting the bottom of the box.

Written correspondence. From Jared Gaines himself.

With shaky fingers, I grab the tiny card and attempt to open the envelope, then tear the single notecard out and study the bold handwriting. He must've wrote it. This doesn't look like an assistant's handwriting. It's too strong, too brash, too confident.

Yes, even his handwriting is confident. Ridiculous, right?

The note is simple. Simple to the point of being annoying because I still don't know if it was actually meant for me or not, even though it says:

For you
JG

That's it. Perhaps his sending me this—*present* was a mistake? Maybe he meant to send it to one of the many mistresses he has on hand. Because he probably has a ton of them. So many, he doesn't know what to do with them all.

Frustrated, I tuck the card into the envelope and drop it back into the box. Then I carefully place the bra and panties inside, wrapping the tissue around them. I slip the lid on. No way am I going to bother to rewrap the box, though. I'll just somehow give this—*gift* back to him. Let him know his mistake and return the items without question.

But for the life of me, I can't shake one niggling thought.

How in the world did Jared Gaines get my home address?

FIVE

RECEIVING mysterious gifts calls for getting together with your friends so you can discuss said mysterious gifts, and that's why I'm sitting at a table in a restaurant surrounded by my friends, who are all watching me, waiting for me to explain exactly why I gathered them here at the last minute in the first place.

It's not like me to call on my girls. My friend Caroline lives for this sort of thing. We are her support group and when she needs us, she never hesitates. We get a text, a DM, and on the rare occasion, even a phone call. A lot of the other women who are part of our friend group do the same thing too.

Me? I'm a little more—independent. I don't like relying on my friends too much. I'm always afraid I might need them *too* much. And we know what happens when we need someone too much.

We lose them.

"Sarah, come on. Tell us what the hell is going on!" my friend Stella snaps, jolting me from my thoughts.

The other women laugh, then turn their curious gazes on me. Watching. Waiting expectantly.

That's another thing I don't like. Being the center of attention. If I had my way, I'd move through life like a ghost. Doing what I need to do, but not wanting anyone to notice me. I'll leave that up for the attention hogs in my life. Trust me, I know plenty of them.

In fact, I'm related to two of the worst attention hogs I know.

But I'm getting distracted. Again. I need to tell the girls what happened. It's late, after all. Past eight o'clock. And while I know we're in our twenties and we should be out partying at all hours of the night, most of us are responsible and have jobs to go to in the morning. Especially Stella, who arrives at work at the ungodly hour of five a.m. so she can serve up her amazing lattes and mochas at the coffee shop/café her family owns.

"Um, remember my weird client?" I finally say, my voice sounding extra loud in the mostly quiet restaurant. Everyone is in the bar at the Italian restaurant, Tuscany, tonight. NBA semi-finals are happening, and the Golden State Warriors are looking to defend their title. Since they've been doing this for the past five seasons or so, all I can think is, what else is new?

"Oooh, yes," Caroline says with a gleam in her eye. I've told her the most about a certain Mr. Jared Gaines, though I've never told her his name. There are some things I keep private, I guess. Though everyone at this table has heard snippets over the last few months, Caroline knows pretty much *all* the dirt. "What did he do this time?"

I launch into my story, trying my best not to leave out a single detail. They need to hear it all so they know what I'm dealing with. It pleases me to see how they're all listening in rapt attention, plenty of nods agreeing with me when I say he's an arrogant prick.

The ultimate detail is the gift. The lingerie set I sold to him earlier, and how he sent it to me.

"It has to be a mistake," I conclude, resting my arms on the table, my fingers linked. I'd kill for a cocktail right now, but money is tight considering it's near the end of the month, so I can't really afford one. Stella's brothers Michael and Tony own Tuscany, and I know they'd give me any cocktail I want for free, but I don't want to look like a freeloader. I don't need a handout.

I've got this.

When I realize my friends remain silent, I glance down the table, noticing how their gazes are...knowing.

"He sent it to me by mistake, right?" I ask weakly, giving in to my urges and reaching for Eleanor's mojito, taking a giant gulp. She doesn't even protest.

"Pretty sure he meant to send you the bra and panties," Stella says with a nod.

"Absolutely not." I'm shaking my head. What Stella just said does not compute.

"Yeah, I'm with Stella," Caroline says, but she's always with Stella when it comes to stuff like this. It's like they share the same brain.

"Come on, Caroline. You know what an asshole he is," I remind her, my gaze snagging on Eleanor's mojito for about the tenth time. Sighing, she pushes it toward me, and I accept her drink eagerly. "He meant to send it to one of his secret lovers, I'm sure," I say after I take another delicious sip.

"Are *you* one of his secret lovers?" Kelsey asks, her tone teasing. She's the newest addition to our friend group, and I really like her a lot.

With the exception of this very moment. Because hell no, I am not one of Jared Gaines' secret lovers.

"No," I practically spit out, picking up the mojito glass and practically sucking it dry. Damn, I'm thirsty. "We don't like each other. Trust me."

"Let's get real here for a minute." Caroline leans across the table toward me, Stella doing the exact same thing. The both of them look like a pair of police detectives ready to interrogate. Their eyes, their expressions, are one hundred percent dead serious. "Does he make you uncomfortable in any way? Give you creepy vibes? Like, do you think he could turn into a psycho stalker who will terrorize you till the end of time?"

I sit in silence for a moment, absorbing what they said. He may be abrupt and borderline rude, but he's never given me full on creeptastic vibes. He makes the occasional flirtatious comment and sends me hot looks almost every single time we're together, but I don't think he's a horrible human being. The most inappropriate he's ever behaved has been today.

If I had to put a label on it, I'd say we've been hostile-flirting these last few months. Does that even make sense?

Hmmm.

"No, I don't think he'd terrorize me," I tell them. "And I don't believe he's an actual creep. He's just very—demanding sometimes."

"Okay, that's good. That's a positive thing." Caroline nods.

"How'd he get your mailing address though?" Stella asks, her gaze sharp as she watches me. "I don't like that."

I don't like it either. "I'm not sure." I think of Bethany. How she rang him up when I had to take Andie's call. Could she have given him my address? That goes against company policy, but I know Mr. Gaines can be persuasive.

Maybe she's the one who sent the box direct from the store and he doesn't know where I live? Though that means she found out he's sending me underwear, and, oh hey, that's not weird at all (insert heavy sarcasm here).

I explain to them how Bethany took care of him with his purchase, and maybe she could be the one who gave him my address.

"That's the only explanation I can come up with," I say once I've finished explaining my theory. "She kind of has a big mouth."

"You should ask her," Caroline suggests.

"Right, and then open up an entire conversation about how my client could be potentially hot for me." I shake my head. "No thanks."

"You have to admit, it's kind of sexy," Stella says, Caroline nodding in agreement.

"What's kind of sexy?" I'm so confused right now.

"The possibility that you two might want each other, and there's been all this build up between you guys for the last few months. The monthly appointments. All that lingerie. The lingering looks you two share across a table, across the store, wherever," Caroline explains. "It must feel like foreplay."

Yeah, no. It doesn't feel like foreplay.

Okay. Maybe it feels a little bit like foreplay.

"I said it before, and I'll say it again," Stella continues. "Maybe you need to hate-fuck him and get him out of your system once and for all."

My mouth drops open, as does Eleanor's. She's the hopeless romantic of our friend group, and I'm sure Caroline using the term "hate-fuck" is about to give her an aneurism. "I don't want to do that with him," I tell Caroline before I meaningfully make eye contact with every single woman sitting at our table. "Really. I don't."

They're all watching me like they don't believe me. At all.

Great.

"You always tell me how hot he is," Caroline reminds me.

Crap. I have told her that.

I squirm in my chair, wishing for another mojito, but 1) I have no cash, and 2) I have to drive home, so no more drinks for me.

"And he requests your help every time he comes in there, which is an awful lot," Caroline continues. "How much lingerie does this guy need?"

"That's my point exactly," I say, fighting the surge of triumph that wants to overtake me. There's nothing better than being validated. "He's a total player, always coming in and buying naughty nothings for his many mistresses."

Stella bursts out laughing. "Naughty nothings, Sarah? Really?"

I wave a dismissive hand at her. "Working at Bliss, we hear all sorts of silly terms referencing underwear, Stel."

"I don't think he's buying all that stuff to give to other women," Caroline says, sending me a meaningful look. "He's constantly coming in there and buying lingerie so he can spend time with *you*."

My entire body goes hot at her words. There's no way that's the reason he's constantly coming into Bliss.

Right?

"He doesn't want to spend time with me." I shake my head. That is the craziest thing Caroline's ever said. "He doesn't even *like* me."

"Uh huh," Stella drawls, the jerk. "Maybe he acts like that toward you because he's sexually frustrated. As in, *you* sexually frustrate him."

"That's no excuse," I protest, but my words sound weak. No way is Jared Gaines sexually frustrated over little ol' me. He could have any woman he wants with the snap of his fingers. Mr. Eligible Bachelor and all that crap. "Besides, he doesn't want me."

"Clearly, he does. He just sent you a pair of assless panties, Sarah. Meaning he wants to see *your* ass in them," Caroline emphasizes. That she can string those sentences together with a straight face amazes me.

"Has the world really come to this?" Eleanor asks, sounding all stressed out. Poor thing. "Have we really come to the point where a man sends a woman an unsolicited lingerie set as a way to seduce her?"

"No," I answer firmly. I've been saying that word a lot tonight, and I'm standing firm behind my thoughts. "He's definitely not trying to seduce me."

"I bet he is," Stella says, sending Caroline a smug smile. When those two are in cahoots, watch out. "Like, I'd bet big money on it."

I don't have big money like Stella, so I wouldn't bet shit on that. But I keep my mouth shut, sending them both a glare that would have my siblings running.

Unfortunately, my evil glare doesn't affect my friends whatsoever.

"You should go to his office and confront him," Caroline says, leaning back in her chair with a smug smile on her pretty face.

She makes it sound so easy. Like I can just walk in and toss that box into Mr. Gaines' face and tell him where to shove it. He doesn't want me. He's *not* sexually frustrated.

He's just an ass who doesn't know how to deal with people on a regular basis. It doesn't matter that he's the CEO of his company—I can't even remember what he does for a living. Mergers and acquisitions? Land development? Something rich and extravagant like that. He probably doesn't even actually talk to people. He just sits in his office and fires off emails and texts his demands. I'm sure no one crosses him. What he says goes.

I seriously can't stand people like that.

No, really. I can't.

"Confront him how?" I ask, sounding tired. Because I *am* tired. The day has been long, my mind is blown, and I want nothing more than to go back home and collapse into bed. I'm absolutely exhausted thinking about bills to pay and hours to work and clients who send me strange gifts.

Seriously. I'm completely over this day.

"Ask him if the gift was really meant for you? He'll either shoot you bedroom eyes and say hell yes the lingerie is for you, or he'll deny it, apologize for his mistake and you both can forget this ever happened," Caroline explains, sounding one hundred percent logical.

I can't imagine him apologizing to me. I don't think he knows how to utter the words *I'm sorry.* Plus, we couldn't forget this ever happened. I know I couldn't.

I have a feeling he couldn't either.

The mistaken gift would loom between us every time he came into the store. He'd have to start dealing with someone else, considering how awkward it would be for us...

Wait. That idea could actually work.

"Okay. I'll go to his office," I finally say, my voice the slightest bit shaky. I clear my throat, wishing I didn't sound so unsure. The idea of going to his office, to confront him in his territory, so to speak, is nothing short of terrifying. But I could overcome my terror if it meant pushing Jared Gaines out of my life once and for all. "I will," I say, my voice the teeniest bit stronger. "Maybe even tomorrow."

"You should definitely do it tomorrow," Caroline encourages with a faint smile. "The sooner, the better."

"Fine. I'll do it tomorrow," I say with all the confidence I can muster.

All while trying to ignore the way my stomach pings nervously, like there's a bouncy ball inside desperate to make its escape.

"Yay!" Stella says, and they all start clapping.

Smiling, I nod, my cheeks growing hot, but deep inside, the nervousness kicks in full force.

I feel like I'm going to throw up.

SIX

JARED

I'M SITTING at my desk trying to compose an email I don't want to send when my phone buzzes. I hit the speaker button, but don't say a word. This is how I usually operate with my assistant, Denise, and she knows it.

"Someone is here to see you," she announces, all brisk efficiency. The woman is no-nonsense, and I appreciate her mightily for it. I show my appreciation by giving her a hefty salary. She's worth every single penny.

"Who?" My heart—yes, I have one, though it's tiny, like the Grinch's—drops at Denise saying someone is here to see me. Drop-ins are rare, considering that I refuse to see pretty much everyone unless they have an appointment. Could it be Miss Harrison?

My skin goes hot at the thought.

"It's your sister," Denise says, and I immediately make a face at the phone, thankful no one can see me. Disappointment makes my stomach sink like a stone and I sit up straighter, tugging on my tie, tightening it.

Candice. My younger sister. I don't want to deal with her right now. Lately I've been avoiding my entire family and I'm sure Candice has figured this out. She always proves herself smarter than anyone ever gives her credit for.

My mouth opens, ready to utter the words *Send her in*, when the double doors burst open and in strides Candice with a sunny smile on her pretty face as she makes her way toward my desk.

"*Jar-ed.*" She draws out my name in a sing-songy voice that's reminiscent of our mother's. Does Candice realize this?

Probably not.

I hit the button on the phone to end the call before rising to my feet. Our mother always told me I should stand for a lady, and my sister is no exception. "Candice. What a surprise." I sound annoyed, and I clear my throat.

"A pleasant one, I hope." Ignoring my obvious annoyance, she offers me a quick hug, her potent perfume making my nose twitch. "You've been a bad brother," she tells me as she sits in the chair across from my desk.

I settle into my chair, quietly contemplating her as she checks her phone. Candice is twenty-three, and she's a very attractive woman. Men trip over their feet trying to catch her attention in any way they can, and she humors them for all about five minutes before she moves on to the next one. It usually never gets beyond flirty conversation at a party— Candice is at every party and social event you can think of on the Monterey Peninsula, swear to God—and then she's done. Over it.

How do I know this? Candice confesses all every time we get together, whether it's just the two of us, or the entire family. She holds nothing back.

Some might call it oversharing.

"How have I been a bad brother?" I ask once she's slipped her phone back into her Gucci bag. She's dressed from head to toe in designer clothing, and she doesn't even work. When our mother passed fifteen years ago, she left a trust fund no one knew about in Candice's name only. Our brother Kevin and I would be just fine, our mother's will said. The trust fund had been left to our mother from her mother's side of the family. Women taking care of women and that sort of thing.

I remember being pissed at the will reading, but I'd only been nineteen and a complete idiot. Traumatized by the sudden loss of the woman I loved more than any other human being alive. That trust fund had felt like a betrayal at the time. Now I see it for what it really was. She was taking care of her only daughter in the best way she knew how. Passing down the legacy, so to speak.

The pain in my chest over the loss of my mother still lingers, though. I absently rub at it now.

"You've been avoiding my calls," Candice accuses. Correctly, I might add. "And Kevin's. Daddy's too."

She's right. I know what they all want, and there's no way I'm giving it to them. "I've been very busy at work."

"Oh yes. You look so incredibly busy." She glances around my empty cavern of an office, her amused expression slowly turning into a frown the more she studies the room. "Your walls are so blank."

"That's considered art, Candice." I point at the abstract paintings on the wall.

"Art painted in various shades of cream and beige." She rolls her eyes. "There's no warmth, no color anywhere in this room. Don't you find this place...depressing?" she asks in a hushed tone, leaning forward like we're about to share some deep, dark secret.

"I don't mind," I say with a shrug. "I'm barely here

anyway." Lately I have been in the office more. Not that I'm telling Candice that.

"You're avoiding our calls because of Kevin's engagement party. Right?" Candice raises her brows, uttering the three words I've been trying my best to forget.

Kevin's engagement party.

Our brother, the middle child of the Gaines children, is getting married. To Rachelle. Rachelle just so happens to be the younger sister of my ex-girlfriend. Wait. It gets worse. Let me correct my statement—my ex-*fiancée*. Yes, for a period of time in my very early twenties, I'd fallen for a girl who made me starry-eyed with lust. I confused that with love and asked her to marry me with a giant ring and a grateful heart. Six months later, four months before the wedding, she broke it off.

That was the last time I had a serious relationship. Ten plus years ago.

"I'm not going," I tell Candice, keeping my voice, my expression grim. Serious. She needs to know I mean business.

Candice's face falls. "Why not?"

"Why should I? Kevin doesn't need me there. He won't even miss me." I don't doubt that for a second. We come from a large extended family—plenty of aunts and uncles and cousins will be there in support of the happy couple. Lots of friends and business associates will surely be there too. And don't get me started on his fiancée's family. They're very well-connected. Maybe more than we are.

Candice's eyes narrow as she contemplates me. "Is this about Evelyn?"

God, why must she utter her name? "No, this isn't about Evelyn," I practically spit out, immediately disgusted with myself. I sound pissed off. Worse, I sound like I *care*.

And I don't. That ship sailed long, long ago.

"Then come to the party." Candice's face lights up like it does when she gets excited, which is often. "It'll be fun!"

"We've been to the city countless times," I tell her, sounding bored. "We used to live there, remember?"

"Not really. I was too young to remember when we moved." She watches me, her head tilted, her long, dark brown hair spilling past her shoulder. Again, she reminds me of our mother right now. She'd be so damn proud of Candice. People might think she's useless, but she's really not. She throws herself into charity work. The extensive time she puts in is all volunteer-based. She doesn't do it for the accolades. Candice volunteers and helps and gives her time and her money because she actually wants to.

"I can't take that weekend off," I tell her, and she slowly shakes her head, like she doubts what I say. No one else talks to me like she does. No one else would dare cross me.

Candice flat out doesn't give a shit. I don't scare her. I never have. Sometimes she'll call me a softy, just to piss me off.

"You are so full of crap, Jared. You're your own boss. You can take off time whenever you want." She waves a dismissive hand. "I promised I wouldn't tell you this, but you *have* to know."

My stomach knots and I swallow hard. "I have to know what?"

The smile on her face is giant, and she's practically bouncing in her seat. "Kevin is going to ask you to be his best man," she announces.

"Why the hell would he do that?" I ask incredulously.

The smile fades, replaced by a frown. I've disappointed her yet again. Something I'm quite good at—disappointing my family. I sometimes wonder if they'd rather pretend I didn't exist. "He's your *brother,* Jared. He's always looked up to you. And he wants you to stand by his side and show your support during the wedding. This is a major moment for Kevin. We have to be there."

I prop my elbow on the edge of my desk, running my hand through my hair in frustration. I know how close Rachelle is to her sister. Evelyn. My ex. If I'm going to be the best man, most likely Evelyn will be the maid of honor, and that means we'd walk into the ceremony together.

Fuck that.

"I don't want—"

Candice cuts me off. "Don't say you don't want to go yet. Think about it. This will mean so much to Kevin, to the entire family, if you're there. I know you two have grown distant over the last few years."

Because he's befriended the enemy—fallen in love with her, really. Not that I ever had a problem with Rachelle when I was with Evelyn. It's just strange that he would end up with my ex's sister. That he would actually want to marry her.

Kevin is going to have the life that I thought I'd have. With a different woman, yes, but still. He's marrying not only Rachelle, but her entire family. A family I'd grown close to once upon a time. His sister-in-law will be the woman I once believed I'd loved. A woman I've had sex with. A woman I was vulnerable with, to whom I'd confessed all of my hopes and dreams and fears and...

Shaking my head, I force the memories out, focusing instead on the here and now. I was a different person then. Young and stupid and drunk on lust. That's all it had really been between us. Love doesn't exist.

Love is utter bullshit.

"...and I think Kevin is secretly hoping his wedding—

and you being in his wedding—will bring the two of you closer together," Candice continues, and I realize I haven't been paying attention to a word she's said until now. Too lost in wasted memories. "So give it some thought, okay?"

My sister's gaze is imploring, as was her tone. I find it hard to believe Kevin actually gives a shit whether I'm there or not. He has lots of friends who would stand by his side, I'm sure.

"I'll think about it," I finally say, making her clap in delight. I roll my eyes and glower at her, but it doesn't faze her in the least. "Just don't pressure me about it. The more you ask, the more inclined I'll be to say no."

"Jared, you can't say no to family. It's not the proper thing to do," Candice says primly as she rises to her feet. "Let's go have lunch."

I check the time on my computer screen. "It's not even eleven."

"Let's have an early lunch then." She smiles, clutching her Gucci bag in front of her with both hands. "Come on. You need to get out of here. I think this blank office is permanently ruining your mood."

Without a word I stand, grabbing my phone and shoving it into my pocket. I don't have the heart to tell her that my mood was ruined years ago.

And I'm afraid I'll never be in a good mood again.

SEVEN

SARAH

I HAVEN'T GIVEN Mr. Gaines his gift back—yet. Today got away from me, and blah, blah, blah. You've heard the excuses before. I woke up late and rushed to get ready, leaving me no extra time to do...whatever. Work was busy. Of course. Once I was off, I had to go straight home to make dinner because Andie was having her friends over to study for their big chemistry test and she somehow conned me into actually making them a homecooked meal.

Okay, fine, rushing home to fix dinner was the perfect excuse as to why I couldn't stop by Mr. Gaines' office and throw that box straight at his too smug, too handsome face. That and maybe I want to actually...

Keep the gift?

I'm probably going to hell for even thinking this, but deep down, I want to keep it. The sexy little gift from Jared feels like flirtation in materialistic form. I can't remember the last time someone gave me a gift, with the exception of my brother and sister or my friends. They don't count.

Listen, I'm not whining and saying, *oh please pamper me,* but seriously. I never treat myself. I can't afford to beyond the occasional nice bra or pair of panties because I got it on major discount thanks to Marlo. Otherwise, all my extra money goes toward my sister and brother or household items. Or food.

You know, the necessities.

Currently, I'm puttering around the kitchen making chicken enchiladas like the domestic goddess I am most assuredly not. Which is probably some sort of metaphor or something because hey, I'm not only cooking chicken, I'm a *total* chicken.

That's probably not a metaphor. I have no idea what I'm talking about, clearly.

Putting together the enchiladas allows for a lot of thinking time. And if I'm being completely truthful with myself, the mere idea of going to his office and confronting him with the gift, makes me a little woozy.

Instead of dealing with it, I shoved that stupid Bliss box full of sexy lingerie onto the top shelf of my very small, extra messy closet and tried my best to forget it existed.

But it's hard, forgetting about the box, and the contents inside. That bra was pretty cute. And the panties—while completely impractical—were also super cute. Not that I have anyone to wear the set for. Maybe I could wear it for Jared?

Oh boy. Here comes that woozy feeling again.

I'm hopelessly single. There's no time to date, what with work and taking care of my sister and the household duties that pile up whether I'm around or not. With our parents gone and me being the oldest, all that stuff lands squarely on me. My brother does what he can to help pay the bills, and Brent has a pretty good job as a server at a very busy restaurant on the wharf in Monterey. He also goes to college part time, and somehow he's still pretty social. Always out drinking with his friends, or banging plenty of babes.

Those last few words come from him, not me. Sometimes, he is the absolute worst. And when he is, I call him out on it.

I'm rolling tortillas, knuckle-deep in cheese, olives and enchilada sauce when my phone starts ringing, indicating someone is trying to FaceTime me. It's Stella.

With the least stickiest finger I've got, I answer the call, and a few seconds later Stella and Caroline's faces fill the screen. Both of them are smiling, their eyes wide as they start calling my name.

"What?" I ask irritably as I make my way to the sink and quickly wash my hands. "I'm in the middle of making dinner."

Ooh, I sound rude. But I'm grumpy. Tired. Hungry.

"Did you go by you-know-who's office today?" Stella asks, sounding coy.

I go to my phone so I can look at them while shaking my head as my answer. The immediate disappointment on their faces is obvious.

"But you said you would," Caroline whines, a little pout on her face.

"Work kept me busy." That isn't a lie. "And I had to make dinner for Andie and her friends." That's not a lie either.

"Please, you could've ordered them a pizza," Caroline says, and deep down, I know she's right. "You purposely avoided him."

"Nope." I grab a pile of grated cheese and sprinkle it over the prepped enchiladas. I still need to add a few olives on top of the dish as well, and then I can pop the pan into the oven and bake it for twenty minutes. "It's been a crazy day."

"And tomorrow will be crazy, and so will the next day," Stella says. "A week will pass and then you'll miss your chance."

Yay. Maybe that's my plan.

"Until he comes into the store again," Caroline points out.

My stomach bottoms out at the thought of him coming in so soon after I just saw him. "He usually only pops in once a month." Lately it's been about every two to three weeks, but I don't want to think about that.

"He might come in sooner, especially if he gets no response about his present," Caroline says with a knowing smile. "Watch out. I bet he'll show up."

"No way." I wipe the excess cheese bits off my hands and grab a handful of chopped olives, scattering them across the thick layer of cheese. "He probably had a twenty-four-hour deadline on me and since I didn't make it, he's moved on to the next woman."

Hmm. That sounds like something he might do, doesn't it?

"So you *do* think he's interested in you then," Stella says, sounding smug.

I pause, letting her words sink in. Letting my own words sink in as well. "I didn't mean it like that. He's just—he has no time for bullshit. If that lingerie gift was some sort of message or test for me, then I'm fairly certain I just failed it."

Which is a good thing, right? Then he'll move on. Leave me alone. Maybe he'll even stop coming to Bliss.

When I realize I'm frowning, that I actually feel sad at

the idea of him not coming into Bliss anymore, I tell myself to get over it.

"This is so disappointing," Caroline says, and I can actually detect a hint of sadness to her voice. "I was hoping you'd tell us a sordid tale of you showing up at his office and him stripping you naked right there on his desk."

The visual instantly pops into my head. Me. Completely naked and sprawled across Jared Gaines' massive desk. He's standing in front of me in one of those impeccable suits, his expression unreadable as he drinks me in. He'd reach out, his hand resting gently on the inside of my thigh just before he pushed it to the side and he—

I close my eyes for the briefest moment, fighting the image. Ignoring how hard my heart is pounding and that my skin's grown uncomfortably warm. The warmth isn't from our old oven that tends to blast the kitchen with heat either.

No, I'm warm from my overactive imagination.

"I don't plan on being naked on Jared Gaines' desk any time soon," I say with a nervous laugh. "I mean—ever."

"Uh huh. You should head over there tomorrow," Caroline says, Stella looming behind her and wagging her index finger right at me. "Give him a piece of your mind. We think he likes it when you're mean to him."

They laugh. I pretend to laugh too.

Then I end the call before they can say another word.

Wiping my forehead with the inside of my arm, I blow out a harsh breath. Survey the mess that I made in the kitchen thanks to the rigorous prep that comes with making enchiladas. I'm using our mom's old recipe, and while I've been making them for years, tweaking them and trying my best to have them turn out just like the ones she used to make, I can never get it quite right.

Much to the disappointment of my brother and sister.

Andie suddenly bursts into the kitchen, like she knew I was thinking about her, stopping short when her gaze lands on me. "Sarah. Are you okay?"

I nod, trying my best to smile as I grab the baking dish crammed full of enchiladas and head for the oven. "Of course. Just cooking dinner. Everything all right?"

"We're all starving, and I was sent in here to see when dinner would be ready." Andie tilts her head, watching me closely as I shove the baking dish into the oven and slam the door shut with a loud thwap. "You're all flushed. Your cheeks are red. So is your chest."

God, did imagining Jared touching my naked body really make me flush that hard? This is ridiculous.

"It's hot in here," I point out, which isn't a lie. The room is so steamy I go to the small window above the sink and push it open, then wash my hands for what feels like the fiftieth time in the past hour. Making enchiladas is messy business.

"True." Her face brightens when Brent enters the kitchen. "Hey! I didn't know you'd be home tonight."

"I didn't either, but I won't be here long," he says as he drops a box he was carrying on the kitchen counter. He glances at me. "This was outside on the doorstep."

"Thanks." I pull a pan out and set it on the stove, then go to our small pantry and grab a box from the shelf. Any other night, I'd make my—excuse me, our mother's—home-made Mexican rice, but that takes too long. So tonight, it's Rice-A-Roni. "Are you eating dinner with us?"

I seriously hope he doesn't want dinner. I don't think I made enough for him to eat too.

"Nah, going out with the boys." He smiles at me as he opens the refrigerator, grabs a bottle of water and then slams the fridge door shut. "I'll be out late."

Nothing new there. "Don't you ever have homework or essays to write or tests to study for?"

"I got that under control. Trust me." He presses a kiss to Andie's cheek and gives me a quick side hug. "Don't wait up. See you chicas later."

And with that, he's gone as fast as he entered the kitchen. I hear Andie's friends all call out his name in greeting as he walks into the living room, then dissolve into giggles when he makes his way down the wall toward his room. They all probably have a crush on him. Why, I'm not exactly sure, but then again he's my brother so I don't think about him in that way.

"He's never home." The disappointment on Andie's face is obvious. She loves Brent so much, but he barely makes time for her. He's the fun sibling. The one who takes her cool places and buys her junk food.

I'm the boring sister who makes sure she eats her vegetables, cleans the bathroom and does her homework. Most of the time, I'm fairly certain Andie doesn't really like me.

That sort of breaks my heart.

"I know. But he's busy with work and school." I sound like I'm making excuses, so I clamp my lips shut. "You should ask him to go to the movies with you this weekend. Like you guys used to do."

Like we all used to do.

"Every time I ask him to do anything, he says yes, then has something else come up and he can't make it," she says bitterly, shaking her head. "He's always breaking his promises. I'm tired of being turned down."

Welcome to the real world, little sister.

"Dinner will be ready in twenty minutes," I tell her, and she smiles, ready to say something—what I'm not sure—but then one of her friends calls her name and she's gone. Back out in the living room and so she can supposedly study for the chemistry test.

Honestly, I think they're just gossiping. But whatever.

I've just set the rice to simmer when I remember Brent brought in a package for me. Curious, I wipe my hands on a dishtowel and stare at the medium-sized, plain brown box. I can tell from the label that it came via Fed Ex. My name and address is printed out, and there's a return address from Monterey, but I don't recognize it.

Plus there's no name included with the address. No business name either.

Weird.

Suspicious, I grab a pair of scissors and cut the tape open, then carefully pry the box open. Inside is another plain brown box, with white lettering scrawled across the top.

The lettering actually says *Christian Louboutin*.

I suck in a breath when I realize what this means. Shoes. And not just any shoes. Louboutins are expensive. No way could I ever afford these. Who the hell is sending me such a pricey gift?

Hmm. I have a sneaking suspicion.

Slowly I pull the lid off the box, gazing at the thick white tissue paper that hides what's inside. Before I burn the rice, I go to the pan and give it a quick stir, wipe my hands on the dishtowel, and then return to the box, where I peel back the tissue paper to reveal the shoes.

They're black. Patent leather. Peep toe with the slightest platform. And that famous red sole that lets everyone know exactly what—or who—you're wearing. They are gorgeous. Like, "stuff my fist against my mouth to contain the squeal that wants to escape me" gorgeous.

I don't even want to touch them. I'm afraid I'll get them

dirty since I've been cooking all evening. But come on. I *must* touch them. Try them on. See how they look before I shove them back into their box and send them back to you-know-who. Because we know who sent these shoes to me.

I'm not stupid.

No way can I keep them, but I'm definitely trying them on. This might be my only chance to wear authentic Louboutins, even for just a few minutes. I kick off my old Victoria's Secret slippers that I got for five bucks last Christmas—don't tell Marlo I wear them!—and then I slip on one of the shoes.

It fits perfectly. Of course it does. I turn my foot this way and that, admiring how the shoe looks, a little sigh of pure happiness escaping me. My head is filled with images of the many outfits I could wear with these shoes for work. Marlo has Louboutins. So does one of the other sales associates I work with—but she's currently dating a very wealthy, much older man who enjoys showering her with very expensive gifts.

Looks like you've found an admirer who enjoys showering you with very expensive gifts too.

Ugh. I hate that the knowing voice in my brain sound suspiciously like Caroline.

Deciding to hell with it, I slip on the other shoe, then take a few tentative steps around the kitchen. I don't even wobble, because I wear heels at work every day. Plus, I feel so freaking tall, thanks to the five-inch heels. These shoes fit like a dream. They look like a dream. They *are* a dream.

I feel like I'm dreaming, like I'm freaking Cinderella. But Jared Gaines is not my Prince Charming.

With a sigh, I take the shoes off and set them into the box, careful not to scuff them against each other. I drape the tissue paper over them, place the lid back on, and I'm about to put the shoebox into the shipping box when I notice the small notecard.

Nerves clamoring inside of me, I pick the card up and flip it over to see that now familiar, bold handwriting.

You're ignoring me. What will it take to get a response?
JG

MY HEART THREATENS to burst out of my chest as I reread the words he's written. I'm ignoring him? He's right. I am. Realization dawns and I want to smack my forehead.

He *wants* me to respond. He wants me to come to his office or call him—I do have access to his phone number, we have it on record at Bliss.

Huh. So what will it take to get a response from me?

Definitely not a pair of Louboutins.

EIGHT

BEHAVING like a woman who doesn't have a single care in the world—or one who gives zero fucks, according to Stella —I show up at Bliss the next morning in my favorite black pencil skirt, my black shirt with the white lace collar and pearl buttons down the front, and the new Louboutins on my feet. I know, I know, I said I'd return them, but screw it. He gave them to me, after all.

These shoes give me power. Who knew a pair of shoes could make a woman feel this way? It's freaking amazing. I feel like a goddamn queen as I stride into the back room of Bliss, heading straight for the timeclock so I can punch in.

"Nice shoes."

I turn to see Bethany watching me. Arms crossed, thin eyebrows lifted. I don't dislike Bethany per se, but she's not what I would call my cup of tea. We've never gone beyond surface conversations when we're together. It's always been that way. We get along fine at work, but I couldn't imagine her being a close friend. Certainly couldn't see her in my girl gang.

Which is fine. I know Bethany has her own girl gang.

Plus, I'm pretty sure she has a tiny crush on a certain Bliss client. Jared, cough-cough, Gaines.

Wouldn't she just die if she knew who gave me these shoes?

"Thanks," I finally tell her, offering a quick smile as I stash my bag in a desk drawer. I hope she doesn't ask where I got them.

"Where'd you get them?"

Damn it.

"Um." My brain scrambles. "A gift from a friend."

Not exactly the truth, but not exactly a lie either.

"That's some friend. I wish I had friends like you," she says sarcastically. "I hate to ask, but are those even real?"

I'd probably ask too, if Bethany suddenly appeared in a pair of Louboutins one day. We know each other well enough. "I'm not sure," I say, my voice hesitant. "She said she got them on eBay."

I hate that I'm lying, but how can I tell her the truth?

"Fake," Bethany says with all the authority in the world. "I mean, I hope they're real, but you have to be really careful with anything you buy on eBay, you know? There are so many scammers out there."

I say nothing. I'm tempted to ask her about her interaction with Jared the other day. What did he do? What did he say? Did she give him my address?

But I remain quiet. Just watch her as she walks away, heading out into the store, most likely off to fold panties and rearrange bras.

I decide to wait a few minutes, going to the cracked full-length mirror that hangs on the wall. It used to be in one of the dressing rooms, but once it broke, Marlo brought it to the back room so we could use it. The crack runs along the right side, so it doesn't interfere too badly when you want to check yourself out.

And I am blatantly checking myself out. My outfit is freaking on point. My hair looks good today too. I washed it the night before last, and it always holds curl better when it's a little dirty. Thank God for dry shampoo.

Smiling, I enter the store and head for the front, keys dangling from my fingers. "Are we ready?" I ask Bethany as I pause in front of the doors.

Bethany adjusts a pale pink bra on one of the displays before answering, "Yep. I'll go turn on the music."

She's gone by the time I've unlocked the doors. I push one of them open to check the weather. Gray skies. Misty. Dreary. Welcome to the Monterey Peninsula, where you can almost always count on fog to greet you in the morning.

I'm about to shut the door when I notice a woman carrying a giant bouquet of flowers headed in my direction. They're gorgeous. One of those farmhouse flower arrangements I always see on Instagram. I don't know how else to describe them. They're in an extra tall mason jar, a straw bow wrapped around the top of the glass, the flowers bursting in a multitude of colors and sizes. I spot sunflowers. Roses. Lilies.

It's beautiful. Whoever is receiving the bouquet is going to be so happy. If the woman were delivering them here, I'd guess the flowers are for Marlo. She receives bouquets on occasion. From clients. Other businesses. Mystery people she won't tell us about.

"Hey!" the woman calls when I've got the door more than halfway closed. "Can you hold the door open for me?"

I do as she asks, surprised when she enters the store. Maybe I was right and they're for Marlo. "Are you delivering the flowers to someone here?" I sound incredulous, because I am incredulous.

"Yeah." She makes her way to the counter where the register is, setting the arrangement down before she turns to face me, pulling her phone out of her pocket. She taps away at the screen, squinting. "Does a Sarah Harrison work here?"

My mouth drops open and I squeak. I can't help it. I sound like a mouse. Or an idiot. Actually, it really doesn't matter what I sound like, I am in complete shock and cannot form words.

The woman stares at me for a moment. "Are *you* Sarah Harrison?"

I nod, still unable to speak.

"Here." She thrusts her phone toward me. "Sign on the line with your finger."

I do as she asks, keeping my gaze averted so I can't see the flowers. Or the card nestled within them that's taunting me.

"Thanks. Have a great day," the woman says before jetting out of the store.

Releasing my pent-up breath, I turn and study the arrangement. They're even prettier up close. And so fragrant. I don't have to lean in to breathe their scent. I can smell them from where I'm standing.

I take the card from its little holder, anticipation curling through me as I clutch it between my fingers. I almost don't want to open it. There's something to be said for waiting...

"Whoa. That arrangement is, like, ginormous," Bethany says when she reenters the room. She approaches the counter, reaching out to drift her fingertips across the flower petals. I'm tempted to tell her to back off, but I remain quiet. "Whose is it?"

Somehow, I find my voice. "Oh, they were sent to Marlo. Aren't they gorgeous?"

"Amazing." She leans in and sniffs. "They probably cost a lot of money."

I can't even fathom how much this arrangement must've cost. "I'm sure they did."

"You going to take it back to her office?" Bethany reaches for the mason jar, ready to lift the arrangement but I shake my head and start to babble.

"No, no, no. I don't want to take them to her office yet. Let me tell her about them first. Don't you think that's a good idea? Maybe she'll want to keep them out in the store?" At Bethany's questioning look, I continue, "Or maybe you're right, and she'll want them kept in her office. I don't know. Let me ask and then I'll let you know."

I go to the back room before Bethany can question me any further, still annoyed with the stupid things I said to her. I'm still clutching the card in the palm of my hand, so hard the sharp edge is digging into my skin and making me wince in pain.

Ugh. See what this man does to me? Sends me beautiful flowers, makes me trip over my own tongue trying to explain them, and now he's actually hurting me. Well. The card he sent me is hurting me.

Same diff.

I rush into Marlo's tiny office and collapse in one of the chairs. "I need your help."

She keeps staring at her iMac screen. "With what?"

"I have a situation." She glances up, her gaze curious, and I go on. "Someone sent me flowers. They were just delivered. Here."

Marlo tilts her head, waiting for me to explain further.

"And I told Bethany they were for you."

"Lucky me." She presses a hand to her chest in mock surprise.

"But they're not. They're for me."

"Right." She nods.

"So I don't want you to tell her they're mine." I send her a pleading look. "Can we keep the flowers in your office for the day? Please?"

"Of course." She doesn't even hesitate and doesn't ask questions either. God, I love my boss.

"And you won't let it slip that they aren't yours?"

"Not at all. I'm a most excellent liar when I need to be." She purses her lips. "Not that it's a skill anyone should be proud of. But I do know how to keep a secret."

"Great." I rise to my feet, the card still clutched in my hand. "Thank you."

"Who are they from?" Marlo asks as I'm just about to exit her office.

I glance at her over my shoulder. "What?"

"Who are the flowers from?" She raises a brow. "Anyone I know?"

I am not a most excellent liar. I'm not the best at keeping secrets either. Should I tell her? Probably not. "Um..."

"A secret admirer?"

"I know who it is." My palms start to sweat, and I swear the envelope is getting damp.

"But you don't want to tell me?"

I send her an apologetic look. "It's probably best that I don't."

"I see." She leans back in her chair, her assessing gaze drifting down the length of me. "Don't you look extra professional today. Very polished."

"Thank you." It's a rare and wonderful thing when Marlo compliments your outfit. She is a paragon of fashion.

"And those shoes." She tips her head, her gaze locking on my feet. "Louboutins?"

Gosh, now my entire body is sweating. "They're fakes. From eBay."

"Hmm. Interesting. Those are the best fake Louboutins I've ever seen." She waves a hand, shooing me out of her office, and I really hope she doesn't question me further. "Go back out there before Bethany sets a negligee on fire."

A laugh escapes me as I leave, and then I'm pausing in the back room a few seconds later so I can tear into the envelope and see what Mr. Gaines is saying now.

Call me
JG

HUH. Like I'm going to call him. I mean, seriously, what I am supposed to say? "Gee, thanks for all the expensive gifts! No, I am not going to sleep with you on the first date"?

That I'm contemplating going on a date with him, let alone many dates, tells me I'm taking his expensive seduction into consideration.

This isn't like me at all.

I shove the card into my purse, take the bouquet back to Marlo's office and set the vase on her desk, then purposefully start my workday. I clean like a fiend. I rearrange every single one of the bra drawers in record time, something Marlo has been nagging all of us to do for weeks. I dust with a vengeance. I greet customers like they're my long-lost friends and I'm dying to help them find the bra or panties of their dreams (weird). I ring up purchases and do my best not to react when men try to flirt with me.

Now trust me, I don't think I'm a special case. They flirt with all of us at Bliss.

I'm so caught up in my focus-on-work-and-nothing-else mode that when the phone rings, I answer it in the most efficient, brisk tone I can muster. "Good afternoon, thank you for calling Bliss. Sarah speaking."

"Well, well, well. Miss Harrison." My heart drops. I know exactly who this is. "You are a very hard woman to get a hold of."

Hearing his deep voice makes every single hair on my body stand on end. Oh God, now he's the one calling me? This can't get any worse.

Turning so my back is facing anything and everything, I whisper into the phone, "Please don't call me at work."

"I don't have your phone number so there's no other way I can get a hold of you." He sounds so completely logical I almost want to agree with him. Almost. "Did you like the flowers?"

"They're beautiful." I clap a hand over my mouth.

Why the hell did I just say that?

"I knew you would like them." His tone is smug. The bastard. "I also told you to call me."

"I've been busy." This is the truth.

"So busy you can't manage a thank-you call?" He exhales loudly. "You've hurt my feelings."

"I'm sorry." I can't believe I just apologized to him. "But I might know other JGs. If you don't sign your full name, how am I supposed to know you're the one I should thank?"

He ignores my question. "You didn't thank me for your other gifts either."

I clutch the phone tighter. "I don't want them."

"Really." His voice is flat. Like he doesn't believe me.

How can he tell that I'm lying?

"Yes, really."

"Then why are you wearing the shoes I sent you?"

A gasp escapes me and he laughs. Oh my God, he is *such* an asshole. "Are you—are you *spying* on me?"

"Of course not," he scoffs, like I offended him. I swear I hear him chuckle. He's not one to laugh, so the sound is shocking. "Just a lucky guess. And don't bother denying that you're wearing those shoes. Your gasp gave you away."

I really need to learn how to control myself. Especially around him.

"Why are you doing this?" I need to know. Is he just toying with me? It feels like it. There's nothing serious behind his extravagant gestures. He's the type of man who can waste thousands of dollars on a woman and then forget all about her a week later.

"Why am I doing what?"

"Sending me such expensive gifts. Paying attention to me." I hesitate, unsure if I should say the rest. I decide to go for it. "It's almost as if...you suddenly like me."

He's quiet for a moment. Contemplating my words? Or planning on what he would say? I'll never know.

"I'm giving in to my urges, Miss Harrison," he finally says. "Don't you think it's time you did as well?"

"When it comes to you, I have no urges." Ah, maybe I *am* a most excellent liar.

"Liar."

I say nothing. Neither does he. This goes on for approximately thirty seconds—which is a long time, trust me, when he finally breaks first. "I'd like to meet with you. Soon. At the store."

No. No, no, no. I can't take an appointment with him right now. He was just here. And I can't face him, not yet.

"I'm afraid all of my personal shopping appointments are booked into next week." Again with the lies. Marlo would be so proud.

Or totally pissed because I'm desperate to turn down business from one of our best clients.

"Bullshit." He has zero problems calling me on my bluff. It's always been that way between us. "Tomorrow at one. You are working tomorrow, aren't you?"

"Yes," I admit, my voice weak. I don't even bother protesting the appointment.

"Perfect. See you tomorrow. One o'clock. You know how I feel about punctuality, Miss Harrison."

"Uh huh." He's a sucker for punctuality. I think he gets off on it. The pervert.

"And one last thing," he says right before I hang up the phone.

"What?" I sound exasperated. Annoyed. Defeated. I am feeling all of those emotions, along with a healthy dose of nerves, excitement and anticipation.

God, what in the world is wrong with me?

"Wear the shoes."

He ends the call before I can manage another word.

NINE

WHEN TIMES GET TOUGH, you have to call in rein-forcements. That means begging Caroline to skip out on her dinner date with her sexy boyfriend so she can be at the apartment she shares with Stella. That way I can come over and share my problems with them.

More like my one particular problem.

It didn't warrant a full-blown girls' night out. I'd have to explain too much to the gang, and I bet some of my friends would think I'm a total idiot for wearing the shoes, accepting the gifts, meeting with him, etc. etc. Which I probably am. Actually, I can admit that I am. But I don't want to face that situation right now. I'd rather wallow in my idiocy with my two closest friends and ask their opinions on it.

Once Stella has finished blending us delicious margaritas and we're all settled—me and Caroline on the couch, Stella on her papasan chair from World Market—I recount to them the twisted tale of Jared Gaines and his many abundant gifts.

"Where are the flowers?" Stella demands to know when I'm finished.

"I told Marlo to take them home." I take a sip of my margarita and wince. It's icy cold, tangy—and chock full of liquor.

"Total waste," Stella mutters, shaking her head.

"You should've brought them here," Caroline adds.

I stare at both of them, fighting the irritation that wants to burst forth. But it's too large to contain. "Seriously, guys? I tell you what's going on and you can only focus on the stupid flowers?"

The flowers weren't stupid. They were beautiful. And I should've taken them home and enjoyed them, but Andie would've asked about a billion questions, and Brent would've too, and I don't have any explanations to offer them that don't sound sordid. It's not every day that a client of mine sends me freaking flowers.

So I gave the gorgeous arrangement to Marlo. Because yet again, I'm a total chicken. I'd rather avoid what's going on than deal with the truth.

"Sorry, sorry." Caroline sits up straighter, takes a deep breath, and contemplates me with that questioning look she's so good at. "You want my opinion?"

That is the entire reason I'm here. "Please."

"He's trying to seduce you."

Stella nods her answer, since her mouth is currently full of slushy margarita. She even offers a thumbs-up when Caroline looks over at her.

I roll my eyes, disappointment washing over me. "I already know this."

"Then why are you complaining about him to us? Do you actually want him to stop with the gifts?" Caroline asks.

"I don't know how I feel about the gifts," I admit,

though I'm not being one hundred percent truthful. "I love everything he's sent me. But I don't feel right in keeping it all."

There it is. I *want* to keep everything, but I don't know if I'm doing the right thing. Yet I'm wearing the shoes. I gave the gorgeous flowers away to my boss, and I doubt I'll give him back the lingerie any time soon.

God, what am I doing? I'm so confused.

"Do you think he's trying to—buy your services, so to speak?" Caroline asks, leaning over so she can rest her hand briefly on my knee. A reassuring gesture from my touchy-feely friend that makes me more emotional than I care to admit.

When was the last time I had a man hug me? Kiss me? It's been forever. No mom or dad to hug me either. Oh, Andie will throw herself at me on occasion and give me one of those brief, tight embraces she's so fond of. My friends are an affectionate bunch too.

But it's not the same.

Is that why I'm attracted to Jared? Am I so deprived of any sort of sexual contact that I'm drawn to this man? Who's possibly showering me with expensive gifts for the sole purpose of getting into my pants?

Is that really all he wants from me?

"She's not a hooker, Car," Stella drawls, making all of us laugh. She looks at me, our gazes locking. "This is his way, right?"

"His way?" I wrinkle my nose.

"From what you've seen, when he comes to Bliss, he's buying lingerie as gifts for the women in his life," Stella explains. "Right?"

I nod.

"I'm assuming he's doing the same to you. You got

lingerie. Shoes. Flowers." She smiles, her eyes twinkling. "What's next? Jewelry?"

"Ooh, that would be awesome." Caroline rubs her hands together. "Maybe he could go into Amelia's store and she could help him pick something out."

Amelia is part of our friend group. She works at a fine jewelry store that's in the same shopping complex as Bliss.

"I don't want jewelry from him," I say.

They raise their eyebrows, disbelief written all over their faces. "Uh huh,"

They are both completely unsympathetic. I think they're enjoying my misery.

"Honestly? I wish it could all go back to the way it was." When he was the grouchy client and I was the nervous sales associate and we circled around each other like wary dogs.

Not the prettiest description of my early relationship with Mr. Gaines, but it's apt.

"So you're resisting his pursuit because...you're not interested?" Stella asks.

And here's where it gets sticky.

"I—I don't know if I'm *not* interested." The moment the words leave me, I cover my eyes with my hands and shake my head. "I shouldn't be interested in him. I've told you both countless times that he can be a jerk. He's insensitive. He's also very demanding."

"Isn't he also hot, young, and insanely rich?" Caroline asks.

"That shouldn't matter." I drop my hands into my lap to find both of them watching me. "I don't want a guy whose only redeeming qualities are that he's hot and insanely rich. I want a *nice* guy. A guy who actually cares about me, and about my family, my situation. My life isn't typical for a woman in her twenties. I need a man who will understand what I'm going through, you know? And that is *not* Jared Gaines."

They both are still just looking at me. Not saying a word.

"Besides, I'm not interested in a boyfriend right now," I continue. I'm going to babble. I can just feel it. "I have too much going on in my life, what with work and taking care of Andie and the house. I'm carrying too much responsibility, you know? What guy would want to deal with that anyway? Andie has two more years of high school after she finishes this one, and then she'll go away to college. She's too smart and we don't make a lot of money, plus she's an orphan, so she'll get into a great college, I know it. Once that happens..." I take a deep breath to stop myself from talking, exhaling slowly before I continue. "Then I can finally concentrate on me."

I have been waiting to concentrate on me for a long time. Years, really. Ever since our parents died, I've put my life and my ambitions on hold so I can focus on my brother and sister. Brent can take care of himself, and he has for years. Andie is still totally dependent on me. Once she moves out after high school, then I can figure out what I should do next.

I have no clue what that is, but I'm sure I'll come to some sort of conclusion in the next two years or so.

My best friends send each other a look before turning their attention on me.

"Sarah. We're not saying this guy is going to be your *boyfriend*." Heavy emphasis on that last word from Caroline. "He doesn't sound much like boyfriend material. But maybe he could be a—distraction." She smiles.

"A distraction?" I grimace.

"What Caroline is trying to say, though she isn't doing a

good job of it, is that you should treat this guy like a fling," Stella adds.

"Remember how we said you needed to hate-fuck him to get him out of your system?" Caroline asks, her voice sweet despite the words she just said.

Horror courses through me, making my blood run cold. Uh-uh. There will be none of that between Jared and me.

"I don't want to *hate-fuck* Jared Gaines," I say primly. Just saying the words makes me squirm a little inside.

Yet I'm also squirming the slightest bit with excitement at the idea of having sex with Jared.

"Come on." Caroline's firm voice makes me jump a little, and when she slaps the edge of the couch, I jump again. "You sooooo want to hate-fuck that guy. Just—go for it. Clearly he has a thing for you. We're guessing you have a thing for him too."

Now it's my turn to remain quiet. I don't know why I'd rather think he *doesn't* have a thing for me. Maybe because it would be easier? Living in denial isn't necessarily a bad thing, right?

"No man sends a woman fancy underwear, expensive shoes and flowers in a matter of a few days just because he thinks she's cute," Stella says, keeping it real. "He *wants* you."

A shiver moves down my spine and I tell myself to chill.

"If I give in to him, then he'll just toss me aside like he does with all of his other women," I say, my voice low. I take a sip from my margarita, then another one. I think I'm going to need this tequila to get through tonight's line of questioning.

"So? Who cares if it's just a quick affair? That's what you want too, right? You know he's not 'the one'. But he can be the 'right now.'" Caroline smiles, appearing mighty pleased with herself. "Stella and I think he would make a most excellent right now kind of guy. We also think you should totally go for it."

"And when you see it start to dwindle between you two, dump him first," Stella chimes in. "Beat him to the punch."

"Seriously?" I can't imagine doing that. He's probably the one who does all the dumping. In fact, I'm fairly certain he's always the dumper, not the dumpee.

"Oooh, that's such a great idea, Stel. You could always ghost him," Caroline suggests eagerly.

"Yeah. Fuck his brains out for a couple of weeks, then just stop responding to his texts." Stella's practically bouncing in her papasan chair, making it rock back and forth. "That'll drive him crazy."

They make it sound so simple. Yet it's not.

"I can't ghost him. He comes to my place of business on a regular basis. He's one of my clients."

"I bet he'd stop going to Bliss once you ghost his ass," Caroline says. "He'll never want to face you again."

Oh my God, why does the idea of never seeing Mr. Gaines again make me feel...sad? I'm losing it. There's no other explanation.

"I can't ghost him," I repeat before taking a big drink from my glass. "That's rude. I couldn't ghost anyone."

"If he acts like a dick to you, I bet you'd ghost him in a hot minute," Stella says.

The both of them laugh, and then they start sharing quick stories about the guys they've ghosted in the past. Or the guys who've ghosted them.

Me? I sit on the couch and slurp the last dregs of my margarita, the liquor already taking effect. I'll Uber home, since I took an Uber here, knowing full well I'd end up having a drink or three.

As we drink and chat and laugh, all I can think about is seeing him tomorrow. What should I wear? I had on my best outfit today, damn it. Maybe I could wear the pencil skirt again, with a different shirt. Yeah, that should work. I'm sure no one will notice. Bethany's not scheduled tomorrow, thank goodness, so I won't have to deal with her and her silly crush on Mr. Gaines.

I'll wash my hair as soon as I get home. Maybe even curl it tonight before I go to bed so it has that freshly fucked look to it so many men find sexy.

Hmm. At least, that's what I read in some article on the Cosmopolitan app once.

Yep. I've got this all under control. Under complete control. When I meet with him tomorrow, I'll feel him out, so to speak, see what sort of mood he's in. And if he's receptive, if I'm feeling receptive, then yeah.

Maybe he can be my "right now" guy.

TEN

"SARAH."

I practically jump out of my skin at the sound of Marlo's soft voice calling my name. I'm hiding in the back room, waiting for my one o'clock appointment to show up. I'm also a bundle of nerves, I have been all day, and I've also been a clumsy mess.

Hence the reason I'm in the back room, retagging clearance panties with their sales prices instead of knocking into displays out on the sales floor. Marlo's the one who's worked with customers today, which she doesn't do very often anymore, considering she owns the place.

That goes to show just how ridiculously bad I've been acting all day.

"Yes, Marlo?" I smile up at my boss, a mountain of lacy panties piled in my lap.

"Your appointment is here. Mr. Gaines." She moves closer to me, her voice lowering to just above a whisper, her crimson lips curled into a frown. "This is unlike him. Wasn't he just in here last week?"

"Um, yes. He was." I toss the panties into the box I

picked them out of, and rise to my feet, my ankles wobbly. I am nothing like the confident, purposeful woman I was yesterday, strutting around the store in my power Louboutins. See what this man does to me? He zaps me of my strength. No man should have that kind of power. "I guess he needs something else? Found another paramour in a week's time, perhaps?"

"Mmmhmm." Her skeptical expression tells me she doesn't believe my explanation for a second. "I think he might be here for—*other* purposes."

I don't respond. How can I when she's right? Instead, I shake my hair back, tug my pencil skirt into place and, without another word, stride out into the store, my gaze scanning the room for my client.

I find him within seconds, standing near the front by the doors, yet I see he's already found me. His gaze is on my feet, specifically my shoes, and I straighten my spine, increasing my pace as I make my way toward him.

"Mr. Gaines," I say, pasting on my best customer smile when he lifts his gaze to mine. His dark brown eyes flash with an unfamiliar gleam and my breath catches in the back of my throat. "Back so soon, I see."

"You know I can't resist you, Miss Harrison." His smile is slow. Wolfish, if that's really a thing. I read it in a romance novel once, thought it was kind of silly, but right now, it's working for Jared.

His entire demeanor right now reminds me of a predatory creature. His face is all hard lines—stern, straight nose, granite jaw, sharp cheekbones, steely eyes. Yet his mouth, his lips are soft. Full. Lush.

Kissable.

Shaking my head at the wayward thought, I return his smile, trying my best to remain polite. Professional.

"Is there anything in particular you're looking for this afternoon?" I'm surprised by how steady my voice is, considering I feel like my insides are sloshing back and forth, like I'm on a boat in the middle of the ocean.

"You don't have anything pulled aside for my appointment?" He raises a single brow, the expression on his face practically daring me to say no.

Well, guess what? I'm about to say it.

"No, I didn't pull anything aside." I shrug when he glares at me. "You never told me the nature of your visit."

He glances about, making sure no one is around, I'd assume. And lucky for him, there's no one in the store currently. It's the middle of the week, early afternoon. We normally don't get too many customers at this time.

We are the only two people in here. Even Marlo has disappeared.

"Perhaps you can show me some of your newer items," he suggests.

"I can do that." All new arrivals are at the front of the store, so we're in the right spot. I lead him to a table showcasing our latest bra and panty design. "Celestial is the theme for spring into summer."

I point to the bras made of thin, sheer netting and pink silk, tiny pale pink stars stitched in a scattered pattern across the tulle fabric. They leave nothing to the imagination, and the panties are the same.

"They hide nothing." He holds up a pair of brief-cut panties, turning them this way and that. Every time he holds underwear in those big hands of his, I melt a little inside. I don't know why he affects me like this.

"You're right. They don't," I agree, grabbing a thong and flipping it over to the thin string of lace that makes up the backside. "But they're terribly sweet."

"Sweet?"

I glance up to find him watching me. "Sweet yet sexy," I counter, my cheeks going hot from the way he's studying me so carefully.

"You like the celestial theme?"

I nod. Press my lips together so I don't say something I regret. Like, *I love this theme,* or *Do you want me to model the panties for you?*

Yeah. That's a bad idea.

"What's your favorite piece?"

Without hesitation I reach for the teddy that's part of the collection. Thin, lacy pink straps. Pink lace bands the leg line, and there's a pink silk sash belt to tie around the waist. The teddy is one hundred percent see-through, the scattered pink stars not large enough to hide anything. Not a nipple, not a pubic hair, nothing. It's a beautiful piece. Completely impractical. Utterly sexy.

Outrageously expensive.

"It's—interesting." He takes the piece from me, his fingers brushing against mine, and just like that, I feel the jolt. An electric current that starts at the tips of my fingers and rushes up my arm, travels across my chest, down my stomach, settling...

Between my legs.

My knees are wobbly, and I shift my weight from one foot to the other.

"It's also pricey," I tell him, my voice weak.

"I don't mind the cost if I like it. You should know this by now, Sarah." He sends me a stern look, but the way his voice caresses my name when he says it, oh God.

This isn't good. Not good.

Or maybe it *is* good. According to Caroline and Stella,

it's perfect. This is what I want. What he wants. That "right now" moment could be happening.

My problem? I'm clueless when it comes to handling this type of stuff.

I watch as he checks the price tag, his lips pursing as he emits a low whistle. "Four hundred dollars."

"I told you it was pricey." I clear my throat, hating how shaky my voice has become. He's standing so close, I can feel his body heat radiating toward me, and I can smell him. Clean. Like the ocean. Like clean, fragrant man. I inhale as discreetly as possible, taking in his scent, and I'm so thankful he doesn't seem to notice.

"You want it?"

I lift my head, our gazes meeting. "Excuse me?"

"I want to buy this for you." He glances at the tag once more, his gaze narrowing. "Is this the correct size?"

It's a medium. I paw through the remaining sizes, breathing a quiet sigh of relief when I find what I want. "This one is."

He takes it from me. "Right. A small." His gaze goes to my chest but doesn't linger. Is he actually turning into a gentleman? Miracles can happen. "And what's your bra size again?"

"A thirty-four C." I fight the embarrassment that wants to take over me. It's hard to change. To be bold and tell him that I want this—whatever this is that's happening between us. Being so close to him unnerves me. Makes me think I don't want this at all. That I'm just playing a game that I know I will definitely lose. "You shouldn't buy it for me."

"You're contradicting yourself," he points out.

"Because you confuse me. I don't understand why you're doing this."

"I like buying you things." His voice is a low growl, vibrating across my skin.

"Oh, trust me, I know." It's fairly obvious.

"And you like receiving them." His gaze drops to my feet. "I see you're wearing the shoes. They look good on you."

"I love them." That I won't hold back on. Honesty. Because I do love these stupid shoes, even though I know I should've returned them to him. "They're gorgeous."

"Have you worn your first gift yet?"

I drop my head, suddenly unable to face him. I touch the closest pair of panties on the table, my fingers sliding across the embroidered stars. "No."

"You didn't like the set."

I'm wimping out. I can't keep this up. He's too much for me. "I can't accept it, Mr. Gaines. What we're doing is..." My voice drifts and I heave a big sigh, shaking my head. "This shouldn't be happening."

Reaching out, he traces his finger along the edge of my jaw. I suck in a harsh breath at his delicate touch, my lips parting. Without thought I reach out, gripping the edge of the table next to us as he tucks his finger beneath my chin and tips my face up so I have no choice but to look at him. "Do you want it to happen?" he asks softly.

I stare up at him, my voice gone, my thoughts scrambling. His thumb skims back and forth beneath my chin, making me tremble, and his gaze settles on my lips. God, it's almost like he's moving in so he can kiss me. Do I actually want this? If this would've happened immediately after the encouraging pep talk from my friends last night, my body fueled by tequila, I would've said yes without hesitation.

But now it's the next day. I've had a little distance, some sleep, a minor hangover and a chance to worry nonstop the entire morning. With him standing right here, right now, staring at me, touching me, those dark, all-knowing eyes boring into me as if he can see my soul, I hesitate. He scares me.

So much.

"I know you want it. I can see it in your eyes," he murmurs, his mouth hovering above mine. I can feel his warm breath drift across my lips and I close my eyes, anticipating that first delicious contact of his mouth on mine.

"Sarah dear, are you still with—*oh*."

Jared's fingers drop from my chin and I turn away from him to find Marlo standing there, watching us with a shrewd gaze, her lips tilted up in the barest smile. Did she see the way he touched me? How he was about to *kiss* me?

God, I hope not.

Leave it to my boss to quickly regain her composure and act like she hasn't seen a thing. "Mr. Gaines," Marlo says warmly as she comes closer to us. "So good to have you back in the store yet again." Oooh, she said that last bit on purpose. Probably wants to know what he's up to, considering how often he keeps coming by.

"Sarah was showing me your newest line," he says, his voice as smooth as ever.

"You like it? We all think it's absolutely adorable," Marlo says, clasping her hands together.

"Adorable is one way to put it." His tone is teasing, and I wonder what his expression looks like.

I wouldn't know, considering at this particular moment, I can't face him.

"Are you going to pick something up for one of your lady friends?" Marlo asks innocently.

Ha, one of his lady friends. Let's see how he answers that.

"As a matter of fact, yes. I do need to pick up something for one of my...lady friends." He chuckles, his gaze flashing toward me for the briefest moment. "Such a quaint way to phrase it, Marlo."

"We are always searching for fun ways to describe what we sell and who we sell it to, Mr. Gaines." She points to the table. "Which piece do you like in particular?"

"All of it," he says without hesitation. He's not looking at me any longer. He is one hundred percent focused on Marlo, and she is one hundred percent focused on him.

I take a step back, wondering if I should hightail my butt out of here.

Of course, I don't move.

"Which bra style do you prefer?" Marlo asks. "The full or the quarter cup?"

"Quarter cup, please." He smiles, and it's almost like I can see the image inside his brain. "Thirty-four C." And that scene in his brain is of me, standing in this very same spot wearing that bra, my breasts threatening to spill out.

Lord, let me just dissolve into tiny little pieces where no one can ever see me again.

"Thong or brief?"

"Brief. Size small." Hmm. I figured he'd go for the thong.

"And what about the teddy? It is *such* an exquisite piece, though I must admit, it's rather expensive." She laughs, and he joins in. "Look at me. I shouldn't try to discourage you, should I?"

"It wouldn't work anyway." His laughter dies and he is all business. "I definitely want the teddy. Size small." He sends me another quick look, his smile sly, his eyes twinkling, and I bite my lower lip.

He's buying over six hundred and fifty dollars worth of

stuff. Stuff that is beautiful, don't get me wrong, and I would take all of it if I could, but I shouldn't let him keep buying me gifts.

Yet he's so hard to resist...

"Do you mind taking care of Mr. Gaines' transaction, Sarah?" Marlo asks me, her right hand full of the lingerie Jared wants.

For me.

"Of course. Right this way, sir." I offer her a bright smile and head for the sales desk, sensing when Jared falls into step right behind me. I put a little extra swing in my hips so I can give him a show, and I hope like hell he appreciates it.

I ring up his purchase, swallowing hard before I tell him the total. He doesn't so much as bat an eyelash as he reaches for his wallet, extracts his credit card and hands it to me. I take the credit card and push it into the card reader, tapping my fingernails against the edge of the counter. "Would you like me to wrap this?"

"Please. I'm sure she'll appreciate the gift."

I'm annoyed at the idea of having to wrap my very own present.

"Very well." I snip off the price from the tags, then fold up each item, wrapping each of them in a single piece of white tissue. I put together one of our gift boxes, then set the items inside, careful to not look at him as I go about my business.

Dude. You have to admit this is super weird, right? Or am I the only one thinking this?

"Do you have a card I can write her a note on?" he asks, and I nod, handing him one of our blank cards and an accompanying envelope.

He writes a message on the card while I pull his credit card out of the reader and print out the receipt for him to sign. We go about our business normally, like we do this sort of thing every single day, and truthfully, I do. He's here often enough that I'm sure it feels like habit for him too.

We are ridiculous.

I pull out one of our bags and shake it open, then slide the wrapped box inside. I hand him his receipt, then the bag. "Hope you enjoy."

My cheeks go hot the second the words leave me. I said that automatically, without thought. And by the look on his face, I'm sure he's eating this up.

"I plan on it. Eventually." He nods once in my direction, his fingers making contact with mine when he takes the bag from me. More electricity shoots up my arm, and I wonder what might happen if he actually touched me in a sexual manner.

I'd probably die.

"Have a good afternoon, Miss Harrison," he murmurs, his gaze sweeping over me one more time.

"You as well, Mr. Gaines," I call after him as he strides through the store.

I watch him exit through the doors, sagging against the counter the moment he's gone. I'm not sure if I can continue this façade much longer. We are playing a game and I'm fairly certain...

I will lose.

ELEVEN

JARED

I RECEIVE the call within minutes of my leaving Bliss Lingerie. I'm on such a high from speaking with Sarah, from actually touching her, even for the briefest moment, that I don't bother to check who's calling when my phone starts ringing. I answer with a cheerful hello, which is not like me whatsoever. First, I rarely answer my phone unless I'm expecting someone specifically. Second, I am never cheerful.

The pause on the other end of the call tells me I've momentarily stunned whoever it is.

"Jared? Is that you?"

Shit. It's my brother.

"Yes, it's me," I say, my voice gruff, my insides twisting with regret. The high from being with Sarah comes crashing down all around me.

"Oh. Hey." Kevin laughs, the sound faint. "For a minute there I thought I called the wrong number."

"No, it's me." I chuckle, but it sounds forced, so I go silent.

I've been avoiding him, and his calls have increased in

frequency because he knows what I'm doing. God knows what Candice told him after our meeting. That I planned on not attending his engagement party? You'd think he'd understand, but blood should probably come before ex-fiancées, so there's that.

"It's been a while, right? I've called a few times, but I never heard back from you," Kevin says, his voice pleasant. Like it doesn't bother him that I don't want to chat.

"Been really busy at work." My usual response sounds like a weak excuse.

"Right. Called you at the office too, but you never returned those calls either. Maybe Denise isn't giving you your messages." He pauses. "Makes me think you might be ignoring me."

"Ignore you? Not at all." More forced chuckling. He must know I'm full of shit. "What's going on with you, Kev? Life treating you well?"

"It's been treating me very well, and that's the reason I've been trying to get a hold of you. Though I think Candice told you what's up. About the engagement party? I asked Rachelle to marry me," Kevin says, sounding proud.

I have to give it to my brother. He graduated high school, went away to college and never came back. Thought he wanted to be a doctor, changed his mind in the middle of college and ended up going to law school. Now he works for a medical malpractice firm, and our father couldn't be prouder.

"I did hear, yes. Candice stopped by the office a few days ago to let me know," I tell him, wishing my voice didn't have such a forced quality to it. "Congratulations. I'm sure you and Rachelle are very happy."

"We are. Though I must admit, I'd be even happier if you said you could make it to our engagement party," he says, and the sincerity I hear in his words makes me feel especially bad that I'm going to turn him down.

I can't go. I don't want to face Evelyn. Or her entire family. Or mine, for that matter. I may be a successful businessman, but my personal relationships are in the damn toilet. Most of the time, it doesn't bother me.

But moments like this, interactions become awkward. Uncomfortable. Usually phone calls are avoided so I don't have to deal with it, but I let my guard down, and now look at me. Having stilted conversation with my only brother and pretending to be happy for him when all I can think is he's making the biggest mistake of his life.

Marriage is bullshit. Look at our parents. We lost our mother too soon, and our father was absolutely devastated. Destroyed. It was so hard, watching him live through that. Watching our mother suffer with cancer wasn't a cakewalk either. I was a selfish teenager who wasn't ever around so I wouldn't have to see her slowly wither away.

And after she passed, I avoided my father so I wouldn't have to see him cry. See the confusion on Kevin's face, see the sadness on Candice's.

Love is no guarantee that you'll be happy. Life comes along and kicks you right in the ass when you least expect it. I'd rather be alone than put my heart on the line, only to watch it get broken into a million pieces.

Fuck that.

Kevin doesn't really want me there at his celebration. He just thinks he does because it's the right thing to do. He'll realize soon enough not having me around is preferable to me having hostile interactions with Evelyn and her family.

"Just say you'll come to the party. It's not this weekend, it's the next one, in San Francisco. I've sent the invite to your email, but I'll text it to you too. It would mean a lot to me and Rachelle if you'd be there. Plus, I'd like to discuss a few things with you that I don't want to do over the phone. I'd rather talk to you about it when we're face to face," Kevin explains, sounding like the mature adult that he's become.

"I'll need to check my calendar, but I think I can be there," I say as I make my way to my car. I will really need to check my calendar, but I don't schedule too much over the weekend, and it's not like I currently have a social life. Lately I've become a hermit. There aren't any women I want to take to one of the many social functions I'm constantly invited to, so I end up staying in the office working late, or I'm at home.

Besides, the only woman who interests me is Sarah. Not that she'd go with me...anywhere. I send her gifts and she doesn't respond. I call her and she acts like she wants to hang up on me. I show up at Bliss and she barely looks at me, then sends me those sultry glances from beneath her lashes that set me on fucking fire. And next thing I know I'm spending over six hundred dollars on lingerie for a woman who I can almost guarantee won't show me what she looks like in any of the shit I buy her.

When it comes to Sarah, it's like I can't help myself. She makes me feel like an addict.

"We hope you'll be there. It would mean everything to us to have everyone from our families with us at the party," Kevin says. "Just let me know if you can make it and if you'll bring a date, okay? Rachelle's been on my case lately, something about needing exact numbers for the catering company or whatever."

My brother laughs. I do too. We make idle chitchat, I

promise to get back to him as soon as possible, and then I end the call.

Yeah. Not going. I hate that I'll disappoint him.

But I won't have to see his face or hear the sadness—or anger—in his voice when he realizes I'm not going to show up, so I'll be fine.

Really, I will.

TWELVE

SARAH

I COME home to find a plain brown box already on my front doorstep, waiting for me. Assuming no one's home, I grab it and hurry into the house, lock the door behind me and practically start sprinting to the kitchen so I can open the box and find out what he wrote on that card.

I already know what I'm getting. The real mystery is in the note.

"Wow, you have another package?"

Stopping in my tracks, I turn to find Andie curled up in the corner of the couch. In the dark. I reach over and switch on the lamp on a nearby end table, and the room immediately fills with light.

And I can immediately tell she's been crying.

Forgetting all about the package, I drop it onto the coffee table and collapse onto the couch right next to my little sister. "What's wrong?"

"Nothing." She sniffs. Hiccups. Wipes at her face to get rid of the teary evidence but doesn't do a very good job of it. "Everything," she says with a little laugh, right before she starts to sob.

I pull her into my arms and hold her close, rubbing her back as she cries into my shoulder. I don't say anything, don't ask any questions, just let her get it all out. I've discovered it's better that way. Asking her what's wrong before she's willing to tell me usually ends up with her flouncing off to her bedroom and slamming the door.

And me never finding out what the problem was in the first place.

Dealing with teenagers is delicate stuff. So I keep on holding her, letting her tears soak into my shirt, until finally she shifts away from me, reaching for the box of Kleenex on the end table closest to her so she can wipe her eyes and blow her nose.

"Feel better?" I ask, tilting my head as I contemplate her.

"Sort of. I guess." She shrugs, wadding up the Kleenex and tossing it onto the coffee table. I'll end up picking up that tissue later, I just know it. Andie and Brent are both slobs. "I hate boys."

Ah. Boy problems. I should've known. "What do you mean?"

"I thought I was over Brenden, you know?" Brenden is her ex. They were off and on throughout their freshman year and into their sophomore one before they finally broke up a couple of months ago, right after winter break. "But I just heard Bella is going to ask him to the Sadie's dance, and I don't know." Her face crumples and tears spring to her eyes. "Maybe I'm not over him at all."

Bella is more an acquaintance than a friend, but I'm sure this still hurts. Obviously, considering how much she's cried in front of me. I pull her into my arms once again, but we keep it brief since she pulls away and sits up straight before I say a word. And I was about to say words like *he's not worth your tears.* Or *forget that asshole, you broke up with him for a reason.*

But I say none of that. I can't. Teenage love is powerful stuff. I remember how I felt about my high school crushes and boyfriends. It was all-consuming, all the time. Shoot, I last had a boyfriend when I was in high school. Once we graduated, he broke up with me in the middle of summer, then hightailed it out of here to go away to college. Haven't heard from him since.

Haven't had a chance to try my hand at a serious relationship since then either. How pitiful is that? Oh, I've dated here and there. Did some steady dating with a couple of guys over the years, but nothing for long.

In the last few years, Andie has had longer relationships than I have.

"What do you think I should do?" Andie asks once she's got the weeping under control. "Should I tell him how I feel?"

"Well, how do you feel about him?" I ask.

"I don't know." She shrugs again. "I totally hate hearing he might go with Bella to that dance."

"So she hasn't asked him yet."

Andie slowly shakes her head.

"Who told you she's going to ask Brenden?"

She launches into a "she said" and "she heard" type of story that has me sighing by the time she's finished explaining herself.

"I say wait and see," I suggest. "Maybe Bella will ask him to the dance, maybe she won't. Is there a boy you're interested in asking to Sadie's?" The Sadie Hawkins dance is the one time of year the girl has to ask the boy. When I was a teen, the possibility both gave me courage and scared me to the death.

"Maybe." Andie draws the word out, her eyes beginning to sparkle. "If I ask someone else, maybe that'll make Brenden want me back!"

I was trying to distract her from Brenden with another guy, not suggest she use the other guy to make Brenden jealous. I'm about to explain myself when she leaps to her feet and darts to off toward her room, patting me on top of my head like I'm a pet dog as she passes by me.

Sigh. Teenagers.

Deciding that I've waited this long, I may as well wait a little longer. I go to my room and change my clothes. Start a load of laundry. Go to the kitchen and check out the prospects for dinner. Decide I'm going to fix myself a sandwich since we don't have much in the fridge.

Only after I've made the sandwich, poured myself a glass of lemonade and tore into the bag of barbecue kettle chips do I finally go to the living room and grab the box from Jared Gaines. Take a pair of scissors from the knife block and cut the tape open. Inside is the very box I wrapped at work earlier, and I take it out to find the card at the bottom.

I pull the card out of the tiny envelope and hold my breath as I read it.

When I look at the stars, I'll think of you.
JG

OH SHIT. He just got romantic on me.

Of course, he's also referring to the fact that the lingerie he sent is covered in stars, and he's hoping that the next time he sees those stars, I'll be the one wearing them. And that's not particularly romantic, right? More like it's just lustful wishing on his part.

Sighing, I shake my head. I don't know what to do about this. I'm tired of asking my friends. They're probably just as tired of hearing me complain about him and my wishy-washy ways. I'm turning into that woman who protests too much—I gripe about how awful he is, yet I won't tell him to leave me alone.

Clearly, I make no sense. My feelings toward him make no sense.

So if I'm this confused, if I'm this distressed about the situation, then I should end it. Just—cut him off. Tell him I'm not interested, he needs to stop, we need to pretend we've never had these conversations, and that he's never given me these gifts. I should probably return those shoes too, as much as it might pain me to do so.

We can do that, right? Forget what happened these last few days? Yeah, I doubt it, which is fine.

Really.

As I eat my dinner, my imagination starts to get away from me. I can picture myself now, marching into his office, tossing the boxes of lingerie onto his desk and demanding that he stop. Letting him know that he's crossed a line that we can never go back to, and that our professional relation-ship is finished.

He can find someone else to help him at Bliss. My tenure as Jared Gaines' personal shopper is...

Over.

THIRTEEN

JARED

"MR. GAINES, you have an unscheduled visitor who would like to speak with you."

Irritation fills me at the hushed, slightly panicked sound of Denise's voice. My assistant is tough. That's the reason why I hired her in the first place. She never lets anyone get past her desk if she doesn't know them or if they don't have an appointment. She's strict to the point that I expect her to crack someone's knuckles with a metal ruler—hell, sometimes I'm afraid she'll do something like that to *me*. So who the hell is trying to see me unannounced at—I check the time—just past eight thirty in the morning?

"Who is it?" My voice is brusque as I tap out a quick text to Candice. We're supposed to meet for lunch at one, but I'm cancelling on her since I have a conference call scheduled at the same time and I need to prepare for it. My sister will be disappointed, but she'll survive. I'm sure there's some sort of charity luncheon scheduled today that she can attend instead.

"The young woman insists she knows you." Denise

lowers her voice until it's the barest whisper. "Says she works at...Bliss Lingerie?"

The hairs on the back of my neck stand on end and I know without Denise having to say another word that it's Sarah Harrison. She must've received her latest gift.

"Send her in," I say gruffly.

There's the briefest moment of silence before Denise rushes on. "Are you—Mr. Gaines, are you *sure?*"

The shock in her voice is undeniable. I'm not one to see unexpected visitors. Drop-ins rarely get past the security desk—or Denise's desk—with the exception of Candice.

"Positive. Send her in." I end the call and rise to my feet, straightening my jacket, smoothing my fingers along my gray silk tie. I had a secret feeling I'd hear from Sarah today, but I assumed she'd call or possibly even text with her thanks, not that I have her personal number. Unfortunately.

It is, after all, the polite thing for her to say thank you, what with me sending her such extravagant gifts. Not that they're the most *tasteful* of gifts, considering I hardly know her. Yet I'm sending her underwear. Shoes. Flowers.

More underwear.

But I couldn't resist. The more I think about her, the more I wanted to keep sending her things, especially when she doesn't respond. She's so intriguing. Such a mystery. And a feisty little thing. What does it take to make a woman like her finally give in and acknowledge my generosity?

Finally I must've hit her breaking point.

I can't stop thinking about our near kiss at Bliss yesterday. When she was showing me the Celestial Collection, something flickered in her eyes. A hint of—wanting. Desire. A feeling that I've experienced for her as well. That I've been feeling every single time I so much as catch a glimpse of her. Or even think of her.

I almost kissed her yesterday, before Marlo interrupted us. I would've done it too. Kissed her right there in the middle of the store. I was that taken with her.

Still am, if I'm being truthful.

The door opens and Sarah enters my office, clad in a black pantsuit that fits her to perfection. She's wearing a crisp white button-down shirt beneath the single-buttoned jacket, her thick, dark hair pulled into a low ponytail. On her way to work, I assume, my gaze landing on her lips—they're shiny with pink gloss. Tempting me as usual. Of course, those sexy shoes are on her feet—the shoes I bought her. My cock jerks beneath my fly, letting me know he's extremely pleased to see her.

"Mr. Gaines." She comes to a stop, like she doesn't want to get any closer to me, and that's when I realize she's clutching a black box in her hand. Wait, she's clutching *two* boxes.

Shit. Is she here to *return* my gifts?

"Miss Harrison." My voice is gravelly, and upon clearing my throat, I stand up straighter and walk around my desk so I'm in front of it and cross my arms. "Definitely not used to seeing you in my office."

She glances around the room, her eyes widening as she takes it all in. It's impressive, I know it is, just by its sheer size, and considering I spent a fortune on one of the best interior designers in the area, it better be.

Though Candice believes it plain. And maybe she's right. There's not much warmth in the room. Not any personal photos or favorite pieces of art. Everything's harsh lines and abstract paintings. Clean white and sharp silver and the blackest of black.

Sort of like a mental institution?

Sarah's gaze finally returns to mine, her expression vaguely—disgusted? "I received my package yesterday."

Guess she's not going to beat around the bush. "You did?"

"Yes, of course I did. I can't accept it. I can't accept any of the lingerie." She approaches my desk, her gaze jerking away from mine as she stops right next to where I'm standing and drops the boxes on my desk with a loud thump.

Before I can say a word, she's moved away from me, hands resting on her hips, her gaze roaming around the room once more. Like she can barely stand to look at me. "I thought I would return the items to you personally so you can make sure and send it to another one of your—mistresses. I don't think I'm up for the job, Mr. Gaines. No matter how tempting it may be."

The last sentence is spoken sarcastically, I know it is, but I can't help but wonder if I do tempt her. At least a little bit?

"You think I'm going to send the gifts intended for you to someone else? Really?"

"Isn't that what you normally do?" she asks, her eyes wide, lips parted, looking like a sweet little innocent girl.

She's goading me on purpose. To annoy me. And it's working.

Irritation sparks my blood and I press my lips together for a moment, so I don't say something rude. "I'm not going to send those items to anyone else."

Her head jerks, her gaze meeting mine. She appears confused.

"I want you to keep those gifts. All of them," I admit gruffly.

"I can't."

"Why not? You're already wearing the shoes," I point out. "What's a couple pieces of lingerie going to hurt?"

We stare at each other quietly and I lean against my desk, my arms still crossed in front of my chest as I wait for her answer. Sarah would never make a good poker player. About a thousand different emotions flit across her pretty face until one finally settles in.

And I'm thinking it appears to be good old-fashioned rage.

"What you're saying is that you want me to keep the assless panties so I can wear them for someone else then?" Her voice is extra sharp.

Most women would be thrilled to receive presents from me. They'd ask when we could next meet so they could model everything I gave them. For my eyes only.

Of course, this one isn't thrilled. She doesn't want to model the bras and panties I sent her. More like she looks ready to grab both boxes and hurl them at my head.

Blinking, I realize she asked me a question. "What did you say?"

"You heard me!" She points at my chest. "You're telling me you'll be fine with me wearing all of this sexy stuff for someone else?"

"Absolutely not," I huff, sounding like an old man. Shit, I sound like my father. That sucks.

"Then just take it." She shoves the boxes across the desk, closer to where I stand. "Take it all back to Bliss. I'll personally complete the return for you."

"I don't want to return any of it."

Her hands clutch into little fists, and for a quick moment, I'm worried she might pummel me to death. "You're still trying to—*proposition* me with all of this stuff?"

"Take the message behind the gifts as you will, Miss

Harrison," I say defiantly. I'm being a rude asshole. I don't know why. Maybe it's because she acts like she doesn't care about who I am or what I do.

"Oh my *God*." Her fingers curl and uncurl, and she takes a step toward me, her blue eyes blazing with uncontained anger. "At first I thought you sent me the lingerie by mistake. Then when you sent the shoes, and then the flowers? I figured you were purposely trying to proposition me."

She's not wrong.

"And yes, I shouldn't have kept the shoes. But I keep wearing them because I love them so much," she admits, dipping her head so I can't look in her eyes.

"I'm glad you like them," I say softly, causing her to look up at me, confusion written all over her face.

Sarah's not used to hearing me be so—nice to her.

"I thought." She hesitates and looks away again, staring at that horrible abstract painting I've now come to call *A Study in Beige,* thanks to Candice. "I thought maybe I'd take you up on your proposition. My friends suggested I should."

I love her friends.

"They told me I should have a—fling with you. A brief affair, because that's all you ever want, right?" Her head is still averted, and I stare at her profile with longing.

She is beautiful. And smart. And so terribly, terribly young. If she were to have an affair with me, I would probably chew her up and spit her out, and most likely break her heart.

"But then." She turns to face me once more, her eyes blazing, her mouth drawn into a narrow line. "*Then* I realized you're sending me indecent lingerie and sexy shoes because you think that's all it will take for me to fall into bed with you."

"We don't always have to use a bed," I suggest, my voice

quiet, my gaze locked on hers. We could do it against a wall. On the floor. In my shower. On my couch.

On this very desk I'm leaning against.

Her mouth falls open in shock and her cheeks get pink. She's gorgeous when she's angry. Maybe that's why I antagonize her so much. I like to ruffle her feathers. Most of the time, she's so calm, so quiet, yet when I get around her, snap at her or make a demand, her eyes blaze with anger, and just like that, my body reacts.

No other woman tests my control like this one.

"Well, Miss Harrison?" I taunt when she hasn't said anything. "Do you have anything else to say? Do you still want to return your gifts to me?"

"You're insane," she bites out.

"Nothing I haven't been told before."

She rolls her eyes, sassy as hell. "I don't want the lingerie."

"That's unfortunate." I'd love to see her wear it, though I'd love to strip her out of it more. This idea conjures up all sorts of images, every one of them involving Sarah naked. In my bed. Beneath me. On top of me. Our mouths fused. My hands...everywhere.

She remains quiet, staring at me, and I wonder why she just doesn't storm out of here screaming she never wants to see me again.

But she doesn't do that. Which makes me curious.

"My special little gifts seem to work on everyone else," I say just to bait her.

"Then they were idiots." She takes a few steps toward me, and I can smell her sweet, intoxicating scent. The tension rises, swirling between us, and I wonder if she can feel it.

She has to feel it.

"Why the sudden change? Yesterday at Bliss, you were almost—sweet." She glares and I continue. "Now my gifts really offend you?" I ask, my voice gruff. Having her so close makes me feel...itchy. I flex my fingers, tempted to touch her.

But I don't.

"The more you talk, the more they *totally* offend me. And I'm sure I'm not the first woman you've upset with your poor gift choices. I mean, seriously, how much lingerie does a man need to buy?"

"A man who has plenty of women he sees and who likes to give them presents."

"You're a pig."

Her insult means nothing. I've been called worse. But there's something inherently sexy about Sarah Harrison when she's so thoroughly pissed off. "You really believe so?"

She nods, her ponytail swishing. I want to grab hold of it. Give her silky, thick hair a firm tug. Bring her close and shut her up with my mouth. Even when she's angry—hell, especially when she's angry—I find her completely irresistible.

"You will *never* be able to keep a woman interested in you if you constantly insult her by treating her like a..." Her voice drifts and she throws her hands up into the air, like she's at a loss for words.

"Like a what?" I ask when she doesn't finish her sentence.

"Like a common whore." She lifts her chin, defiant.

"You think I'm treating you like a common whore?" I'm truly horrified at the thought.

"Um, yes. I do." The sarcasm in her voice is evident.

"All you had to say if you didn't like it is, 'I appreciate the gifts, but no thank you,'" I tell her.

She snorts. "I appreciate the gifts, Mr. Gaines, but *no* thank you." With that, she kicks off the Louboutins I gave her, sending them skittering across the floor before she turns and starts toward the door.

Panic races through me. She could walk out that door and I'd never see her again. I could go to Bliss and Marlo might turn me away. Or worse, tell me that Sarah can no longer assist me and offer up someone else.

I need to do something. Say something.

Fast.

"Would you like to accompany me next weekend?" I call after her. It's the first thing that comes to mind.

Sarah freezes, her back still to me. "What did you say?"

Shit. I can't believe I just asked her that. *Let her go. Let her leave. Stop shopping at Bliss and end this right now.*

I'm contradicting myself in my own thoughts. Clearly, I'm screwed.

"I asked, would you like to accompany me out of town next weekend?"

"Where?" She glances over her shoulder, our gazes meeting. Holding.

She's intrigued.

I can tell.

"It's a family gathering, of sorts." I hesitate. What I'm suggesting is fucking crazy. She'll really think I'm insane for even asking. "My brother is celebrating his recent engagement."

"A party?" She turns to face me once more, hands on her hips. She's a tiny little thing without the heels. "An *engagement* party?"

"Yes." I haven't been able to get Kevin's call out of my head. I even had a dream last night that I went to the party —and that I was actually married to Evelyn. We had matching rings on our fingers, and I remember the ball of dread that burned in the pit of my stomach as we milled about like a supposed happy couple. How I was filled with the urge to get Kevin alone and confess I was absolutely miserable, and I needed him to help me get out of this sham of a marriage.

I woke up bathed in sweat and grateful it was all a dream. Or a nightmare.

However you want to view it.

"And you want me to go with you. To this party, where your entire family will be. As your *date*." She's watching me like I've got bugs crawling all over my skin.

"His beautiful future bride Rachelle insisted I make an appearance." Well, that's a lie. "And he really wants me there." There's some truth. "They want both families there to help celebrate the merger."

Well, Kevin didn't actually call it a *merger,* but that's what it feels like.

"Merger?" Sarah asks incredulously. "That sounds horrible."

Shit. I can't admit that was my word choice. "That's what he called it."

"Ugh." She rolls her eyes. "He sounds worse than you."

I don't take it as an insult.

"Where's this party at anyway?" Sarah asks.

"Well." I rub my jaw, hoping like hell she doesn't turn me down after this. "It's in San Francisco."

Her mouth pops open. Damn, she's cute when she does that. "You want me to go to a family engagement party with you in San Francisco."

"Yes." I nod. Why is she so surprised? The city isn't that far.

Sarah's eyes go a little wider, but otherwise, she seems calm. "You don't mind bringing me around your family?"

"Not at all," I reassure her truthfully.

"What are you going to tell them?"

I frown. "What do you mean?"

"When you introduce me to good ol' Mom and Dad, to your brother, to whatever other siblings you have, Aunt May and Uncle Ben, how are you going to introduce me to them?" I do get her Spider-Man reference, which I wholly appreciate. "What are you going to call me?"

I contemplate her, crossing my arms once more. Seems she's making this more difficult than it needs to be. And I don't even bother telling her that my mother died years ago. I'll let her in on that later, if necessary. Right now, that's none of her business. "My date?"

"Okay. This is weird." Her cheeks go pink. She's adorable. And simple. That's not an insult either. There's something so—intriguing about this woman. Sarah can maintain an air of mystery, yet when it comes to her, what you see is what you get. I find that fascinating. When was the last time I had something simple in my life?

"It's as weird as you want to make it be." I send her a look. "And we don't need to make it that weird."

"This entire situation is weird!" She throws her arms up, like she's exasperated with me. She probably is. "Isn't this a serious family event?"

"I suppose." I shrug. It *is* a serious family event—that's why I want to bring Sarah. She's the perfect shield to protect me from the endless questioning from my father, my stepmother, Candice, Kevin. If I have a beautiful woman on my arm, Rachelle's family—especially my ex-fiancée—can't bother me.

"Yet you'll bring some random woman to your brother's engagement party?" She sounds incredulous.

"Trust me, Miss Harrison..." I lower my voice, my gaze lingering on her perfect, plump lips. "You are anything but random."

She stands a little straighter, her cheeks blazing red, but she doesn't say a word.

Unfortunately.

I do love it when she puts up at least a little bit of a fight.

"Let me be honest." I walk around the desk so I can settle into my chair. She stays put, clear across the room, but at least she's still looking at me and not making a mad dash for the door. "I'm not big on romance."

Another snort. "You don't say."

"I don't have to be. Women tend to just fall at my feet and do whatever I want, whenever I want it."

Her delicate brows shoot straight up. "Ego much?"

I ignore her little jabs. "They don't ever play hard to get."

"Really? Well, I'm pretty sure I do," she says with the faintest hint of triumph.

"Yes," I agree. "You do."

And that's what I like the most about her.

FOURTEEN

SARAH

THIS ENTIRE CONVERSATION IS SURREAL. I don't know what Mr. Gaines is wanting from me—well, yes, I do, he wants to take me to his brother's engagement party, which is kind of strange, don't you think?

I'm not sure if I can trust his motives. He's probably saying this so he can still land me in his bed. I mean, the man did send me skimpy lingerie as a gift.

Twice.

Not like that would be a hardship, finding myself in Jared Gaines' bed. I can only imagine how skilled he must be.

My entire body goes hot at the thought.

"You've played hard to get since the moment I've met you, and I must say, I never realized before just how much I love a challenge." He sends me a pointed look. "You, Miss Harrison, challenge me."

I huff out an irritated breath. "If we're really going to an engagement party together, maybe we should at least call each other by our first names on a regular basis?"

"All right...Sarah." A shiver moves through me at the

way he draws out my name, almost as if he's savoring it. "If anyone else spoke to me like you just did, I would've kicked them out of my office."

My stomach flips. "Really?"

He nods, his gaze roaming over me, making me warm. "No one speaks to me that way. Ever."

The stern warning behind his words makes my entire body quiver. "Are you looking for an apology?"

He smiles. Though it's not a real, full-blown smile. More like the faintest upward curve of his mouth, his eyes sparkling. My heart trips over itself seeing him like this. Like he's...happy? This is not the Mr. Gaines I deal with. Not even close. "I assume you won't give me one."

"You're right. Considering you've been blatantly propositioning me for the last week, I think you should be the one who apologizes."

Jared chuckles and the sound resonates within me. Oh, he has a nice laugh. He has a nice everything—except for that monster ego. "You'll go with me to Kevin and Rachelle's engagement party."

My mouth drops open. It's not like he's asking. More like he's *telling* me that he wants to take me.

"It's next weekend," he continues, repeating himself.

"Um..."

"In San Francisco."

"Uh..." Is he freaking for real right now?

"And from what I understand from the invitation my brother sent me, it seems they're celebrating the entire weekend," he adds.

Oh, *hell* no. "I don't thi—"

"Just say yes, Sarah." His voice is firm, like he refuses to let me argue.

I don't understand him. At all. "Why?"

He frowns. "Why what?"

"Why do you want to take *me* to this party?"

"We know each other," he says. I cough, trying to hide my snort of laughter. "Sort of." I roll my eyes in the most *come on* gesture of all gestures. "If we're being completely honest with each other, it's because I can trust that I'll take you to my brother's engagement party and you won't expect...compensation for your time."

"If you're hinting that I might ask you to pay me to go with you, you've lost your damn mind," I retort, highly annoyed and beyond offended. If he really thinks I want money in order to go with him to San Francisco, then he's freaking nuts.

Though really, why would I want to go? He makes me crazy.

With lust.

There goes that nagging little voice in my head that sounds like Caroline.

I don't like really like him.

Liar.

There's something so...curious as to why he would want me to go with him. He's a powerful man who acts like he's scared of nothing. Yet he acts almost intimidated about going to a family party to celebrate his brother's future.

It's weird.

"I would never suggest that I'd pay you." He sounds downright appalled, which is reassuring. "But considering it's a weekend trip, with a few activities planned through-out, I assume I'll need to provide you with certain—things." He shrugs those impossibly broad shoulders, drawing my attention to the charcoal gray suit he's wearing. The man dresses to perfection. I'm sure one of his suits costs more than our monthly mortgage.

"What sort of things?" I ask warily. The last thing I need is more gifts.

"Clothes. Jewelry. Whatever." He waves a hand, like it's no big deal, even though he said the word *jewelry*. That equals expensive in my mind. "You have to look the part."

"What part?" I can't believe I'm seriously contemplating this. Worse, I can't believe he's seriously suggesting it.

"As my girlfriend, of course."

Weirder still, I'm having a total déjà vu moment right now, but not for me. More like for...my friend Caroline. She did something like this with Alex, her boyfriend. Only he took her on a private jet to Paris.

Mr. Gaines is offering a weekend in San Francisco, which sounds pretty fantastic, I can't deny it, but do I really want to spend an entire weekend with this man? What if his family is exactly like him?

I shudder at the thought.

But a weekend getaway sort of sounds like a dream come true. When was the last time I did something just for me? Like take an entire weekend off and go out of town?

I can't even remember. I'm thinking I've *never* done something like this.

The office is still quiet, which I assume means he's waiting for me to say something. He is, after all, watching me expectantly, his brows lifted.

"So what you're telling me is that want me to be your, what—pretend girlfriend for the weekend?" I ask.

"Maybe." He hesitates, then shakes his head once. "Actually, that's *exactly* what I'm asking from you."

I can't help it, I burst out laughing. What he's saying, what he's asking me to do...it sounds straight out of a reality

TV show. Or a really bad movie on Lifetime. I'd say the Hallmark Channel, but those movies are squeaky clean and Mr. Lingerie Fetish over here is not what I'd call squeaky clean.

Not even close.

I notice quickly he's not laughing along with me, so I stop. "You're serious."

"Yes." He doesn't even crack a smile. "I am." He tilts his head to the side, his gaze contemplative. "How old are you anyway?"

"That right there." I point at him. "You're not allowed to do that."

He leans back in his chair, his brow furrowed. "Do what?"

"Ask me how old I am. That's kind of insulting."

"Only if you're pretending to be twenty when you're really thirty-five." He squints, like he's trying to read my mind. Or guess my age. "You tell me how old you are and I'll tell you how old I am."

Hmm. That sounds like a fair deal. "Fine." To draw out the moment I go to one of the chairs in front of his desk and sit, resting my hands in my lap. "I'm twenty-four. Almost twenty-five."

His gaze slides over me again, in that slow, leisurely way that makes me turn to mush inside. He's annoyingly sexy. "You're just a baby," he says. His voice is extra low, and I imagine what it would be like, to have him whisper those same words in my ear.

Now I'm trembling, damn it.

To hide my reaction, I lift my chin, trying my best to appear unruffled. "I'm very mature for my age." Ugh. Just saying that makes me sound like a total baby, even though it's true. I am very mature for my age. I've had a lot thrown on me since my parents died, and I can handle it all just fine.

"I'm sure you are." His placating tone is not helping matters and I glare at him. "Go ahead. Ask me how old I am."

"How old are you?"

"Thirty-four." He smiles again, though there's no teeth. Just that faint curve of his lush mouth again. It's powerful. Imagine what might happen if he flashed his teeth at me? Might drop to the floor in excitement. "See? A baby compared to me."

Ten years older. Why do I find that kind of sexy? Okay, fine. I find it really sexy, which maybe I should be worried about. Like, do I have a daddy complex?

But seriously, all the guys I know around my age are still so immature. A lot of them love to party. Most of them have no idea what they want to do with their life. Not that I have any room to judge.

This man, though. He has a successful career and more money than God. He knows exactly what he wants.

And for some strange reason, I think he wants...

Me?

"Will our age difference be a problem?" he asks when I still haven't said anything.

"No." I shake my head, trying for confident. "Not at all."

"So you'll accompany me next weekend."

"Yes." The word pops out of my mouth before I can stop myself.

What the hell did I just agree to?

Jared grabs his phone, frowning at the screen as he brings up his calendar. "Can I take you shopping tomorrow evening?"

I wrinkle my nose and he glances up, catching my displeased look. "I'm not sure."

"Why? Do you have plans?" He appears genuinely perplexed.

"Maybe." Not really. I think I was going to help Andie with her English project, but that's it.

He growls irritably and glances over his calendar once more. "I need a firm answer, Miss Harrison."

"How about Friday night? The stores are open later, so that would work out better." Our gazes clash once again. He's scowling at me. "And it's Sarah."

"Sarah." He growls my name, sounding irritable. "You work Friday?"

"Till six."

"I'll pick you up at six-ten."

"At Bliss?" I frown. "Maybe..."

"Maybe what?"

I don't want my co-workers to see me meeting with Mr. Gaines—I mean Jared. That's just weird. And I don't feel like explaining to them what we're doing. "You should pick me up somewhere else. Or we could meet."

"Where?"

"In front of the coffee shop down the street from Bliss." Now he's frowning. "Sweet Dreams. Ever heard of it?" Everyone who lives on the Monterey Peninsula has heard of Sweet Dreams. Stella's family has owned that place for generations. It's practically an institution in Carmel-by-the-Sea.

"Noted." He taps at his phone screen and then pushes it away from him. "Ten minutes after six at the coffee shop down the street from Bliss. Correct?"

"Sounds good." I rise to my feet, trying to fight the shock that wants to take over me. I can't believe I'm agreeing to this. Earlier he said that he's intrigued by me, and I have to admit...

I'm just as intrigued by him. And the reason why he wants me to go to this party with him.

He's a mystery I want to figure out.

"Any store preferences? Designers you like?" he asks.

"No, not really." I'm not about to make some gauche recommendation and have him potentially make fun of me. He's the one with sophisticated taste. I'd be perfectly content going to Target and picking out a few things.

"I'll text you Friday morning and confirm our arrangements."

Oh Lord. He just made it sound like we're having a business meeting. "How can you text me if you don't have my number?"

Without hesitation, he demands, "Give me your number."

I automatically do as he commands, as if I have no control over myself while he grabs his phone, and within seconds, I have a text from Jared Gaines' phone number that says this:

Can't wait to see you Friday.

I ignore the warm feeling that emanates through me at his words. He's just trying to charm me. And though I hate to admit this...

It's working.

"Are you trying to flirt with me?" I ask, calling him out.

He shrugs one shoulder. "Perhaps. You should get used to it. You are my pretend girlfriend, after all."

"True," I say, my voice faint.

"Put your shoes back on, Sarah," he quietly commands, and I do as he says, walking across the room where I kicked them and slipping one on, then the other, my mind a whirl the entire time.

How am I supposed to do this? Pretend to be his girlfriend and convince his family we're legit? How can I actually go with him to San Francisco for the entire weekend and play like we're a real couple? This is pure insanity.

Back out, the logical voice inside my head tells me. *Back out, walk out and never talk to this asshole again.*

"See you Friday night," I find myself telling him as I start to leave his office.

Ugh. For once, I'm not listening to that logical voice inside my head.

"Don't forget your gifts," he reminds me.

I go completely still and turn to face him yet again. "You really want me to keep everything?"

"Yes," he says, his voice low, his eyes dark. "After all, you were the one I had in mind when I purchased it all."

Oh. *Oh.* My entire body goes liquid and I rush toward his desk, grab the boxes and scurry out of his office before I do something stupid.

Like jump him.

FIFTEEN

"I'VE DONE SOMETHING CRAZY," I tell Eleanor once we're settled at our table, giant salads perched in front of us. We've grown closer the last year or so, and we try to meet for lunch at least once every other week, sometimes even once a week, since the hair salon she works at is just down the way from Bliss.

Eleanor's fork pauses in her salad bowl, her gaze lifting to meet mine. "Uh oh. What happened?"

I take a bite of my salad. Sip from my glass of lemonade. Do my best to avoid the curious stare aimed straight at me. "I don't know where to start," I finally admit.

Her expression is bright. She's the sunniest, sweetest girl I know, I swear. Wholesome California girl looks, with the long blonde hair and bright blue eyes. She has tan skin and a curvy figure and sometimes I'm incredibly envious of her beauty. But that usually passes considering she's just so incredibly nice. "How about at the beginning?"

Setting my fork down, I clear my throat and ask, "Remember how my client sent me the lingerie set?"

"Of course," she immediately answers, taking a sip of

her hibiscus berry tea. It's such a bright pink, I wonder if it could glow in the dark. "I forgot to check in and ask if you ever went to his office."

"Oh, I went to his office all right," I say, the sarcasm extra thick. "Eventually. After he gave me a pair of Louboutins, a giant bouquet of flowers and another lingerie set."

"Wait, he gave you more stuff? Oh my God." Her gaze drops to my feet. "Are you wearing the Louboutins right now?"

My face goes hot. I have a sneaking suspicion I will wear these shoes until they fall off my feet. "Yeah."

"You actually kept them? Wow. I mean, I guess I can't blame you. They're freaking Louboutins, after all. I bet those cost at least six hundred bucks." Her gaze meets mine once again. "So I assume he's the reason you did something crazy."

I nod, forking up another mouthful of salad, though it feels like it's expanding in my mouth as I chew. So gross.

"Maybe you'll think it's straight out of one of those romance novels you're always reading," I tell her. Eleanor is our sweet romantic of the group. Maybe she'll think it's a good idea, what I agreed to do with Jared.

"Please don't tell me you had sex with him on his desk, wearing the Louboutins and nothing else." Eleanor looks vaguely horrified. "What did Caroline and Stella call it? Hate-fucking?"

"No!" I look around, making sure no one heard what just came out of Eleanor's mouth, but no one is paying us any attention. I lower my voice. "Of course not."

"Oh, thank God." Eleanor rests her hand against her chest, her shoulders sagging with relief. "I was afraid that's what you were going to tell me."

"I wouldn't have sex with him on his desk at his office." Wearing nothing but the Louboutins. Hmmm...

"You're imagining it right now, aren't you?" Eleanor asks, sounding horrified.

"No, of course not." I wave a hand, dismissing her worry.

"Huh. Sure." She points her fork at me. "Now tell me what happened before I stab you."

Dang, she's extremely hostile. "I agreed to go with him to his brother's engagement party in San Francisco next weekend."

Her fork clatters against the edge of the bowl when she drops it, making an extra loud sound. Not that anyone notices in the noisy café we're eating at. "He asked you on an out of town *date* and you said *yes?*"

She sounds shocked. I suppose she should be. I'm still a little in shock as well. "Not really a *date* date, if you know what I mean. More like he asked me to accompany him to be his...fake date. We don't really like each other, remember?" Because of course nothing real could happen between us.

"You don't *like* each other? Keep convincing yourself of that," she says drolly.

"Whatever. He asked me to accompany him to San Francisco, and I said yes." Which means I'm insane. I'm going out of town with a man I don't know very well and I'm going to pretend to be interested in him.

The more I think about it, the more I realize I should probably back out.

"Well, this sounds vaguely familiar," she says, referring to Caroline. "Do tell."

I launch into the entire story. How I went to his office

and he was borderline rude, and I tried to return the gifts he sent to me, but he refused to take them.

The knowing look Eleanor sends my way is so annoying.

I don't leave out a single detail. The argument and him making me feel like a cheap whore for a hot minute and me trying to leave his office when he asked me to accompany him.

"That's how he phrased it," I explain to Eleanor, who's pretty much finished off her salad, what with how long I've taken to tell my tale. "He asked me to *accompany* him."

"For the entire weekend?"

"Yes. Crazy, right?" I stare at my salad, my appetite having long left me. "I'm not even hungry."

"Too nervous about your weekend in San Francisco with your mystery man?"

"He isn't that much of a mystery. I know exactly who he is."

Sort of.

"Well, I don't." Eleanor whips out her phone. "Give me his name."

"Jared Gaines," I tell her, pushing the salad bowl away from me and leaning back against the seat. I feel shaky. A little on edge. I believe I'm still in shock that I told Jared I would go with him. "He's taking me shopping Friday after work."

"Taking you shopping?" Eleanor's brows shoot up as she tap, tap, taps away at her phone screen. "For what?"

"Clothes. Jewels. Furs." I laugh when she sends me a weird look at my mentioning furs. "Mostly clothes. He says I have to look a certain way to play the part."

"Didn't Caroline's boyfriend do that? Took her to

Chanel and bought her a bunch of stuff?" Eleanor's focus remains on her phone as she scrolls.

"I don't want him to take me to Chanel." We don't even have a Chanel store nearby. Unfortunately.

"You already got a pair of Louboutins out of this, so you're fine." Eleanor's brows lift as she reads. Oh no. I hope it isn't anything awful.

"What did you discover?"

"Well, he's definitely a ladies' man." She turns the phone my way, and the screen is filled with images of Jared with a woman by his side. There's a different woman in every single photo.

Every. Single. One.

"I already knew that," I mutter, which I did, but to actually see the evidence is...painful. It would be even more painful to admit my feelings, so I keep my mouth shut.

"Huh." She resumes looking at her phone, tapping away, scrolling, scrolling. "All of these photos are from a year ago."

"Really?" Hmm. That's strange.

"Wait, here's one from about six months ago—oh." Eleanor's face falls. "It's a photo of him and his sister at some holiday fundraiser."

I wave my fingers at her. "Let me see it."

She hands me her phone and my gaze first drinks in Jared, who looks gorgeous in a black suit, his expression impassive as he poses for the camera. His arm is around a tiny woman's waist, and she has long dark hair and a giant smile curving her lips. I can see the family resemblance, in her eyes and face shape, though of course her features are feminine while his are wholly masculine. She's short, like me, and her form-fitting dress is covered in green sequins, which I sort of love. Her full lips are slicked a deep ruby red and she's wearing giant earrings that look like emeralds. Like real ones. The Christmas spirit is strong in this one.

"She looks sweet," I say as I study the photo.

"She looks like a Christmas tree," Eleanor says, making me laugh.

I read the caption. Candice Gaines is her name. Hmm. I'm sure I'll meet her in San Francisco, though from what I can tell, I think she lives here. So why is the party in San Francisco? Does Kevin live there? Or his future wife and her family? Guess I'll find out soon enough.

After handing Eleanor's phone back to her, she keeps scrolling, her frown deepening the more she investigates. "Yeah. That's the last photo of him out on the social circuit around here. Back in late November." Her gaze lifts to mine, her eyebrows raised. "Interesting."

"It means nothing."

"How long has he been shopping with you at Bliss?" she asks.

Oh. Um. Around six months.

"I have nothing to do with him not going out with other women," I tell Eleanor.

"Don't be so sure about that. I think you might." I want to argue, but she keeps talking. "I'm currently checking out his LinkedIn profile. You do know he's kind of a big deal, right? Like he's worth a lot of money?"

I assumed he was, but I don't know much about his career. Like, at all. "What exactly does he do?"

"He acquires failing companies and absorbs them into the family business." She sends me a pointed look. "In other words, he makes a shit ton of money."

"Eleanor," I quietly chastise. She doesn't curse much, so to hear her say shit is a little shocking.

"What? I'm just being honest." She shrugs. "He's also

one of those types who negotiates acquisitions of major companies, and he does it all over the western United States. Like, this guy is serious business."

"Wow." I mean, I knew he was powerful, but I didn't realize the extent of his business acumen.

"He's also thirty-three." Another pointed look from Eleanor.

"Thirty-four," I correct.

"That means he's *ten years* older than you."

"I know." I hesitate, then decide to go for it. "Do you think I might have a daddy complex?"

"I thought you didn't like him." The knowing smile twisting Eleanor's lips is slightly annoying.

"I don't. Not really. I mean, I'm—attracted to him. Somewhat." Those last three words were choked out. It was hard, admitting that.

"Oh, so now we're being a little more honest, huh?" She's still smirking.

"Come on, just answer my question. Do you think I have some sort of weird daddy issue, since I lost mine so many years ago?" God, it pains me to just think I might feel that way. I miss my father. I loved my dad so much, he was so good to us.

He'll be a hard act to follow, I know that.

"What are you talking about?" Eleanor shakes her head. "If this guy was, like, twenty-five years older than you, then I'd say you have a total daddy complex, but ten years difference? Big deal."

Relief washes over me and I sag in my chair. "Okay, cool. You made me feel a lot better."

"I'd say you're focusing on the wrong things." She shakes her head and sets her phone on the table. "This guy is big time. Sounds like his family is too. Specifically, his father. Like they're important, influential people within the community. Well, more his father than him, but you know what I mean." She grabs her phone again. I swear it's practically glued to the palm of her hand. "And his sister is kind of a big deal too. She does a lot of charity work in the area. It's like everyone knows who Candice Gaines is."

"How do you know?"

"I'm Googling her right now, and all of her images are at various fundraisers, smiling with a bunch of people that I actually recognize." Eleanor sends me a pointed look.

The salon she works at is pretty high class. As in, lots of people from the area get their hair done there. Specifically, women who live in Carmel with plenty of money.

"What about his mom?" I desperately want to find out more about the woman who raised him. What's she like? Was she a total witch while he was growing up, and that's why he's so awful to me every time I talk to him?

Eleanor changes up her Google search. "His father recently remarried, so they must've divorced. Oh, wait. His mother—she died. Fifteen years ago. Cancer." The sad look on my friend's face says it all.

She's thinking of my parents.

"Oh." So Jared and I have something in common. We've lost our parents. What a sad thing to share. "That's terrible."

"Yeah." Eleanor offers me a grim smile. "Maybe that's something the two of you could—bond over?"

"I don't plan on doing much bonding with Jared," I say, shaking my head. "He's the last person I want to bond with."

"Ooo-kaay." She draws the word out, and I know she doesn't believe me.

Which is fine, because I don't believe myself. I'm full of crap.

We remain quiet for at least a minute—the longest minute of my life—and finally Eleanor says something.

"Then why are you doing this? Going with him to San Francisco for the weekend as his fake date? It makes no sense, especially if you don't like him. Which, honestly, I don't believe, but whatever. Oh, wait. He's not..." Her voice drifts and her expression slowly turns horrified. "He's not paying you, is he? Are you that hard up for money?"

"I already told you he's not paying me, I promise." I shake my head. "This isn't a *Pretty Woman* situation."

Eleanor makes a face. "I always hated that movie."

I'm seriously shocked. "Are you for real right now?"

"Most definitely. They always try to describe it as the most romantic movie of all time, but please. She was a Hollywood hooker with a heart of gold and blah, blah, blah. And she changes the stiff, wealthy businessman with her magic hoo-ha."

"Her magic hoo-ha?" I ask slowly, my lips twitching with the need to laugh.

"Yes! One minute he's telling her don't kiss me, and the next they're making out and he's buying her jewelry and flying her...to San Francisco." Eleanor pauses. "And he's in...mergers and acquisitions." Her smile grows to huge proportions, and she starts to yell, "You are *totally* in a *Pretty Woman* situation!"

"I am not!" I yell back at her, horrified at the thought. "No way. I'm not the hooker with a heart of gold with a magical hoo-ha."

"Thank goodness," Eleanor mutters, and we both start laughing.

SIXTEEN

JARED

"SO. ARE THE RUMORS TRUE?"

Candice's cheerful voice is going to give me a headache. "Is what true?"

"I hear Kevin convinced you to come to the party."

My baby sister's smug tone is almost more than I can bear first thing on a Thursday morning. I've only been in the office for a few minutes and I just started scrolling through my inbox when the phone rang.

My gaze snags on *A Study in Beige* and I turn my back to the horrible painting. "I responded to his invitation, yes," I tell her, purposely keeping my answer short.

"And you included a plus one." She doesn't even bother to hold back. "Who are you bringing? You have to tell me, Jared."

"Did Kevin put you up to this phone call?" I ask wearily, scrubbing a hand across my face. I'm on my cell phone, and I answered it when I saw her name flash on the screen, despite my reluctance. I figured if I avoided Candice's calls this morning, she'd march down to my office and bust through the double doors like last time.

Better to just get this over with and carry on with my day.

"No. He wouldn't do that. I mean, he texted me a few minutes ago to let me know you were coming, and he mentioned you were bringing a date. So I had to call you directly and find out who this mystery woman is." Candice hesitates for only a moment. My sister is a talker. This is why she's so good at charity work. She can convince anyone to hand over a huge donation after non-stop chatting them up for fifteen minutes.

"Trust me, you don't know her."

"Let me be the judge of that—give me her name. You haven't been seen out with anyone in months, you know. This is kind of a big deal," she says, her voice teasing.

"Her name is Sarah."

"Sarah Morton?"

"No."

"Sarah Hernandez."

"Nope."

"Oh! Sarah Von Wagner? Please tell me it's not her. She's the absolute *worst,*" Candice bemoans.

"It's definitely not Sarah Von Wagner." What a pretentious name. Not that it's her fault, since she was born with it. But the Von Wagners are a pretentious lot, so...

"Are you really saying I don't know this woman?"

"That's what I've been trying to tell you since you've started guessing."

"What's her last name?"

"Harrison."

"Sarah Harrison." She's quiet for a moment, and I hope she isn't trying to Google Sarah on her iPad. "I don't know her."

That's what I've been telling her. "Are you looking her up?"

"Of course I am," she retorts. "But I don't see much information about her."

"She's not part of our social circle." I almost don't want to admit where she works. If I did, Candice would probably go there.

There's no probably about it. She would definitely go there.

"Plus, she's a very private person," I tack on, hoping my sister gets the hint.

"Uh huh." I can tell Candice isn't listening to me. She makes a low humming noise before saying, "Interesting. Her address is listed in Seaside."

"You can actually see her address?" God, the internet is a wonderful and terrible thing all at once.

"No, not her full address, though I could find that out if I wanted to. Would only cost me a total of nineteen-ninety-five through one of those spy sites," Candice says with a laugh.

"Please don't spy on her." A notification pings on my phone and I pull it away from my face to see I have a voice-mail. I didn't even hear the other line ring. "I have to go. There's a call I need to take." Not really, but I do want to know who the voicemail is from. And I do need to actually work, unlike my sister. "Talk to you later."

"Wait! I want to meet Sarah Harrison before we go to San Francisco! Reassure her that the Gaines family isn't so bad."

"No." I'm shaking my head even though she can't see me. "No way. I don't want you two to meet."

"And why the hell not?"

My sister doesn't say bad words very often, so I know I just pissed her off.

Worse? I can't come up with a good enough reason for them not to meet.

When I remain quiet for longer than approximately thirty seconds, Candice just dives in. "Let's go to dinner together this weekend. The three of us. Hopefully I won't be crashing a romantic weekend or whatever."

I almost laugh. "I don't know if we'll have time for dinner."

"Why? You have an action planned weekend or what...*oh*." She swallows so hard I hear it. "Please don't tell me what your weekend plans are. I don't think I want to know."

She's implying that Sarah and I are going to have a sex-filled weekend. And that's the furthest thing from the truth. Unfortunately. "I will spare you the details."

"Thank God. Though I mean it, Jared. I would love to meet her, especially if you have serious feelings for her. You wouldn't take just any woman to Kevin's engagement party, am I right?"

She has no idea.

"Well, I am taking her shopping tomorrow evening..." I let my voice drift, knowing this will tempt Candice.

"Ooooh, really? Shopping? For what?"

"She needs a dress for the party, and she wanted me to go with her so I can give her my opinion while she tries stuff on." That sounds good, right? Something a couple who's steadily dating might actually do.

"I love shopping! You know this! I want to come." Her voice turns a little whiny, and I know I'm going to give in. My sister is a difficult person to resist. "Please, please, Jar? I want to get to know this girl. And I feel like you're holding something back. Are you two serious? Is she your actual girl-friend? How long have you been seeing each other?"

"Calm down, Jesus," I mutter, feeling like a shit for talking to her that way. But hey, she calms down, so it worked. "We haven't been dating that long, so no. It's not serious. And I don't want you making a big deal about us, or ask her a bunch of questions, okay? You need to be relaxed when you meet her. Like this is no big deal."

"I know how to be relaxed."

No, she really doesn't, but that's fine. This is actually perfect. Maybe Candice can be the distraction Sarah and I need when we go shopping tomorrow. A buffer of sorts, so we don't have awkward silences or spiteful arguments.

Having my sister around will also prevent me from dragging Sarah into a dressing room and stripping her naked. Right?

Right.

SEVENTEEN

SARAH

Plans have changed.

THE MOMENT MY PHONE DINGS, I grab it, frowning when I see the unfamiliar number and the text. But then I remember that I didn't put Jared's name into my phone yet and this is from him.

My breaths become short and I tell myself to not freak out. Has he changed his mind? Is he trying to back out of our plan? Did he realize I'm the last person he wants to take to his brother's engagement party and he's canceling on me?

I should be glad he's canceling on me. The more I think about it, the more I wonder what the hell am I doing, going to San Francisco with this man. I threw all my old cautious ways right out the window and decided to be daring for once in my life.

Totally unlike me.

Realizing I need to answer him, I send a quick text.

What do you mean the plans have changed?

He doesn't respond for an agonizing four minutes. Like, what in the world is he doing during those four minutes? I don't understand.

Finally, I receive a text.

My sister is going to accompany us during our shopping excursion tomorrow evening. Candice has fantastic taste, and rest assured she'll help you find clothing appropriate for next weekend's trip.

I stare at his response, frowning. Is he so used to composing business emails regarding all of the corporations he's going to take over that he ends up texting so formally?

You sound like an old man.
  Well, I am ten years older than you.

Touché, Mr. Gaines.

Are we grabbing dinner too?
  Would you like to?

I may as well get a meal out of this.

Usually I'm starving when I get off work.

Then I'll make sure and feed you before we shop. Though it'll have to be somewhere fast.

I love me some Taco Bell.

I wait for his response, laughing when I get it.

:(

I decide to offer another suggestion.

McDonald's?

I'd rather not.

Now it's my turn to send the sad face.

You're no fun.

You should already know this by now, Miss Harrison.

I laugh some more. I don't know if he's being funny on purpose, but he's cracking me up.

Are we back to formality, Mr. Gaines?
Indeed we are.

Should I say what I really think?
Yeah, I'm going for it.

I think you get off on us talking like this.
Like it gives you some sort of perverted
thrill or something.

He doesn't respond for six minutes this time, and I'm disappointed. Did I drive him away? Maybe I said too much.

But finally, I receive a text.

You really believe that?

I respond immediately.

Yes. I do.

Then I add a winky face emoji to keep the moment light.

Perhaps you're right. Good night, Miss Harrison. See you tomorrow.

MARLO LET me clock out ten minutes early as I asked, and so I take those extra minutes and get ready for my shopping date with Jared and his sister. Hopefully it won't be weird with her being there. It has the potential to get awkward, because things are pretty damn awkward between the two of us already.

Hopefully his sister isn't too observant. If that's the case, she'll see right through our charade.

I grab my bag from the back room and lock myself away in one of the store's dressing rooms, staring at my reflection in the full-length mirror. My makeup still looks pretty good, I just need to touch up my lipstick and that's it, so I do. My hair is decent. Curling it the night before usually means it stays curled throughout the next day.

I'm wearing my usual Bliss uniform of black—pants today—and a thin, black short-sleeved sweater that has such a flattering fit. My boobs look pretty great, if I do say so myself, as they're nicely supported by my brand-new Celestial bra.

Yes. I'm wearing one of the bras he gave me. Screw it, they belong to me, so I may as well embrace my new gifts.

I'm keeping the same clothes on, because I don't want to look like I'm trying too hard. This is just a casual shopping excursion, as he called it via text last night. I look professional, put together, and hopefully his sister will like me.

But what if she hates me? What if I hate her? I stare at my reflection, nibbling off my freshly applied lipstick, immediately annoyed with myself. How can she hate me? I'm a decent person. It's her brother who's the asshole.

I wonder if she knows that. I wonder if I have to be the one to break it to her.

Deciding I look as good as it's going to get, I leave Bliss, shouting goodbye to Marlo and Bethany as I walk out the door. They have no idea what I'm doing tonight, because no way am I going to tell them. I was able to get next Friday and Saturday off—I rarely work on Sundays—so I'm set on leaving for the weekend. Marlo didn't even ask what I'm up to.

And I didn't volunteer any information to her either.

I walk down the street, enjoying the warm spring evening, the scent of the ocean carrying on the breeze, along with all of the delicious smells emanating from the restaurants I pass by. I stop in front of the Sweet Dreams bakery and settle my butt on one of the black iron chairs that sit out front, a sigh escaping me. I've been on my feet all day, and while the Louboutins are somewhat comfortable, my feet still ache.

Checking my phone, I see I still have four minutes before Jared has to officially show up and I decide to text Caroline real quick and give her the deets.

Not that I'm trying to brag or anything. More like I need her to know in case anything terrible happens to me. It's like when you go on a date with some strange dude that you met on a dating app. We all keep each other informed when we do stuff like that. I don't want to end up the victim of the next Craigslist Killer.

Not that we're going out with guys we find on Craigslist, but you know what I mean.

Hey! I'm going shopping with Jared Gaines and his sister tonight. Text me on occasion and check up on me, okay?

My phone buzzes within a minute of me sending that text. Now that's how someone is supposed to respond.

Shopping? Oooh, exciting. Too bad he can't take you to a Chanel or Dior boutique.

Rub it in, I respond, adding a smiling faced emoji.

A man clears his throat and I glance up to find Jared standing by the table, towering over me. I forgot how tall he is. How commanding his presence is, too. "Oh. Hi. Where's your sister?" I glance around, expecting to see the adorable woman from the photo Eleanor showed me, but it looks like good ol' Mr. Gaines showed up alone.

"We need to talk. About that." He sits in the chair opposite me, his penetrating gaze meeting mine when I turn to face him. "She thinks we're together."

Duh, I want to tell him, but I don't. "I would assume so."

"That means we need to act like we're—together." His expression is pained. Is it really that bad, pretending to like me? I thought he already did.

Well. Like and attraction can be two different things.

"That's not a problem," I say, keeping my voice calm, my expression solemn. I'm curious, though. Why all the pretending? Why does he feel the need to put on a show for his family? I'd love to know.

I doubt he'd tell me.

"Okay. Good." He nods. Exhales loudly, like he's been holding his breath. Was he worried? That's kind of mind blowing. I didn't think much bothered him, with the exception of me. "She's going to meet us here, but she's always late, so it'll be a while."

Glancing behind me through the window, I see Stella's dad working the counter inside Sweet Dreams. The man is here day and night. Does he ever rest? "We could eat here, if you want."

"I've had their coffee. And their pretzels, though it's been years," Jared admits.

Oh look, he's a normal human after all. "Aren't they delicious?"

"I remember them being pretty good," he says.

"The sandwiches are delicious too. If you, um, like sandwiches. Though maybe you want something fancier, I'm not sure." I sound like a babbling idiot, which is normal behavior when I'm around this man.

He points an index finger at me. "You can't do that in front of my sister."

"What am I doing?" I sort of realize what it is, but I'd appreciate it if he described it to me in full detail.

"Talking to me like you don't know me. We know each other." He sends me a pointed look. "We're supposed to be dating, remember?"

"But we've only ever interacted at Bliss and that's it," I remind him. "I don't really *know* you."

"From those brief interactions, what have you discovered about me?" He crosses his arms, contemplating me.

Talk about putting me on the spot. Taking a deep breath, I decide to be one hundred percent truthful. "I know you're extremely demanding. Exact. Particular. You're always punctual and mostly professional." He's said and done a few things that are the opposite of professional, and he knows it.

He says nothing. Just studies me with that piercing gaze.

"You're generous." Very, what with the gifts he's sent me. "Focused. You, um, go after what you want."

"That's true," he says, nodding slowly. "What you said is all true."

"You can also be very...unforgiving. You have a low tolerance for bullshit," I say in conclusion. I don't bother telling him he's attractive and sexy. He's probably been told that countless times by his many mistresses.

"You're right." He tilts his head, contemplating me. "Can I tell you what I've learned about you?"

"Please. Go ahead." I brace myself for insults.

"You're very...thorough. You're also thoughtful. Observant. Confident. Smart. A little stubborn." He hesitates, his voice shifting lower. "You're also extremely beautiful."

My entire body goes hot at his words, at the way he's looking at me. He's offered me nothing but compliments. And yes, that means I'm taking the stubborn remark as a positive. His words leave me completely shook, but in a good way.

A very good way.

The breeze ruffles his hair, causing a thick lock to fall across his forehead and giving him a boyish appeal. Though there's nothing boyish about Jared Gaines, at this moment, I could almost consider him...

Adorable.

Shit. This means I am in big trouble.

"There. That's it," he says, his voice soft. "That's how you need to look at me."

"How am I looking at you?" I sound horrified, and I clamp my lips shut. Sit up a little straighter.

"Like you adore me," he admits, his lips curling in the faintest smile. "Keep that up and Candice will totally—"

"Candice will totally what?"

We both glance up at the sweet, feminine voice that just interrupted our conversation. Of course, it's Candice Gaines standing in front of us, her expression questioning, her big smile putting me at immediate ease.

"I was telling Sarah how much I think you two are going to get along," he says smoothly, sending me a pointed glance before he stands and presses a kiss to his sister's cheek. "You're late."

"As usual." She's not fazed by his annoyance. I already like this chick. "You should know this by now. And you." She turns her attention to me, her sparkling eyes seeming to eat me up, though not in a bad way. The curiosity is practically causing her body to vibrate. "You must be Sarah."

I rise to my feet only to find myself tugged into her arms. She gives me a big hug, her bold floral scent enveloping me, making my nose itch. I glance over at Jared, who's watching us, a helpless expression on his face, and I realize quick that he's...

Terrified.

Interesting.

His family seems to make him extremely nervous.

Resolve steels my spine and I vow right then to make

our phony relationship as believable as I possibly can. Why I want to help this man, I'm not sure, but that quick flash of vulnerability in his gaze just hooked me.

"It's so nice to meet you," I tell his sister, pulling away and offering her a warm smile. "Jared has already told me so much about you."

"Really? Well, then you're at an advantage. He hasn't told me nearly enough about you." Candice reaches out and playfully shoves at Jared's shoulder, but he barely moves.

Did I mention that he's tall and broad and he towers over both of us? Because he does.

"Ha, ha. Very funny, Candice." Jared shifts so he's standing by my side, sneaking his arm around my waist and pulling me so close, I'm plastered against him. He's warm and solid and he smells so delicious, I'm thankful he has such a tight grip on me. My entire body starts to tingle from his nearness.

It's not a hardship to pretend to be attracted to this guy.

That's because I actually *am* attracted to him. No faking necessary.

Candice is smiling at us as we stand there, and she clasps her hands together in front of her chest like a child. "Aren't you two the cutest? Oh my God, I love this."

My cheeks are warm at her making such a fuss over us, but Jared doesn't appear ruffled whatsoever. "Are you hungry?" he asks Candice.

"Always," she answers with a tiny laugh.

"Are you?" He gazes down at me, his fingers pressing into my side, and I nod. Nibble on my bottom lip for the quickest moment.

"Definitely," I answer, noting how throaty my voice sounds.

I think it's because he's touching me. Looking at me.

As if he actually likes me.

"Please tell me we're going to eat at Sweet Dreams," Candice says as she approaches the front window and presses her hands against the glass while peering inside. "I've always loved this place. I know the owner."

"You do? So do I! His daughter is one of my best friends," I tell her as I shift away from Jared and go stand next to her at the window.

"You know Stella?" Candice asks as she looks at me.

"Oh my God, you know her too? How crazy is this!" I need to calm down, but hey, Jared's sister and I have something in common. Mutual friends. I figured we moved in separate circles. His family is in the rich one and I'm in the poor one.

But Stella comes from a prominent family. They've lived in the Monterey area for generations, and Sweet Dreams is an institution. Her older brothers have carried on the legacy and have opened two restaurants in downtown Carmel, with plans to open a third on the Wharf in Monterey.

"Yes! We had dance together when we were kids. We were on the same competition team for a couple of years." Candice wiggles her hips, making me laugh. "I have the medals and incriminating photographs to prove it."

"Oh, I would love to see those someday. She's never mentioned being on a competitive dance team," I tell Candice as Jared leads us inside the bakery-slash-café. It's quiet, only a few tables are occupied, and there's no one in line at the counter. Sweet Dreams does most of its business in the morning, when there's a line out the door for their delicious coffee drinks and pastries.

Stella's dad Lorenzo comes from behind the counter to

greet me with open arms. I let him wrap me up in a hug, savoring the feeling, hoping I don't get choked up.

Lorenzo hugs always remind me of my dad and make me miss him.

"It's been too long, beautiful girl," Lorenzo murmurs close to my ear before he pulls me away from him. He keeps his hands wrapped around my upper arms so he can examine me. "You never come here anymore."

"I'm here all the time," I tell him with an eyeroll accompanied by a laugh. "It's Stella who usually helps me. You're always in the back, so I never get to see you."

"Tell her she needs to bring you to dinner at our house soon. We get together—"

"—every Sunday," I finish for him with a smile. "I remember."

I've been to my fair share of Ricci family dinners. They're always loud and boisterous, with Lorenzo yelling at his sons and the sons yelling back. Stella usually brings a few tagalongs looking forward to an authentic, home-cooked Italian meal, and her mom is always more than willing to feed us.

"You're too thin," she used to tell me when I was younger. "You need to eat more. Here." She'd shove a bowl of pasta at me, and I'd always take it.

The last few times I went to eat dinner there, though, she didn't remark on how I was too thin. I guess I've finally filled out enough for her approval.

"Do you remember me, Mr. Ricci?" Candice takes a step forward, bestowing Lorenzo with a megawatt smile. "My name is Candice Gaines. I used to dance with Stella at the Dance Studio."

"Of course, of course." He pulls her in for a quick hug,

beaming at her. "Aren't you still the cutest thing?" He glances over at Jared. "And who's this?"

"My brother, Jared. Sarah's new boyfriend!" Candice announces with glee.

Lorenzo's eyes narrow as he contemplates Jared. "New boyfriend, eh?" He's now looking over at me. "Is he doing right by you, Sarah?"

"Yes, of course he is!" I say too brightly, moving so I'm standing right next to Jared. I hook my arm through his, trying to appear united with Jared. "He's the greatest."

Jared makes a little growling noise low in his throat, and I take it as code for *shut the hell up.*

"Why hasn't Stella mentioned this boyfriend of yours to me before?" Lorenzo asks skeptically.

"We've only been dating for a short time," I tell Lorenzo, wanting to laugh at the scowl he sends in Jared's direction. I appreciate Lorenzo's overprotective father act, but I don't want him to blow our cover either.

"But don't they make the cutest couple?" Candice asks with a big romantic sigh.

"I suppose," Lorenzo says as he makes his way back behind the counter. "Now tell me what sandwich you each want, and I'll make it special. Even yours," he says directly to Jared.

It takes everything within me not to burst out laughing.

EIGHTEEN

JARED

THIS EVENING HAS the potential to become a nightmare of epic proportions. This means Sarah and I have to be extra careful.

Candice is her usual over-the-top self. She sucked right up to the old man who owns the Sweet Dreams Café and got herself a free sandwich out of it, including a cup of pasta salad and a drink. Sarah got a free meal as well, though she knows the man through one of her friends, so I don't have a problem with it.

That old man clearly has a problem with me, though. He regards me with immediate distrust, and no matter what I say or do, he shuts it down or throws subtle insults in my direction. I decide it's best to remain quiet instead. Don't want to disturb the old guy and make him think I'm up to no good.

We sit outside, Candice and Sarah chatting away while I eat my dinner—that I had to pay for, by the way. They're acting like they're long-lost best friends, and Sarah keeps sending me looks that clearly say *can you believe this?* and *wow I think she really likes me!*

At least, that's how I'm interpreting them.

I remain quiet throughout dinner, listening to their conversation. Really, what could I say? I should be glad they're getting along so well. But it's also risky, that they're acting this way so quickly. What if Candice reveals bits of information about me that I want no one else to know about? Or what if Sarah blows our cover and confesses that we're not really together? I'm not sure what Candice would do if she found out I lied to her about my and Sarah's so-called relationship.

Truthfully, I didn't even mean for her to get this involved. I should've never answered that damn phone call.

Once we finish dinner, we make our way to the very plaza where Sarah works. All the stores stay open later on Friday and Saturday nights, and it's busier than normal, thanks to the warmer weather and the slow trickling in of tourists.

"Maybe we should go in there," Candice says as we pass by the exterior of Bliss Lingerie. "Though maybe not. I don't want to go bra shopping with my brother. And it would probably make you guys uncomfortable, going into a lingerie shop so early on in your relationship?"

Sarah and I send each other a secret look, both of us smiling ever so faintly. My sister doesn't know the half of it.

"I don't need any new underwear," Sarah says, resting a reassuring hand on Candice's arm. "But I'm in desperate need of a new dress for your brother's party, and the stores close in ninety minutes."

Yeah, it's not suspicious that Sarah knows the exact time this place closes down. Though my sister doesn't even notice. She probably just thinks Sarah's a major shopper like her.

"I know just where to go," Candice says, leading her to the giant store at the back of the shopping plaza.

I follow them, wishing Candice hadn't come with us after all. I'd hoped to use this time to try to get to know Sarah a little better. To try to become more comfortable with her, so no one in my family would suspect us of not being a real couple when we go to Kevin and Rachelle's party.

Not that anyone is going to be paying any real attention to us. They're all going to be focused on the bride- and groom-to-be. If I'm lucky, we'll have to hang out at the party for only a couple of hours, and then we can hightail our asses out of there.

"This place has such great clothes," Candice tells Sarah as we wander inside a giant store. Music is playing in the background, people are milling about, and there are clothes everywhere.

I'm in for the long haul, I know it. And I'm not the most patient person. I can admit that it's one of my faults. Sitting around while watching women shop is not on my list of enjoyable things to do.

"Hey, Jared," my sister says.

I turn to find Candice and Sarah both watching me. "Yes?"

"You should sit right over there." Candice points to a bank of chairs near a doorway that leads, I assume, to the dressing rooms. "And wait for us while we find some outfits for Sarah. Then you'll be right by the dressing room so she can come out and show you."

"I get approval?" I raise my brows, my gaze going to Sarah.

"Sure," she says with a little shrug, looking away from me.

"Aw, look, you two are so shy with each other still! This is soooo cute." Candice waves a hand at me. "Go on. Give her a kiss and wish her luck. We'll be on the hunt for at least a half hour, maybe longer."

Give her a kiss? The panicked look Sarah and I send each other is almost comical, but I school my features into total neutrality, and she does the same. I take a step forward. So does Sarah. We step toward each other until we're close enough to touch and I reach out, gently grabbing hold of her wrist so I can hold her still for a quick kiss on the cheek.

"Make it look more believable than that," Sarah whispers, her wide-eyed gaze meeting mine.

Interesting. She wants me to kiss her again. Well, I aim to please. Cupping her face with both hands, I press a soft, lingering kiss on her plush, damp lips. The soft sound of surprise that emits from her at first contact does something to me. Twists my gut. Steals my breath.

I shouldn't do this. Sarah's not mine to do it with. This is all just playacting. We're putting on a show for my sister. That's it.

But I want more. I'm going to take more too.

Giving in to my urges, I lean in and kiss her again, my lips lingering this time, her mouth clinging to mine before I break the kiss first. "How was that?" I ask.

Sarah blinks up at me, her tongue sneaking out to lick her upper lip. I bite back the groan that wants to escape. "It was—it was good."

Her voice is shaky. I feel shaky.

"Let's go." Candice takes hold of Sarah's hand and starts leading her away. "Have fun waiting for us!"

I watch them leave, shoving my trembling hands into my pockets. My mouth still tingles from that deceptively simple kiss. Sarah glances over her shoulder at me as

Candice leads her away, her eyes extra wide, those lush lips parted.

Did she feel that? The electric current that seemed to spark between us at first touch? Or was it all just one-sided?

Taking my hand out of my pocket, I rub my thumb against the edge of my lips, my gaze locked on Sarah's backside.

This ought to be interesting.

NINETEEN

SARAH

"THIS IS HOPELESS." I stare at myself in the mirror, my expression nothing short of pure horror, because the dress I'm currently wearing is hideous. Like, beyond awful. "Do you really think I'm going to find something tonight? The store closes in less than thirty minutes."

My urgent tone borderlines on terrified. I need to keep it together. It's just a dress. I'll find one eventually. Maybe.

Maybe not.

"Shush." Candice is flipping through the handful of dresses one of the sales associates brought to us only a few moments ago. Most of them are florals, since for some reason I had my heart set on wearing a flowy, ethereal floral print dress.

Yeah. So far that hasn't worked out for me so well. For most of them, I'm too short. Even with the Louboutins giving me an extra five inches, a lot of the longer dresses still hit me at a weird spot, and it's not good.

Not at all.

"Are you really shushing me in the final minutes of this failure of a shopping trip?" I clamp my lips shut. I'm whining, and I don't mean to. Candice is doing her best with the situation at hand, and I can't blame her. She can't help it that my legs are unnaturally short and I'm hellbent on wearing a floral print.

It's also not her fault that all the flowery dresses in this store look like something from the couches our grandmas owned in the eighties.

"Calm down." Candice sets her hands on my shoulders, standing right behind me so our gazes meet in the mirror's reflection. "There's one more thing I want you to try on, but I have to sneak out and go grab it from the rack."

"It's not any one of those?" I wave a hand at the pile of dresses hanging on the various hooks.

"No." Candice slowly shakes her head. "And it looks nothing like any of the stuff you've tried on so far, but I want you to keep an open mind when you see it. Can you promise me you'll do that?"

"I don't really have a choice," I tell her, sinking my teeth into my lower lip. I give her a nod. "I trust you."

Candice straightens her shoulders and actually salutes me. "Aye aye, captain. I'll be right back."

She exits the dressing room and I slump against the wall, annoyed. Frustrated. My original idea isn't going as planned. I sort of blame Jared, which is ridiculous, but I can't help it. He should've never kissed me like he did before we started shopping. The simple kiss on my cheek? That had been enough to practically melt me into a puddle, but when Candice goaded him into actually kissing me on the lips?

His mouth on mine had rocked my world and rendered me stupid. His soft, damp lips. His fingers clasped around my wrist, his thumb stroking the sensitive skin there. And that wasn't even the most overwhelming part. He kissed me again, cupping my cheeks with his big hands, his mouth gentle. Lingering. I could taste him. Was ready to part my lips and let him really kiss me right when he ended it.

I walked away from him on wobbly legs and with a spinning head, Candice taking my hand and dragging me to the back of the store where all the dresses were. My brain was fuzzy when she asked me if I had anything in mind, and I said I wanted to wear a dress with flowers on it. She made it her mission to run all over that store and grab every floral dress or skirt she found in my size.

Maybe that wasn't so much of a good idea, and I can blame that decision on Jared's lips, so see how it became his fault?

My logic is, in a sense, completely illogical.

But it became too much, too fast, all those dresses Candice brought in for me to try on, especially when none of them were working. There was one I sort of liked. The length wasn't too bad, though it was navy with red trim, not a flower in sight. Cute enough.

But it wasn't bold or sexy. It definitely didn't make a statement. My heart was set on wearing something that would impress Jared and his whole damn family. I want to put the dress on and feel like a powerful woman who knows what she's doing.

So far, not one dress I've tried on makes me feel that way.

"Okay." Candice slips back into the dressing room clutching something black. God, boring, basic black. I'm already over it. "I can see your lip curling," she accuses, amusement tingeing her voice.

"I always wear black for—" I was going to say work, but I'm pretty sure Jared doesn't want her to know I'm just a measly sales associate at Bliss. Maybe? I'm still not sure.

Better to keep quiet than blab all my business. "—every social event I attend, I swear. I'm kind of sick of it."

Nice save. If I could pat myself on the back, I would.

"There's a reason we always wear black, right? It looks good on everyone. And this isn't your typical LBD."

I'm frowning. "LBD?"

Candice heaves a tired sigh, like I should know this. "Little black dress?"

"Oh." I nod. "Right."

"The best part? This isn't even a dress," she says with excitement. "And it comes in a petite size! Check it out."

She holds the hanger up and I take it in. It's a jumpsuit, all one piece. Strapless, with a giant bow at the waist on the left side, and a zipper in the back. It's simply cut, no embellishments beyond the bow.

"It looks..." I wrinkle my nose as my gaze meets Candice's. "A little boring?"

"Try it on." She sets the hanger on the closest hook and undoes the zipper on the dress I'm currently wearing. "And hurry. I think Jared is getting ready to leave."

"Seriously?" Oh, what an asshole. He'd actually leave me when he's the one who asked me to go shopping in the first place?

"He's bored out of his mind, and one of the associates said he actually fell asleep while he's been waiting for us. She said she even heard him snore." Candice laughs and I can't help it. So do I.

I hurriedly try on the strapless jumpsuit, getting rid of my bra so I can get the full effect. I'm so grateful for Candice when she zips up the back and adjusts the waist and legs so the fabric falls into place properly. I turn and look at myself in the mirror, sucking in a breath when I see the way this deceptively plain jumpsuit fits me.

"Wow," Candice says softly as she takes me in. "You look amazing."

"Do I really?" I turn this way and that, checking out the jumpsuit from every angle. I have no bra on, so it looks like my boobs are trying their best to make their escape, but otherwise, I do look pretty damn great, if I do say so myself.

And oh my God, it has pockets! I slip my hands into the pockets and strike a pose, smiling at myself in the mirror.

Okay. This is it. I could feel powerful in this. I'd keep the jewelry simple, and maybe try a bold lip. Deep red or bright pink.

"Yes. Get it girl." Candice nods, unable to contain the smile that stretches across her lips. "It fits you like...wow."

She's repeating herself. I take that as a good sign.

Bending my head, I grab hold of the tag dangling just below the bow and check the price. My eyes nearly bug out of my head when I see it. "It costs pretty wow too," I mutter sadly.

Three hundred and ninety dollars, if we're being specific. Talk about wow. Jared just dropped almost twice that on me a few nights ago alone. I really don't want to ask him to pay for it. I already feel like I owe him so much, when he's insisted that's not the case.

But there's no way I can afford this jumpsuit.

"Four hundred isn't so bad," says the woman who's never had to worry about money in her life.

"Sure," I say weakly. "Maybe I should swing by Target after this. See if they have something similar."

"Oh, you're just being silly." She tugs on my hand, smiling at me. "Let's go show Jared what you look like in this."

"Um..." I don't want to. What's the point? I'm not buying the jumpsuit anyway.

"Don't you chicken out on me now, Sarah. We're going out there." She pushes open the dressing room door and grabs my hand, pulling me along with her like I don't have a choice. And I guess I don't. Jared has waited for us for a long time, so I guess he deserves to see me in my outfit of choice.

Though it can't be my outfit of choice. I have no choice but to put it back. I can't afford it. And I'm not asking him to pay for it, either. I wonder if they have something similar on Amazon? Stella has Prime, I bet she'd order it for me...

"Oh, Jared," Candice calls as we draw closer to the open doorway. No one else is around. The store is mostly deserted, except for us and a few employees I see at the sales desk. Even the music has been shut off. I'm guessing they really want us to leave. "Are you ready to see Sarah?"

"Hell yes," he growls, and I press my lips together, wanting to laugh.

Why do I enjoy it so much when he's grouchy?

"Here she is." Candice moves out of the way and I exit the dressing room area, holding my arms out and doing a slow spin before I stop directly in front of him. "Well, what do you think?"

I'm filled with nervous anticipation as I stand before him, slipping my hands in the pockets, striking a pose similar to the one I made in front of the mirror. He leans back in the chair, contemplating me. His gaze is positively scorching as it drifts down the length of me, and my skin grows hot the longer he studies me.

"You're not wearing a bra," he finally says.

That would be the first thing he notices.

"I have a strapless one at home," I tell him, wishing I could reach over and kick him in the shins. The heels I have on are skinny enough; I could probably do some major damage if I aimed just right.

"Good. Wouldn't want you on such public display at a family function," he mutters, shaking his head like he's, oh, I don't know, *disappointed* in me?

What a prick.

"Quit criticizing her and tell her she looks beautiful," Candice practically hisses, glaring at him.

"I like it." He rises to his feet, hiding the sudden yawn behind his hand. "I say get it and let's go."

"But it's four hundred dollars," I blurt, unable to contain myself. His behavior tonight proves yet again what a total asshole he is. I shouldn't like this guy. At all. In fact, I should expose him for what he really is—a total fraud—and run out of here without ever looking back.

"That's not a problem," he says, his voice tight. "I'll take care of it."

I stare at him, words failing me. My chest is heaving, considering I'm out of breath with rage, and his gaze drops to my breasts, lingering there. A disgusted noise leaves me and I run away just as I envisioned, but instead of leaving the store, I head back to the dressing room, slamming the door behind me and collapsing against it. I close my eyes against the sudden swell of emotion that wants to sweep over me.

I'm this close to crying. And I don't cry. Not really. Assholes never make me cry, that's for sure.

So why is this stupid guy the exception?

A knock sounds at the door I'm pressed against, making me startle, and I'm about to tell Candice I'm fine when a man's voice speaks instead.

"Sarah." Jared hesitates only for a moment before he demands, "Let me in."

"No." I sound like a child.

The exasperated breath that escapes him is loud enough

for me to hear, and in reply I give him the finger. "You're being ridiculous," he says.

"Go away," I tell him, giving him the double finger now.

"I want to talk to you."

"I said go away, Jared."

He tries the handle and pushes the door open with ease, despite me pressing my full body weight against the wood. I stumble away from the door as he enters the tiny dressing room, shutting the door behind him. The space is so tiny, it's like he eats it all up with just his presence, and that irritates me beyond reason.

I glare at him the moment our gazes connect and move to the opposite corner of the too-small dressing room, creating as much space between us as I can.

"I'm sorry," he says, leaning against the door. He looks exhausted. His tie is long gone, and he's undone a couple of the top buttons on his shirt, giving me a tantalizing glimpse of the strong column of his throat. His jacket his rumpled and his trousers are wrinkled, and I like seeing him look a mess. Makes him less perfect.

Makes him more human.

"Did Candice put you up to this?" I don't buy his apology for a second.

He sighs. Runs a hand through his hair, turning it into a delicious mess. He blinks slowly as he contemplates me. "Maybe."

"Then your apology means nothing." I point at the door. "I'd like you to leave now."

"Sarah..." He shakes his head. "I didn't mean to hurt your feelings. I've been up since six a.m. and my patience has worn thin. I realize my reaction to your outfit wasn't the best."

"It was *terrible*," I tell him, crossing my arms. The position makes my boobs plump up above the front of the jump-suit, but you know what?

I don't really care. Let him look at them. Let him lust after me. I don't care. He's never going to get to touch them. Like, *ever*. "You're a terrible human being, Jared. Do you know how hard it was for us to find this one stupid jump-suit? How many dresses I tried on before we finally decided on this one? I'm doing this all for you, you know. I come out to show it to you, and it's as if you don't even care. You barely looked at me. And when you did, you only worried if my boobs are going to fall out."

"Are they going to fall out?" His gaze zeroes in on my chest once more, and I want to slap him. Or kiss him. Maybe grab hold of his cheeks and bring his face right into my cleavage. What would happen if I did that? Would he shove me away? Or tug the fabric down and run his lips all over my newly exposed skin...

OMG, I need to stop. Clearly, I have a problem.

"No, they won't. And I will make extra sure they won't fall out when you're introducing me to your parents, okay?" I turn away from him so I can't feel his gaze on my bare skin anymore. Glancing down at my chest, I can see that my skin has turned red.

Ugh. The man is infuriating.

"My parents..." His voice drifts and he clears his throat. Clears it again. "My mother. She, uh, she died."

Oh. That's right. His mother is gone. I knew this already. But I have to pretend like it's news to me. Slowly I turn to find him standing there with his hands in his pants' pockets, looking a little lost. A lot...sad.

It's in his eyes. They find mine and I can see so much emotion swirling there. Emotion I've never noticed before.

But then he blinks and it's gone and I take a step toward him, like I can't help myself.

"I'm sorry," I say solemnly.

He shrugs. "It happened a long time ago."

I work my jaw, ready to confess my sob story, but then it's his turn to shift away from me and I stare at his broad back as he tilts his head back and gazes up at the ceiling. "You have to understand, Sarah. Sometimes when I'm tired or feeling impatient I act like..."

"An asshole?" I supply for him.

Jared glances over his shoulder, giving me the faintest smile. "Yeah. That."

He remains quiet for a while and I'm ready to choke on the words I want to say to him, so I just let it all spill out. "If you want my help, then you need to treat me with respect at the very least, Jared. You keep acting like a total asshole all the time, and I don't want to have anything to do with you," I tell his broad back.

"Yeah. I get that." He drops his head, staring at the floor now, and he kicks at one of the discarded dresses lying on the floor. "That is hideous."

"I know." I wince when he kicks the dress again, feeling bad. When you work in retail, you've seen it all, and you're sympathetic to every other retail establishment you go into. Like this one.

He lifts his head, examining all of the dresses that remain in the room. And there are still a lot of them. "I hate every single dress I see in here."

"Thanks for your honesty," I say, heavy on the sarcasm.

"Hey, I don't want to lie." He turns so now he's fully facing me. "Was it Candice's idea? The flowers?"

"No, actually that was my idea. She's the one who brought me this." I pull my hand out of my pocket to indicate the jumpsuit I'm still wearing. "I think she made the right call."

"Definitely." He moves closer, so close I can feel him exhale when he breathes. "I really am sorry, Sarah. I didn't mean to hurt your feelings."

I lift my chin, my gaze meeting his. I can't tell him I forgive him. I'm not ready for that yet. "I accept your apology."

He extends his hand, like he wants me to shake it. "So we're good?"

"I suppose so." I let him take my hand and he pulls me into him, making me gasp. I reach out, bracing my hands flat on his solid wall of a chest, and just like that, my heart starts to race. "What are you doing?" I ask, my voice shaky.

"Checking to see just how indecent this jumpsuit is," he admits, his gaze directed down the front of my top.

I should be mad. I'm about to call him out for being a jerk yet again but then...

But then.

He touches me there, his index finger tracing the edge of the fabric, right across my chest, the top of my breasts. His barely there caress causes tingles to sweep all over my body, leaving me breathless. Making my heart beat uncontrollably.

"Maybe you can get away without wearing a bra," he tells me.

"Okay." I swallow hard, surprised I could choke that one word out.

"I can feel your heart racing," he whispers.

My lips part, but no words form. The man renders me stupid every chance he can get. One minute he makes me want to smack him, and the next I want to kiss him.

He makes no sense. Us together, we make no sense.

Jared hooks his finger, sinking it beneath the fabric, and I close my eyes, anticipation making my blood run hot. I lick my lips, waiting for the moment when he touches me with real purpose when suddenly there's a rapid knock on the door.

"Are you ready to make your purchase now, miss?"

We spring away from each other, my eyes popping open to find he has his back to me once more, and he's fumbling with one of the dresses on the hanger. Like he's trying to help me put this stuff away, I guess?

Silly man.

"Yes, I'm sorry," I call, swallowing hard. I wish I had something to drink. My mouth is suddenly so dry. "I'll be out in just a minute."

"Please don't take long. The registers will go offline in fifteen minutes."

"What the hell? I've never heard of such a thing," Jared growls once the sales associate walks away. He's facing me once more, giving up the pretense of trying to help hang up the dresses we're leaving behind.

I grab my bag and glance at my phone for the time. "It's nine-fifteen, so I'm guessing the system shuts down at nine-thirty?"

"Ridiculous," he mutters under his breath.

"Or they say that as an excuse to get us out of here," I say.

"That's more like it." He sends me one of those I-can't-read-him looks, reaching for the door handle. "I'll get out of here so you can get changed."

"Wait!" I practically scream before he opens the door. He turns to look at me, his brows lowered in question. "Um, could you help me?" I turn so my back is to him. "I need you to unzip this."

He says nothing. Not a word. He merely steps forward, his hand going to the spot directly between my shoulder blades. Slowly, he undoes the zipper, the fabric parting, revealing my bare back, maybe even the top of the panties I'm wearing.

The panties he bought for me.

"There," he says when he's done. He pauses for a moment, and then he asks, "Are you wearing the stars?"

Nodding, I remain where I'm at, my head bent, my stomach fluttering with nerves. He touches me there, his fingers drifting across the waistband of my panties for the quickest moment. "Too bad I have to go," he murmurs.

And with that, he leaves the dressing room.

TWENTY

THE WEEK FLIES BY, and the next thing I know, it's Friday afternoon and I'm waiting for Jared to pick me up at my house so we can finally head to San Francisco.

Yes, can you believe it? I'm letting him come to my house, but the only reason that's happening is because Brent is at work and Andie's at school. Neither of my annoying siblings are around to ask endless questions.

Well, my siblings aren't annoying, but the questions they'd ask Jared would be. And I can't deal with that right now. I'm already freaking out enough. I don't need Brent and Andie to make everything worse.

Glancing around, I take in the worn-out couch, the dated look of the room in general. Am I little embarrassed by the shabby condition of our house? Maybe. I've never seen Jared's giant mansion by the ocean, but I'm sure it's freaking amazing. I'd guess our house looks like a shack compared to his. But it's all ours and I can't imagine not living here, so it'll have to do. I'm not here to impress him.

Not really.

I packed for this weekend trip all week long, and it

stressed me the hell out. All I had on hand were duffel bags of various sizes, and I knew none of them would work. I had to borrow one of Stella's suitcases, a blush pink hard-cased number that rolls so smoothly I can tell she spent a lot of money on it. And since it was so large, I filled it with a variety of outfits, more than I would've brought if I were stuck with one of my bags. That made things easier, considering how unsure I was about what to bring. I don't know exactly what we're doing or what's been planned beyond the party.

I'm going into this trip mostly clueless, but so incredibly grateful I'll have at least one ally by my side.

That would be Candice.

We've kept in constant contact since our Friday night shopping date. More so than Jared and I have, which is kind of wild, though he warned me he'd be busy with work all week so he could take the extended weekend off.

Candice, on the other hand, has texted me every day and we chat nonstop. We even met for drinks Thursday night at a cute little bar in downtown Monterey, far from where my friends like to hang out.

It's not that I don't want Candice to meet my friends, it's just that...there would be so much to explain. Like how I work at Bliss, and my parents are gone and I'm raising my teenaged sister pretty much on my own, with my brother's help. That I'm not some spoiled rich girl like all of Jared's other women.

I am the furthest thing from that.

Plus, how do I introduce Candice to my friends? They all know about Jared, but the majority of them think he's some sort of twisted pervert with a panty fetish. I can't bring his little sister around and expect them to not ask any questions.

For now, I figured it was best to avoid them. Really, I'm avoiding everyone, and that's probably not a good thing, but I'll worry about that later.

We had the best time, Candice and I, drinking wine and eating happy hour appetizers for half price. She told me all sorts of stories about the family, about Jared specifically, and about their mother. How she left Candice a secret trust fund that ensured she would never want for anything for the rest of her life, and how Candice is trying her best to live up to her mother's legacy by giving so much of her time to charitable organizations.

"My mother died of breast cancer," Candice admitted near the end of the evening. "And I want so badly to help with the various breast cancer charities we have in the area. Do you know we have three? Three. And I can't make myself go to any of them." Her voice lowered, her eyes full of fear. "They scare me. Every single one of them. I'm scared I'll get it. And I'll end up dying young just like my mom."

Her confession had broken my heart, and all I could do was squeeze her hand in sympathy. I wanted to tell her about my parents, how devastated we were when we lost them, how angry Brent had become and my sister had been so young still, and so confused. It was a tough time, but I didn't share. I couldn't.

Sitting there, squeezing Candice's hand and murmuring words of comfort to her, I still felt like a liar.

I shove the memory from my brain and focus on the here and now, pacing the length of the living room as I wait for Jared to show up. I'm nervous. Scared out of my mind, actually. The party is tomorrow night, so I'm a little unsure as to why we need to get there this evening. Plus, I forgot to ask if Candice had an itinerary for the weekend, which was my bad.

Maybe I can text her. Yeah, that's a good idea. I grab my phone and I'm about to send her a quick text asking if there was a schedule, when there's a knock on my door.

My stomach twisting and my text forgotten, I go to the door and open it to find Jared Gaines standing on our front porch.

His expression is serious, his dark hair a mess, and there's a hint of stubble already lining his jaw, which is totally unlike him. He's wearing dark jeans and a gray hoodie sweatshirt, and he looks so unexpectedly and deliciously casual that I want to throw myself at him.

But I don't.

"Hey." His voice is devoid of emotion and I frown at him. "Are you ready?"

"I am." I try to smile, but he doesn't return it, so I end up watching as he grabs my suitcase and takes it to his car. I follow after him once I shut and lock my front door, making my way to his Tesla. It's a gorgeous vehicle, white and sleek and modern. I'm excited to finally be riding in it.

I still can't believe we're doing this. It's mind blowing.

"You're just bringing this?" he asks as he shoves Stella's beautiful pink suitcase in the trunk. "Is there anything else you need to grab before we go?"

"Nope." I shake my head, pat the bag slung over my shoulder. "I'm ready to go."

With a nod, he slams the trunk shut and then heads to the right side of the vehicle to open the passenger-side door for me. I slip inside, smiling my thanks at him before he shuts the door. I study him as he rounds the front of the car and opens the driver's side door, slipping into the seat and slamming the door with a muffled thud. He starts the car, sending me a curious look when he discovers I haven't taken my gaze off of him.

"What?" he asks when I don't say anything.

"You're quiet," I tell him. "You also seem—tense."

And we know this is a bad sign, am I right?

He laughs, though there's no humor in the sound. "Tense. That about describes it."

"Why? What's wrong? Is your family really that bad?" I start to envision all sorts of horrible, abusive scenarios, though honestly that makes no sense, what with how sweet Candice is. Though Jared does act like a control freak. What if his father is ten times worse than he is?

Oh God, what if I'm walking into some sort of horror situation and I'll need to call my friends on the downlow and beg them to come save me. I can take an Uber from San Francisco to Seaside, right?

Reaching out, Jared clutches the steering wheel with both hands, staring straight ahead, even though we're not moving. "They're not bad people. They're actually—pretty great. My father is a good man. My stepmother is...okay. We've never been particularly close, but that's my fault. My brother is a nice guy. He's a lawyer, and he's going to be a great success, I know he is. And you've already met Candice."

No red flags, family-wise. At least according to Jared. Though if he had anything to hide, he'd do exactly that. Hide it. "Then what is it? Clearly something is bothering you."

"It's nothing." He shakes his head, his jaw tight. "I just... I always get this way before I go see my family. It's my own weird thing."

He's being very real with me right now, and I appreciate

it more than he could ever know. "Do they all live in San Francisco?"

"No, my father and his wife live here. Well, in Pacific Grove." He pulls away from the curb and drives through the city streets, headed for the northbound Highway One on ramp. I hate how silent we are. There's not even any music playing, and I'm twisting my hands together like a Nervous Nellie.

"Go ahead and ask more questions," he finally says, amusement tingeing his voice. "I can tell you're dying to say more."

I breathe a sigh of relief at his permission. I didn't want to pry but... "Do you work with your father?"

"I do, though he works mostly out of his home office now. He's semi-retired. I'm the one who's handling most of the day-to-day business," he says as he merges onto the highway.

"And, um, what is it exactly that you do?" I'm trying to make conversation, but I'm also trying to get him to tell him me stuff. About himself.

I want to know more.

He chuckles. "I buy and sell companies in the hopes of turning a profit."

"And do you usually turn a profit?"

"Definitely. Though there's been the occasional purchase that hasn't turned out exactly how I wanted." He shrugs. "Sometimes we win, sometimes we lose."

"Why didn't your brother go into the family business?" This is so awesome. He is my captive, and I plan on asking him as many questions as he'll allow me to during our two hour-plus drive.

"He's always wanted to help people, ever since he was a kid.

I was the one buying bulk candy at the store and selling it for twice what I paid for it at school. Kevin was the one offering free advice and defending kids from bullies. It makes sense that he became a lawyer. Though he originally wanted to be a doctor."

And he goes on like this for over an hour. It is so great. I'm storing all of the information he's revealing for later, when I can lie in bed before I go to sleep and go over everything he's told me. About his father, his sister, his brother, his mother. She sounds like she was a lovely person. Sweet and gentle and kind. A little overprotective. The classroom mom, the one who was there for every field trip and every holiday party.

Kind of like my mom.

"I'm tired of talking about myself," he finally says, shooting me a quick glance. "I think it's your turn."

"Maybe we should listen to some music," I suggest hopefully.

"Nope. Now I get to ask twenty questions."

"Oh, did you play that game too when you were a kid?" I ask, trying my best to distract him.

"I just played it right now with you, Sarah. Now spill. Brothers and sisters?"

Great. I guess I'm going to spill all of my sordid (not) secrets. "One of each." I slump in my seat.

"Like me."

He's right. I guess that's the other thing we have in common.

"What's the birth order?"

"I'm the oldest, then my brother Brent and my sister Andie."

"Again, like me." His expression is thoughtful as he studies the road ahead. Traffic is getting heavier, which tells me we must be getting closer to the city. "What about your parents?"

My heart clenches and I rub a hand against my suddenly aching chest. "What about them?"

"Are they still together or are they divorced?"

"They're, um..." I swallow hard. May as well just say it. "They're dead."

His head swivels hard to the right, his eyes wide as he stares at me. "What? Are you serious?"

"Yes, I'm serious." I wave a hand at the windshield. "Maybe you should keep your eyes on the road, Jared."

He does as I say, his mouth open and closing like he's not quite sure what to say next. "How—what happened?"

"They were in a car accident. Four years ago."

His expression is pained. "You were only twenty."

"Yeah." I nod. "It was tough. My brother was a senior in high school when it happened. Andie was only twelve. It was really..." I blow out a harsh breath. "Difficult."

"Did you have other family come in and help you?"

"No."

"No?" He sends me a quick, horrified glance. "Then who helped you?"

"No one. I did it all. I mean, Brent stepped up as best he could, though it took him a couple of years, what with him still being in high school when it happened and really pissed off that our parents had to die like that." It's been such a long time since I've told someone my story. No guy has really stuck around long enough for me to get to this point. This is what I would consider make or break time.

Not for us, though. What Jared and I are doing is...not real.

"Sarah, that's just so...how devastated you must've been."

"It was pretty devastating," I agree. I sound almost nonchalant, but I'm beyond the point of always wanting to cry when I think about those early days after the accident. The confusion and the pain and the horror of knowing that your parents are just...gone. I was so young, my brother and sister even younger, and we were three kids cast out to sea all by ourselves. Adrift, trying our best to survive. My parents' friends rallied around us for a while, but eventually they all faded away. They had their own lives to live, though I didn't understand it then.

My father's parents were older when they had him, and they were both gone by the time the accident happened. My mother's parents weren't happy that she married my dad and essentially cut her off before any of us were even born. My grandmother sent me a letter after the funeral— that they didn't bother to attend—saying they would be more than glad to take us all in and take care of us during our time of need.

I didn't waste my time answering that letter. Just tossed it in the trash, and no surprise, we never heard from them again.

It was just us. Alone. I stepped up and worked as much as I could. My parents had small life insurance policies, but I ended up having to use a lot of that money to pay for their funerals. Once Brent came around, he started working too, and I encouraged him to go to college, to the local university in Monterey, so he could at least get an education. Our parents would've wanted that.

They would've wanted that for me as well, but I had to put my life on hold. Brent and Andie needed someone to take care of them, and that someone was me.

I tell Jared all of this, not leaving out a single detail. It feels almost cathartic, unloading on him. He's a good listener, remaining quiet as I spill my guts. Making appropriate noises at the appropriate times and asking gentle questions when I drift in my storytelling.

"Once Andie graduates high school and goes away to college, then I'll focus on myself," I say, leaning my head to the right as I gaze out the passenger-side window. "Then I'll take care of me."

"And what do you want to do?"

"I don't know. When I was in high school, I always thought I wanted to be a nurse." I turn to look at him. "But I watched some reality show that filmed at a hospital ER and I realized I couldn't handle that. I'm not a fan of blood." It also triggered memories of when the accident happened. I want to help people, but I can't work a job where I freak out at the sight of blood or when someone comes in after a horrible traffic accident.

We have to recognize our limits.

"Most people aren't fans of blood," he says, and I can tell he's trying to make me feel better. "I know I'm not."

Unable to stop myself, I reach out and rest my hand on Jared's knee, giving it a squeeze. "Thank you for listening to me rattle on. I can babble sometimes, and that was one big babble overshare."

"I didn't mind," he says.

"Really?" I turn my head, really looking at him. He glances in my direction, catching me staring. "Or are you just saying that?"

"I'm glad you trusted me enough to share your story with me, Sarah," he says, his voice soft, his gaze full of understanding. This is a version of Jared Gaines I've never seen before in any of our previous interactions.

And I like it. I like *him.*

What a scary feeling.

TWENTY-ONE

JARED

I CAN'T STOP THINKING about what Sarah told me about her parents. What a horrible tragedy, to lose your parents at such a young age. I know what that feels like—almost to the exact age—but I only lost one parent.

What would I have done if I lost them both?

Her words stick with me the rest of the drive. Long after she's fallen asleep in the passenger seat, all curled up like a little girl, her arm tucked beneath her head, her forehead pressed against the glass. Normal me would've been irritated, seeing her face pressed against the window of my precious Tesla. I get this car cleaned once a week and pay lots of money for someone to wipe down every inch of surface.

But now, I don't care if her forehead leaves a smudge on the window, and it will. I know it. Fuck it. No way am I going to wake her up. It's like she told her story and was so exhausted after sharing so much information, she passed out within minutes.

She's adorable too, when she sleeps. Her breaths are shallow, and I wish I could touch her. Run a hand over her soft hair, stroke her cheek. Offer her any bit of comfort that I can.

I can't. I'm driving. We're in the city now, traffic is at a standstill and I need to get to the hotel so we can check in before we meet my family for dinner. Rachelle isn't coming —she has other family coming into town and she can't get away to come with us, which is a goddamned shame.

Ha. Even my thoughts are sarcastic. I don't want to deal with Rachelle. She probably hates me. God knows what Evelyn's told her to poison her thoughts and make her despise me, but I'm sure they've shared a few good stories about me over the years.

I hate being made to look like an ass, and that's exactly what Evelyn did to me. She should've told me no when I asked her to marry me. It would've been painful, and I would've been angry, but I would've eventually gotten over it.

And it would've been better to be rejected right from the get-go rather than her dumping me only a few months before the wedding. Her parents lost money on the deposit they put down on the hotel ballroom they reserved for the reception. Evelyn had already bought a dress, not that I ever saw it. I wonder if she was able to return it.

I doubt it. That thing was probably custom and I'm sure it cost a fortune.

Thank God we hadn't sent out the invitations yet. Talk about humiliating.

We come to a sudden stop and I hit the brakes, so hard I jolt Sarah awake. She lifts her head, looking around with sleepy confusion before her gaze finds me. "Oh." She glances at the window once more before she returns her attention to me. "I think I drooled on your window."

Jesus. Normally this would send me over the edge.

"It's fine," I tell her, calm about this sort of thing for once in my life. "You all right?"

"I actually slept." She stretches, thrusting her chest out as she wiggles in her seat, and I can't help but sneak a look at her chest. She has a great body. One I wouldn't mind exploring with my hands and mouth sometime soon—

Nope. There is no way I'm going there. Not now. Not after hearing her tragic story. This woman is still in a delicate state. I don't care if she always mouths off at me and intrigues me beyond reason.

She is fragile. And still healing, even though it's been four years, I know that feeling never really goes away. The loss of a parent. Times that by two? It's twice as intense. I'm not so much of a bastard to dump my bullshit on her.

I am flat-out not worthy of her affection.

"Where are we headed to first?" she asks once she's resettled herself in her seat.

"We're staying at the Wilder Hotel in downtown San Francisco, so we'll check in first, then meet my family at a nearby restaurant for dinner," I tell her.

"Oh. My friend's boyfriend is Alex Wilder. His family owns those hotels," she says.

Huh. I know vaguely know Alex too. But I don't want to think about him at the moment. All I can focus on is the nervousness in Sarah's eyes.

"Um, what should I wear? To dinner tonight?" she asks. "I brought a couple of dresses. Stuff I normally wear to work."

"A dress will be fine. We're going to a French restaurant. My dad loves it, we've been going there since I was a child, so it's kind of a tradition for our family," I explain.

"I've never eaten French food before," she confesses. "Is it good?"

"I'll make sure you order something you like. Candice will help you as well." I pause, checking over my shoulder before I switch lanes. Why is the fast lane always the slowest in a traffic jam? "I hear you two have been keeping in touch."

Her face brightens. "We have. I really like your sister a lot. She's so funny and sweet. I think we could be great friends."

Dread tugs at me, and I know that's not a good thing, Candice and Sarah becoming closer. What's going to happen when Sarah and I, and I quote, "end it"? Will Sarah tell Candice the truth? How we're not even involved, yet I'm bringing her to Kevin's engagement under the pretense that we're a couple?

Candice will be infuriated. Ever since she was a child, she's had a real problem with liars, as well she should. She flew into little fits of rage when she found out the Easter Bunny and Santa Claus weren't real. Finding out her brother is lying will make her extremely angry.

Something I really don't want to deal with.

It's also something I can't really focus on right now. I need to get through this weekend first.

And I'm going to need all the strength—and most likely alcohol—I can get.

TWENTY-TWO

SARAH

AFTER MANEUVERING through agonizingly slow rush hour traffic, we finally made it to the Wilder Hotel, and it is *gorgeous.* Glittering chandeliers, the scent of fresh flowers filling the lobby, soft piano playing the background—there is an actual person who is playing an actual piano—and everyone who works at this hotel is eager to help you. A guy around my age took my suitcase like I was doing him a favor, an older gentleman held the door open for me, tipping his hat in my direction as I passed. And yet another one who passed me by in the lobby wished me good afternoon. The woman at the front desk had been so courteous while we checked in, dutifully answering all of Jared's persistent questions with a smile on her face, and I tell her thank you multiple times to make up for Jared's overly stern behavior.

Not that he was an asshole to anyone, he was just so... Jared. Serious Jared. Quiet Jared. *I will stare you down as an intimidation tactic* Jared. To the outside observer, he's a bit of a jerk, I'm sure.

To me, well. I'm starting to understand him.

Isn't that terrifying?

We take the elevator to the very top floor, where there are two penthouse suites. Yes, I said *penthouse* suites. We are sharing one of them, which is more than fine with me. We each get our own bedroom and bathroom, and I am beyond stoked about this. No awkward *oh gee, do we have to share a bed* moments, like I always see in those fake relationship movies on the Hallmark Channel. No wait, more like on the Lifetime Channel.

We're nothing like the Hallmark Channel, which I've already clarified. We're not wholesome enough.

Trust me.

The suite is huge, probably as big as the house I currently live in. I get a king bed all to myself, a closet that's larger than my bedroom, and a bathroom with a giant tub next to a wall to ceiling window that overlooks the city.

I am in heaven.

"What time are our dinner reservations?" I call to Jared as I'm bustling about my room, hanging up my clothes that I brought so I hopefully most of the wrinkles will fall out.

"Not till seven-thirty," Jared says, his voice sounding far away. Considering how large this suite is, I'm not surprised. His bedroom is clear on the other side, though he gave me the room with the better view.

Isn't he a gentleman when he wants to be?

I feel more confident about being here tonight. Sharing our personal tragedies seemed to bring us closer together. Not that I want to use what happened to my parents as a way to get closer to Jared, but it certainly broke down some walls and allowed us to share our commonalities. And that's a good thing, right?

"I'm going to take a quick shower." He appears in my open doorway. "Just wanted to let you know. In case you look for me."

"I think I'd figure it out when I heard the running water coming from your bathroom." I smile at him and he ducks his head, a tiny smile curling his lips.

My heart goes pitter-patter in my chest. I wonder what would happen if he flashed a full-blown smile in my direction. I'd probably drop to the floor, rendered powerless by its extreme potency. I haven't seen one of his genuine, full teeth showing, flashing smiles yet.

I wonder if I ever will.

"You like your room?" he asks, lifting his head.

"Who wouldn't?" I glance around, wholly impressed all over again. "And there's a full kitchen, right?"

He nods. "Partially stocked too."

My mouth drops open. "Really?"

"Yeah. Check it out when you get a chance."

"I'll take a shower when you're done," I tell him right as he's about to leave.

He pauses, frowning at me. "You don't have to wait."

"Sure I do."

"No, you don't," he insists. "This is a giant hotel. There are people taking showers at the same time at all hours of the day and night. Go for it."

He leaves before I can say anything in response, and I feel like an idiot. We can't have two showers running at the same time at my house because it affects the water pressure. And all the hot water runs out faster. My house is old. And I'm so used to that, I assume all places are the same.

Clearly, they're not. And I'm a big dork for not realizing it.

Pushing my faux pas out of my brain, I go into the dark bathroom with my phone, wanting to capture the city lights in their semi-full glory. It's still light out, the sun is slowly setting, and the buildings are already lit. I snap a couple of photos and send one to a group text I have with Brent and Andie, reassuring them I made it here safe (they think I'm on a girls trip with a couple of friends—I couldn't tell them the truth, they'd flip), and then I share the rest on my Instagram private story, which includes all of my girlfriends.

My view is what I caption the photos, along with heart eye emojis and San Francisco-themed gifs. I may as well play this trip up. Not all of my friends know I'm here with Jared, but they're going to find out now.

The messages start coming in at a rapid-fire pace, no surprise.

From Caroline: **Please tell me you two are sharing a bed.**

Ha, she wishes.

From Stella: **Nice view, but where's the better view? AKA Mr. Hot Stuff.**

And she makes fun of me for saying stuff like *naughty nothings*.

From Eleanor: **How romantic! I love San Francisco so much!**

Typical response.

And from Kelsey: **Wait, are you with that perverted lingerie guy right now? WTH???**

Guess I'll have to fill her in when I get back home.

I grab a fresh pair of panties and a matching bra, and make my way to the bathroom, where my toiletry bag and makeup bag are already waiting on the counter. I take a quick shower, not washing my hair because I plan on refreshing my limp curls with the curling iron I brought.

The shower's water pressure is freaking amazing. I crank the temperature to as hot as I can stand it and just let the water pound my skin, closing my eyes and tilting my head back, thankful for the shower cap the hotel provided. Steam fills the bathroom, and when I finally get out, I have to take an extra towel and wipe the mirror so I can actually see myself.

I do all the usual after-shower prep. Moisturize my face, body lotion, deodorant. I slip on my panties and bra, annoyance filling me when the mirror starts to fog back up.

Irritating.

To help get rid of the steam, I crack the door open and then brush my teeth, making weird faces at myself in the mirror while drooling toothpaste foam.

Classy.

As dinner draws closer, I'm starting to get nervous all over again, feeling a little jittery. I'm trying to calm myself down by being silly, but I don't think it's working.

Once I finish brushing my teeth, I plug in the curling iron, hating how hot I already am. I don't want to start sweating this soon after taking a shower, so I kick the door open even more before I start curling the ends of my hair. I'm halfway done when I hear Jared call my name.

And realize he's super close. Like, in-my-room close.

Kicking backward, the door is nowhere near my flailing foot, and I lift my gaze at the same exact moment Jared appears in my bathroom doorway, fully dressed.

While I'm standing in the steamy bathroom wearing a black lace bra and matching pair of panties I bought on clearance at Bliss, plus my discount (score!).

And that's it.

"Oh shit. I'm sorry." He quickly averts his head, placing his hand over his eyes.

Okay, this is silly. I wear bikinis that cover me just as much as my bra and panties. I mean, the man has basically touched my breasts already. And I'm fairly certain he's fantasized about me in lingerie.

I'm not bragging here. You know he has.

"It's all right," I tell him, still watching him in the mirror as he keeps his hand over his eyes. "You don't have to cover your eyes. It's nothing you haven't seen before, am I right?"

Um, where is this coming from? I know I'm speaking the truth, but I'm acting pretty bold right now.

Slowly, he drops his hand, his eyes wide with shock. He keeps them locked with mine in the mirror, never letting them drop. "I didn't mean to barge in."

"The bathroom was too hot. It's my fault for leaving the door open." I left the bedroom door open too, whoops.

"Oh." For the first time ever, I'm witnessing an uncomfortable Jared Gaines, and it's kind of amusing. I didn't put him on the spot on purpose, and I'm not trying to tempt him by parading around in only my underwear. I hope he doesn't think that.

We're adults. We can handle this. Right?

"Were you going to tell me something?" I ask when he remains silent. I continue curling my hair, knowing that time is ticking away and we'll need to leave soon to meet his family for dinner.

That realization sends a fresh set of nerves washing over me.

"Will you be ready to go in about fifteen minutes?" His gaze still never strays from mine when he asks the question.

"Definitely. I can get ready pretty quickly." It's true. I'm not one to take forever and put on a ton of makeup. I don't do a good job anyway, not like my little sister. She watches all kinds of YouTubers who give makeup tutorials, and she's really good at it.

Me? I don't have the patience. I'm always in too much of a hurry.

"Okay. Great. I'll, uh. Leave you alone." His gaze finally drops, slowly drifting down the length of me, and my skin tingles as if he actually touched me.

The moment he's gone, I press my lips together, my eyes wide as I stare at my reflection. I may act like I'm playing it cool, but secretly, I *wanted* him to look at me. I wanted to see if I'd get any sort of response, and while he didn't say anything, he definitely checked me out.

And I think he enjoyed what he saw.

I'm playing with fire, I know I am. And I'm either going to enjoy the heat this weekend or I'm going to get burned.

We'll see.

WE ENTER the crowded restaurant twenty minutes later, Jared sticking close by my side as he looks around for his family. Candice had texted me earlier, asking if we'd arrived yet, and I told her we'd made it to the hotel. She replied with an emoji-filled text saying she couldn't wait to see us, and right now that's who I'm searching for.

I need someone who's going to make me feel normal tonight, and Candice has that ability. She already feels like an old, familiar friend. I know Jared is watching out for me —we discussed our plan in the Uber on the way to the restaurant, how we need to stick close and act like a giddy new couple—but he's kind of a nervous wreck himself.

Even after our confessional car ride, I still feel like he's hiding something from me. What, I'm not sure. Hopefully I'll figure it out soon. Maybe I could even ask Candice...

But that might turn into me finding out something I'm

not supposed to know. I definitely don't want to put myself in that situation. Not right now.

"Sarah! There you are!"

I hear Candice's squeal and I turn to find her coming at us, her arms open wide, a giant smile on her face. She embraces me tightly, pressing a sticky-with-gloss kiss to my cheek, and the overwhelming scent of her perfume almost makes me sneeze.

"You look beautiful," she whispers in my ear before she pulls away and hugs her big brother.

"I don't even rate anymore, do I?" he asks in a teasing voice I've never heard before. "You called Sarah's name and didn't even mention me."

"She's my new favorite," Candice says as an older couple approaches, stopping just behind her. "Kevin's running a little late, but he'll be here soon."

"He'd better," Jared says gruffly as he goes to the man standing directly behind his sister. "Hey, Dad."

"Jared. Good to see you." They embrace in that typical manly way. Quick hugs, loud slaps on the back before they pull away. His father tilts his head, contemplating me with interest lighting his brown eyes. Eyes that remind me of Jared's. "Is this your girlfriend?"

I stand a little straighter, keeping myself composed even though I'm shaken by the term *girlfriend*.

But that's what I am, at least for the weekend. Jared's girlfriend.

Wild.

"Yes, this is Sarah." Jared returns to my side, nodding toward his dad as he makes the introduction. "Sarah Harrison, this is my father, Marcus Gaines."

"Nice to meet you," I tell him as I reach out and we shake hands, Jared's dad nodding and offering me a warm hello. I assume it's Jared's stepmother who approaches me next, and I'm right.

"Lovely to meet you, dear. I'm Mitzi, Marcus's wife." She smiles, her eyes, her entire demeanor open and friendly.

I immediately like her.

We wait in the restaurant lobby for another ten minutes, until Kevin finally shows up. I'm a little dazzled when I first meet him, because he's the younger version of Jared, no joke. They look so much alike, it's a little disconcerting. Though Jared is taller, and he has brown eyes versus hazel, and Kevin is not as broad-shouldered.

Not as hot, not as sexy, not nearly as a commanding presence as my Jared. Ha, look how possessive I am.

Kevin has the potential to be just as hot, though. His fiancée is a lucky woman.

We're seated at a table with a spectacular view of the city spread out before us, though I'm fairly certain I'm the only one who notices. I can't help but sneak glances out the window when I'm supposed to be concentrating on the menu. But it's hard to concentrate when the entire menu is written in French.

Unfortunately, I took Spanish in high school, so that isn't going to help me. Though I can pick out a few words...

Jared leans over, his mouth right at my ear, his breath fluttering against my skin as he says, "Don't worry. I'll order for you."

I turn to smile at him, startled that he's so close. Kissing close, as I like to think of it. "Thank you. I like chicken, remember?" I also gave him a list of my food preferences while we took the Uber to the restaurant. I'm kind of a picky eater.

He chuckles, his eyes gleaming in the dim light of the restaurant. "I remember."

"No seafood." I hate the stuff.

"Funny, considering we live in an area that has some of the best seafood restaurants in the world," he teases.

Yes, teases. He's teasing me. Who knew he could act this way? Certainly not me.

"My loss, right?" I smile and he leans in even closer, his cheek pressed to mine as he whispers, "I think we're pretty convincing as a couple, don't you?"

My heart falls and I fight the disappointment that surely must be written all over my face. I compose my features, hoping he can't tell since our cheeks are pressed so close together. "Definitely," I tell him with all the confidence I can muster.

He pulls away, his gaze warm, his hand on mine for the briefest moment before he releases it. I return my attention to the menu, fighting the emotion that suddenly fills me. I swallow hard, pissed at myself that I can actually feel tears threatening to fill my eyes. I can only assume I'm having a major PMS moment.

I need to remember that this isn't real. Jared and I are playing at a couple, and his only goal is to convince his family and everyone else who'll be at the stupid party Saturday night that we're together.

Why, I don't know.

But I'm determined to find out.

TWENTY-THREE

"CAN I CONFESS SOMETHING TO YOU?" I ask Jared
as we enter the dark suite.

Jared makes his way to an end table and switches on one
of the table lamps. "We forgot to turn on a light before we
left."

"Yeah, we sure did." That felt like him dodging what I
asked him, which I don't like. Did he mean to do that? Or
did he not hear me? "Can I tell you something?"

He feigns a yawn, covering his mouth with his fist. "Can
it wait until tomorrow?"

He's purposely trying to avoid my question. Whatever.
I'm still saying it.

"Your stepmother is really nice." I sat next to her during
dinner, much to Candice's disappointment. She wanted me
to sit next to her, but I couldn't leave Jared's side. That's the
whole reason I'm here. And Mitzi was on the other side of
me, who I was curious to get to know, so I stayed where
I was.

Poor Candice. I'll sit with her tomorrow.

"She's all right," Jared says dismissively, like he's not

even paying attention. "You want something to drink before we go to bed? There's a fully stocked bar."

"Okay," I tell him, lifting my chin, determination steeling my spine. Maybe I can get a couple more drinks in him and use the alcohol like truth serum. The man is so close-lipped. He doesn't want to talk about anybody or anything personal in his life, beyond his confessions in the car earlier. At dinner, he'd made small talk with everyone, even his brother, who he hadn't been face to face with since last Christmas. And I'm not talking the holiday that happened five months ago, but the one that happened the *year* before.

They don't live that far apart, so that's a long time.

He talked business with his father but avoided or diverted all of the personal questions his dad asked him. Mitzi would try to make conversation with him, and he shut her down with short, one-word answers. The only one he was kind to was Candice. Oh yeah, and me. But that's all bullshit.

He's super frustrating.

"What do you want to drink?" Jared asks once he's at the bar that's tucked away in the wall. Unbelievable. This suite is full of surprises. "Vodka? Tequila? Whiskey?"

"No, no and no." I shake my head. "Is there any rum? I'd take a rum and Diet Coke." I shouldn't even be drinking. I should go straight to bed.

But I'm too curious to sleep.

"Done." He starts making me a drink and I wander around the living room, stopping at the window so I can stare out at the glittering city below. It's a beautiful night, clear with the stars twinkling in the sky, and I press just my fingertips against the glass, taking it all in.

I may be spending the weekend with an extremely frustrating man, but I'm going to make the most of it. And if I'm lucky, I'll break him down a little bit more and get him to tell me what's really going on.

"Here you go." He's standing right next to me, a drink in each of his hands, and he lifts the one closest to me, offering the glass. I take it from him. "Toast to tonight being such a success?"

I lift my glass and clink it against his, and then we both drink. He mixes a delicious rum and Coke, I'll give him that. The liquor isn't too strong, but I can definitely taste it. A couple more sips and I'll be good and warm and ready to go to sleep.

"I'm pretty sure I convinced my dad we're the real deal, and I was worried the most about him," Jared continues. "He's way too perceptive. That's why I couldn't get away with shit when I was a kid. He always figured me out."

His dad still has time to figure him out, but I don't bother pointing that out. There's no need to freak him out tonight. He's pretty skilled at doing that to himself.

"You think Candice believes us?" I ask.

"Definitely," he says after he takes a healthy sip from his glass. He seems rather...excitable. On a high from pulling one over on his family? I suppose that could be it.

"What about Mitzi?"

He grimaces. "I really don't care what she thinks."

"Really?" I lift my brows. "Maybe you should."

"Why?" he asks incredulously. "She doesn't matter."

"She's the closest person to your father. No one else has his ear like her, you know what I mean? I'd guess she wields major influence over him," I point out.

"Doubtful," he scoffs. "My dad is his own man."

He's not going to listen, no matter what I say. He's determined to hang on to his hatred for Mitzi. "She's really not that bad," I say softly. "I mean, I know I just met her, so what do I know? But it's clear your father loves her. She dotes on Candice. And it seems like she has a close relationship with Kevin." I don't need to continue talking. He can assume what I was about to say.

Everyone seems to like Mitzi except for you.

"We've never been close," he says with a shrug. "After my mom died, I moved out of the house. Kevin and Candice were still at home, and within a year of our mom passing, Dad had a girlfriend. Mitzi. How was I supposed to accept the woman who replaced my mother so easily?"

I understand what he's saying but...

"She's very close to both Kevin and your sister," I tell him.

"She is," he says, pushing away from the window and making his way over to the couch, where he collapses on it, his almost-empty drink dangling from his fingers. He lifts his head, his gaze meeting mine. "Mitzi knows how to put on a good act to get everyone to like her. She's been working on it for years."

Most people do put on an act when you first meet them. We're all trying to be on our best behavior to make a good impression.

But there was something so warm and genuine about Mitzi. How she seemed to want to get to know me, asking me lots of questions, but none of them too intrusive. She kept a polite distance and I appreciated that.

"It's okay to admit you didn't like her because you thought your dad was replacing your mom with her," I tell him as I go to the couch and sit on the opposite end, hating that I'm still in a dress. I'd give anything to dip out on the conversation and change into my pajamas.

But all of this needs to be said. I can't leave now.

He completely ignores what I said. Instead, he finishes the last of his drink, rattling the ice in his glass as he asks, "You want another one?"

I shake my head, studying my mostly full glass. "I'm good."

I watch as he stands and goes to the bar, mixing himself another drink. Whiskey.

"It's a waste of your time, you know, holding on to all of those resentful feelings," I remind him.

He sends me a dark look, pouring extra whiskey in the glass before he returns to his spot on the couch. "What are you talking about?"

"You're mad at Mitzi for replacing your mother. A lot of time has passed, Jared. You should let it all go. The only one you're hurting is yourself."

"Are you trying to convince me she's a good person? Because it's not going to work."

"She seems really nice."

"Says you."

"Says everyone in your family," I counter, frustrated. "Your dad is so happy he couldn't stop smiling through the entire dinner, and same with your brother, though we know why he has a permanent grin on his face, considering he's celebrating his engagement this weekend. Candice is probably one of the most giving, well-adjusted people I've ever met, and you know who I think she can owe that to?"

"My father?" Jared asks with a frown.

"Well, yes. And your mother, of course." I send him an imploring look, hoping I can get through to him. "But also Mitzi. She's the one who helped raise Candice after your mom was gone. I'm sure she had some influence."

His gaze is incredulous, like I'm speaking a foreign language. "Candice is just like our mother. Sweet and fun and willing to help anyone in need. She talks like her, looks like her, even makes little gestures like our mom. I don't see how Mitzi had any influence with that."

"She did—she nurtured those traits in Candice. She was there for her when your father couldn't be, and that was a lot, considering the nature of his business. He was out of town all the time, he said so himself at dinner. So Mitzi stepped in and she was a mother to a young girl who wasn't even hers. That takes a lot of guts."

Jared's gaze is flat, his cheeks ruddy—from the alcohol, I'm sure. He's either not comprehending what I'm saying or throwing up a wall so my words won't penetrate.

And we know how much he loves throwing up walls...

"If you could just let go of that giant grudge you're holding onto, you'd see I could be right," I tell him as I rise to my feet. "I'm going to bed."

"You didn't finish your drink," he accuses as I walk over to the bar and pour out my drink in the tiny sink.

"Wasn't thirsty after all." I start to leave and I hear him get up from the couch, hear his footsteps sprinting across the room and down the hall toward my bedroom to catch up with me.

He places a hand on my arm, stopping me, and I whirl on him, hoping he realizes I mean business, but he's the one who speaks first. "You act like you know so much about my family when you just barely met them."

"Sometimes it takes is an outside observer to see what's really going on." I point a thumb at my chest. "And that's me."

He stares at me for a moment longer, taking a deep breath before he exhales raggedly. "You're saying this is all my fault."

"No. Not at all. You clung to what you believed, and I

understand that." I lower my voice. "Better than anyone else."

He nods slowly, his hand going to his jaw where he rubs it absently. "It's hard, tearing down resentment."

"I know."

"You're right. I know she's not so bad, I just—that was my mom, you know? And it felt like my dad replaced her so damn fast. Too fast." He drops his head into his hands, running his fingers through his hair before he lifts his head once more, our gazes meeting. "I forgave him because he's my dad. To me, Mitzi is just a stranger. I didn't have to forgive her."

He didn't want to either.

"If you start getting to know her, she won't be a stranger any longer," I point out with the gentlest smile I can muster.

"That'll take time."

Hope sparks within me. His words are a good sign. "Are you saying that you'll give it a try?"

"I can't make any promises."

"You can," I say firmly. "You're just not ready to with this one. Right?"

He barely nods. "Right."

"Maybe you should actually start talking to her tomorrow. Make conversation like a normal human being. Ask her about the weather. Or what her favorite TV show is. Something, Jared, to show you care."

"You really think you can change me in a weekend?" He sounds doubtful.

I step closer to him and run one hand up his chest until my palm is resting in the center, right above his beating heart. "I'm going to do my damnedest to try," I whisper.

I walk away from him and quietly close my bedroom door before he can say or do anything else.

TWENTY-FOUR

"WHAT WAS up with Jared last night?" Candice asks, her tone conversational as she pours herself a cup of hot water and then dunks a tea bag in it.

Saturday morning. We're at breakfast in one of the hotel restaurants. Candice's parents are out to breakfast with old work colleagues of Marcus's. Kevin is with his bride-to-be and her family somewhere, and Jared is...

Still sleeping.

So Candice and I decided to make it a date and get breakfast. I thought about waking Jared up and letting him know, but when I peeked in on him in his room, he was sound asleep, the covers pushed down to his hips, his bare back on display since he was sleeping on his stomach.

I stood there with my head around the door like some sort of peeper, staring at him. Trying not to drool. Once I gained some control over myself, I snuck away and sent him a text to let him know where I'm at once Candice and I met at the restaurant.

He still hasn't responded. I get the sense he's not the type to sleep in, like, ever. He must've been exhausted.

"What do you mean?" I finally ask Candice, unsure of what she's referring to. There were many things up with Jared last night. His hostility toward his stepmom. The way he avoids personal questions his own family asks him. How we're faking a relationship and if anyone looked just a little closer, they could probably tell.

"He's so touchy. Worse than usual." She glances over her shoulder at the giant buffet line behind her. "Should we do the all-you-can-eat breakfast or order off the menu?"

"I'm never good at buffets," I tell her, hoping I won't have to answer her question about Jared. "I never feel like I get my money's worth."

"Same," she says with a sigh as she cracks open the menu. Her eyes grow larger as she reads over the items. "Though maybe we should reconsider. The regular breakfasts are more than the buffet."

"Then the buffet it is," I say as I push the menu away from me. Our server approaches, asking if we'd made our decision, and Candice informs him that we're doing the buffet. Once he's gone, I lean back in my chair, ready to take my time.

"That line is still mega long," I tell her, frowning at my cup of coffee. I'd rather have a latte, but they didn't have specialty coffee drinks on the menu. I need to mention that to Caroline so she can talk to her boyfriend. His family owns the Wilder Hotel Corporation, so she has some pull.

"We can wait for a few minutes." Candice pours milk into her tea and then stirs it with a spoon. "Was Jared in a bad mood last night or what?"

Crap. I was hoping we could avoid this. "I think the traffic made him cranky."

Such a lame excuse, but it was all I could come up with.

"Everything seems to make him cranky. Except for

you." She sends me a knowing smile. "You two were quite cozy last night at dinner."

He was all over me at dinner. I'm scared he'll do it again tonight. Every time I'd look at him, the look in his eyes, on his face, was so intimate. Like we shared a naughty secret. And I suppose we do, though it's not what you think it should be.

"I've never seen him act so affectionate toward a woman before," she continues. "He's not one for public displays of affection."

"Why does this not surprise me?" We both laugh when I say that.

And I can't help but wonder if I shouldn't have said that. How does he want me to act around his sister? She makes me so comfortable, I let down my guard. Not that I'm going to let it slip that Jared and I aren't a real couple or anything like that, but I do feel like she's a friend. A real one.

"I'm glad you two are together. I've never really liked any of his past girlfriends," Candice tells me. "Not that he had a lot of them."

I lean forward, ready to glean a few gossipy bits out of her. "Really? Do tell."

Candice laughs, shaking her head. "I don't know if he'd want me to talk about his love life. You know he's such a private person."

Great. So he has his sister trained to throw up walls around his personal life too? "I won't tell if you won't."

Candice looks around, as if Jared is lurking behind that giant potted plant in the corner behind her. "Well, he hasn't had a serious girlfriend that I know of for a couple of years at least."

I'm frowning. "A couple of years?" I guess this makes

sense. He's been a client at Bliss Lingerie for at least that, maybe longer. He's been around as long as I've worked there. And he's been coming in regularly, buying sweet little nothings that us sales associates figured he gave to the women he was actively involved with—right before he dumped them.

But maybe we were wrong. Not like I'm ever going to work up the nerve to ask him about it.

"Yeah. Crazy, right?" She's nodding, her expression eager, looking ready to spill. "Ever since what happened with—"

"There you guys are. I've been looking for you." Jared's voice sounds from above me and I nearly scream. The wide-eyed look Candice is sending my way is relaying one message and one message only.

Busted.

"Oh. Hey." I glance up to find him standing directly behind my chair, smiling down at me, ever the dutiful boyfriend. I rise to my feet and turn, looping my arms around his neck and tilting my face up to receive a kiss. "Good morning, sleepyhead."

I am trying my best to distract him. Hopefully he wasn't standing there too long and overhead what Candice was telling me.

He doesn't miss a beat, this guy. He rests his hands on my hips and dips his head, brushing his mouth against mine. Tingles erupt all over my body, and I can't help but smile at him as he pulls away. "Good morning," he murmurs, that *let's go back to our room and have sex all morning* look in his eyes as he gazes at me. Warm. Attentive.

The perfect boyfriend.

Damn, he's good.

I glance down, taking in the red Nike T-shirt he's wearing, the black athletic shorts. "Going for a workout?"

"Planned on it." He kisses my forehead, his lips lingering, and I swear I can feel him inhale. "Thought I'd stop by and see what you two are up to this morning first."

"We're having the all-you-can-eat breakfast buffet. There's a waffle bar." I turn just in time to see Candice beaming at her brother, trying to tempt him to stay. I'm sure she wants to distract him as well. "You should join us."

"Waffle bar?" He makes a face, like he doesn't like waffles.

I mean, seriously. Who doesn't like waffles?

"There's an omelet bar too," I add.

"I can do that." He gives my hips a squeeze. "I'm going to go check out what else they have. I'll be right back."

The moment he's gone, Candice is practically jumping in her chair. "Do you think he heard what I said?"

"I don't know." I reach for my coffee and take a sip, grimacing. Still too strong despite the creamer and sugar I dumped into the cup earlier. I'm dying for a Starbucks. I think there's one down the block. "He's acting okay. Not like you really said anything." Damn it.

"True. I don't think he heard me. Though he can't blame me for spilling family secrets to a friend, right? You're practically family yourself, since you're dating him. And by the looks of things, you two are pretty into each other," Candice says.

Yes. Because we're most excellent actors, I want to tell her, but I don't.

Jared returns in moments, pulling the empty chair out at our table and settling himself in it. "I think I'm staying. I'll work out after I eat."

"I don't know how you do that. I'm always too full." Candice clutches her stomach and makes a face.

I'm laughing. So is Candice.

"That's because you eat too much bacon and waffles," Jared says, his tone borderline judgmental.

Candice's laughter dies. She pushes away from the table extra viciously and rises to her feet. "I'm going to the buffet."

Once she's out of earshot, I grab hold of Jared's arm and give him a shake. "That was rude of you."

"I'm just speaking the truth," he says with a shrug before he grabs my cup of coffee and takes a sip. He immediately looks like he wants to spit it out. "This tastes awful." He sets the cup back onto the saucer. "Too sweet."

"I'm sure you're the serial killer type who likes to drink his coffee black." I slump low in my chair, crossing my arms. He was so freaking rude to his sister just now, and he acts like he did nothing wrong.

I need to break him of this awful habit. That's the very least I can do before he ruins every single relationship he has with his family, all because of his uncensored mouth.

"I do like to drink my coffee black," he says, raising his hand at the server as the man walks by. He stops, Jared lets him know he'd like a cup of coffee and that he's doing the buffet, before the server is on his way.

Notice how he mentioned nothing about the serial killer comment.

Whatever.

"You want to go get in line?" he asks. "I'm starving."

I sit up straight, astounded by his complete obtuseness. "Jared."

"Sarah." He mimics me, a faint smile curling his

perfectly shaped lips. Who knew such beautiful lips could say such hurtful things?

Has no one ever called him out on his shit before?

"You just hurt Candice's feelings with your comment. Or did you not realize that?" I glance over my shoulder just in time to see Candice avoid the waffle bar completely. From what I can tell, her plate looks pretty pitiful—a couple slices of fruit and a dry-looking piece of toast. Poor thing. "She's not even going to eat waffles because of you."

"Good. She needs to take better care of herself."

I roll my eyes, hating how he thinks he's said the right thing to Candice. "I'm sure you're just watching out for your sister's best interests, and that's terribly—sweet of you. But the way you say things to her could be a little...oh, I don't know? Nicer?"

"Sometimes the truth hurts," he says evenly, murmuring a thank-you when the server appears and pours him a cup of coffee.

"Especially when it's delivered in such an asshole way," I tack on once the server has walked away.

Jared scowls at me, the first real emotional reaction I've seen from him all morning. "I can talk to my sister however I want. She's *my* sister. And she's nothing to you. When we return home, you and I are going to 'break up.'" He makes quotation marks with his fingers. "And then you'll never have to talk to her again, while I still have to deal with her for the rest of my life."

I'm horrified by the things that come out of his mouth. Does he really not care about anyone? I don't get it. "I don't understand you." I stand, grabbing my purse and slinging it over my shoulder. "You can't just treat people like they're meaningless, Jared. Eventually, you're going to end up all alone."

Before he can say another word, I leave the restaurant. I hear him call my name, but I don't look back. I swear I hear Candice call my name as well, but I ignore her, as much as it pains my heart to do so.

With determined strides fueled by anger, I march out of that hotel, until I find myself on the sidewalk directly in front of it. The air is cool, I'm only wearing jeans and a long-sleeved T-shirt, and I shiver as the breeze hits me. I could go back in and fetch a sweater. Or I could just hide out in my room in the suite and order room service. Make sure to charge it up so Jared is stuck with the bill.

That would show him.

But I'm not petty, so I do none of those things. Instead, I make my way to the Starbucks that I see on the corner, breathing a sigh of relief when I enter and smell that familiar scent of coffee beans and hear the whir of the blenders making Frappuccinos. Cheerful music is playing over the speakers and the barista currently making drinks glances up, offering me a pleasant good morning.

Ah. Right now, I feel like I'm with my people.

I order a venti caramel macchiato and sit at a tiny table, waiting for them to call my name so I can get my drink. I'm not even that hungry anymore, I just need the caffeine to hit my system and make me feel semi-human.

Scrolling absently through my phone, I contemplate if I should tell my friends what happened with Jared. Maybe I should just go home. This isn't going to work. He can't pretend to be with me, all lovey-dovey cuddlebug shit, and then turn around and snap at his sister like a tyrant. It's totally unbelievable.

Makes me realize that maybe all that cuddlebug stuff is a big fat lie. Which I should already know, but hey. A woman can still think he might really be like that with the one he loves, right?

I'm starting to wonder if he even knows *how* to love. It's as if Jared is a robot. Moving through life completely unfeeling. He's like a cranky old man, yet he's not even thirty-five. Imagine what he might be like when he's *seventy*.

I shudder at the thought.

The barista calls my name, and I go and grab my drink, about to settle back into my chair when I feel someone stop just behind me. It's probably Candice. I noticed she wasn't smothered in perfume this morning, so I can't smell her before I see her. I'm sure she's wondering what's wrong with me.

Turning, I stop short when I see it's actually Jared standing in front of me. His face is pink from the cold, which doesn't surprise me considering he's just in shorts and a T-shirt, and I swear he just shivered.

Good. I hope his nuts freeze up and fall off.

"What do you want?" I ask wearily, taking a sip from my drink. "Ow." Great. I think I burned my lip.

This day just keeps getting better and better.

"I'm sorry." He swallows hard, resting his hands on his hips as he glances around the café. No one is paying attention to us. I don't know why he's so worried about what other people think all the time.

This feels like a repeat. I keep getting mad at him and he keeps apologizing to me. "I'm guessing Candice put you up to this. Again." I set my drink on the table beside me and cross my arms, wishing he'd just leave. I want to drink my coffee in peace. "Your apologies are meaningless, Jared, if you can't come up with the words to say to me on your own."

"You're right. I know you're right." His head is bobbing

up and down, like he's some sort of mechanical doll stuck on one setting. "I get what you're saying, and I know I'm a total asshole. Candice already told me that when I tried to apologize to her."

I can't keep up with all of his apologies, and I'm guessing he can't either. No wonder he stopped caring what people thought when he spoke. This shit is exhausting.

"Maybe you should just go," I tell him, my voice small. I pull my chair out and settle in, glaring up at him when I realize he's not going anywhere. "We can talk about this later."

More like never.

"I want to talk now." He pulls the other chair out and sits right next to me, so close our arms brush against each other. Despite the cool temperatures outside, his arm is warm. Solid. Muscular. I hate that I notice that.

I also hate that I notice the dark stubble shading his strong jaw, giving him a roguish look that is massively appealing despite my anger towards him. We're so close, I can almost count all the eyelashes surrounding his dark brown eyes, and he has a lot of them, which is so annoying. Us women pay big money to have thick eyelashes like his, and we still can't duplicate his look.

The most frustrating thing of all? I'm so pissed at him, yet I can't help but be drawn to him. He appeals to something deep inside of me that I don't get. Is it because I can see a glimmer of hope in him? Clearly, he needs nurturing. I do too. Maybe we're kindred spirits.

I'm just the nicer one.

"Then go ahead," I tell him when he still hasn't said anything. "Talk away."

He rests his forearms on top of the table, his large hands clasped together, fingers loosely linked. My gaze falls to those sexy hands and it takes everything within me not to let out an irritated sigh. I mean, yes, I'm irritated by his behavior, but I'm even more irritated by my reaction to him.

"I really am sorry for what I said. I just...I can't explain why I am the way I am. Or maybe I can. I don't know." He drops his head, clenching his hands together, his fingers flexing. "For the longest time I was pissed off at the world."

He remains quiet for a while so I ask, "Because you lost your mom?"

His focus still on the table, he nods. "Then I fell in love."

My heart sinks. I don't want to hear this. Though I do. I so do. I want to know who he fell in love with, when did it happen, how long were they together, and where is she now? I want all the details.

Yet I also don't. I might end up hating her. Or worse?

Being envious of her.

"What happened?"

"She dumped me. And it was like a kick in the ass." Exhaling loudly, he lifts his head, his gaze meeting mine. "I realized then that I was—unlovable. I was so in love with her, I showed her every flaw I had, confessed every secret, shared with her my every dream. I saw a future between us. I believed we were going to be together forever. But then out of the blue, she broke up with me. Told me she didn't feel the same way. I felt destroyed all over again."

My heart is now cracking.

"I was angry. So fucking angry." A ragged exhale escapes him. "So I put up a wall and I didn't let anyone in. I still don't let anyone in, not even my family. It really is a lot easier being a complete jerk, speaking my mind and not giving a shit what people think about me. Everyone leaves me alone when I act like that."

"Is that what you really want, though? To be alone?" I ask softly. I feel like we're having this life-changing moment in the middle of a Starbucks in downtown San Francisco, surrounded by strangers. It's a total surreal moment.

"That's what I thought." He drops his head again, and I wish I could look into his eyes. "Then I met...you."

TWENTY-FIVE

JARED

I PROBABLY PLAYED my hand too quickly, but I am a desperate man. Back in the hotel restaurant, cranky from lack of sleep and dealing with a hangover, I didn't even realize at first what I said or what I did to offend Candice so badly.

But that wasn't even the worst of it. Candice will forgive me. She's my sister. She always forgives me. It's *Sarah* I offended the most. When she left the hotel, I panicked and chased after her, losing her once I got outside. Candice followed me, demanding I go find Sarah before I "screw up a good thing" and I quote.

Now Sarah and I are sitting at the table for two like we belong together, and damn it, I'm going to be honest with her. Real. Raw. I haven't done this since I was with Evelyn, and that was over ten years ago.

Meaning I'm a little rusty at this confess my feelings thing

"What are you trying to say, Jared?" Her voice is soft, her blue eyes wide, her demeanor unsure. I keep her on edge, and she doesn't like it.

She keeps me on edge too.

"I—like you." Okay, that sounded lame. Like I'm confessing a middle school crush. "I care about you."

"Like how?"

She's not going to make this easy, is she? Well, I guess she shouldn't.

"I want to be with you," I admit, my voice low.

Sarah leans across the table, her gaze falling to my lips. "What did you say? I'm not sure if I heard you right."

Is she playing me for a fool? It did just get busier in here. A big group of kids just came in, and they're all so damn loud, I can hardly hear myself think.

"I said." I clear my throat and start talking louder. "That I want to be with you, Sarah. For real."

The moment I started making my confession, the teens quieted, shushed by the adults accompanying them, and I'm fairly certain everyone in the damn Starbucks heard me say I wanted to be with her.

Talk about putting me on the spot.

She's smiling. Grinning, really. "You don't have to yell at me, Jared."

Growling, I give in to my urges and reach for her hand, lacing our fingers together. I need to cut to the chase. "Do you want to be with me?"

Her smile fades, her expression growing serious. Maybe even a little shy. "I do, but...not like this."

"Not like what?" Fear makes my skin run cold and I grip her hand tighter, scared she might yank hers away and tell me to go fuck myself.

I'd deserve it for all I've put her through.

"You're going to have to apologize to a few people before you're off the hook with me," she says.

I stare into her beautiful blue eyes, hoping she can see the sincerity on my face, hear it in my voice. "I'm sorry."

"I know you are, and I believe you, but I'm the least of your troubles." She withdraws her hand from mine and starts ticking off everyone I need to acknowledge. "You need to apologize to your sister."

"I already did," I start, but Sarah shakes her head, cutting me off.

"I want to witness that one."

"Fine," I mumble. It's not easy for me to apologize. I don't say sorry very often, so this is going to be a major moment for me.

"You need to apologize to your stepmom for not letting her get to know you." She holds out another finger. "To your father, for being rude to his wife all these years."

I grimace. I don't want to apologize to Mitzi or to my father about Mitzi. Why should I have to?

"I know what you're thinking, and you're wrong," Sarah says, her voice stern. Now she's the one laying down the law. "You've shunned her for years, which means you've also shunned your father. She's a part of his life whether you like it or not. He *loves* her. You need to learn how to accept her and care about her as well."

That sounds impossible, but no way am I going to tell her that.

"And you need to apologize to your brother."

I'm incredulous. "What did I do to Kevin?"

"Candice told me how you always avoid his calls. He's your *brother,* Jared. He's the only one you've got. Why would you cut off your family when they love you and want you to be a part of their lives? That's not fair to them, or to you." Her expression turns sad, and seeing her like this makes my chest ache. "You know what it's like to lose someone. Why would you deprive yourself of spending time with your family, when we only have so many years on this earth? You could lose your brother tomorrow. What would you do if that happened? How would that make you feel?"

She's right. I know she is. Everything she says makes perfect sense. But this shit is going to be hard. I've cut everyone off for years. I can't just walk into that engagement party tonight with open arms, an open mind, and open heart.

"This is going to take baby steps," I tell her, hoping like hell she'll understand. "I'm not making excuses. I'm just trying to be real with you."

"Thank you for being honest." Her eyes are positively glowing. I think she likes that she's getting a commitment out of me.

Not a commitment to her, but a commitment to myself. And my family. What she wants is totally selfless.

I can't help but admire her.

"I won't be able to ask for everyone's forgiveness tonight," I tell her. "That will be—too much for me."

"I know. But just seeing you making an effort and trying to be nice to everyone will be so worth it. It'll make my heart happy." She's smiling again, a faint curl of her lips, and I love seeing her like this.

I remember how she greeted me in the hotel restaurant earlier. That easy smile, how she wrapped her arms around my neck and waited for me to kiss her. I want that. I want that every day, if I can get it.

"I can do it." I reach for her hand once more and give it another squeeze. "I'll do that for you."

"You shouldn't do it for me, you should do it for your-self." It's her turn to squeeze my hand and we sit there for a few seconds, me losing myself in the depth of her eyes, until I finally shake my head.

"Can we get out of here? I'm freezing my ass off," I admit, making her laugh.

If I had my choice, I'd do whatever it takes to make her laugh like that as much as possible.

TWENTY-SIX

SARAH

My brother begged for your forgiveness, right?

I SMILE at the text Candice just sent. Talk about restraint. What happened in the hotel restaurant was hours ago, and she's only just now asking me about it?

Jared and I left Starbucks and went back to the suite, where he changed into warmer clothes. Then we snuck off by ourselves and had an early lunch at a cute little Italian place not too far from the hotel. The food was delicious, as was the company. We didn't talk about family or mistakes or any of that kind of stuff. Instead, we chatted about the most trivial things you could imagine. Favorite sports team. Favorite movie. Favorite TV show. Favorite color.

You know, the stuff you talk about when you first start dating and you're trying to get to know each other.

We kept it light and easy, and I had the best time. I think he did too. We walked around for a bit after lunch, holding hands and looking in store windows, before we finally made our way back to the hotel.

Realizing I need to answer Candice, I send her a quick text back.

He did.

Her response is immediate.

Good. I told him he had to go fix things before you left him forever. That seemed to light a fire under his butt.

I'm glad you told him that, I type. Would he have chased after me without Candice's encouragement? I think so, but...

Then again who knows? He's very stubborn.

Candice sends me another text.

You forgave him?
    Yes. He groveled and there's more groveling involved, but we're good.

I smile and send my text, giddy that I can actually mean what I'm saying.

This isn't pretend, what's happening between Jared and

me. He actually likes me. And I like him. I might be setting myself up for failure, but I really don't think so. I think in the end, he's going to be worth it.

So worth it.

Another text arrives from Candice.

Yay! So glad. See you at the party?
Yes Can't wait.

"Who are you texting?"

I glance up as Jared approaches the couch where I'm sitting. I set my phone on the end table and smile up at him. "Your sister."

He frowns. "What's she saying?"

"That she's glad I'm making you grovel." I laugh at the scowl that appears on his face. It's like he can't help himself. Though I wouldn't change his growly ways. I think he's cute when he does this.

"She *would* like that," he mutters.

"Don't forget you're apologizing to her again tonight," I remind him.

"Oh, I won't forget. I know you won't let me." He lifts his chin in my direction. "Can I sit with you?"

"Sure."

He sits on the couch, and not on the other end either. Not in the center. No, he plants himself right next to me. So close, he's pressed up against my side, and I'm pressed up against his. He lifts his arm, stretching it out on the couch behind my head, and I glance up at him, then drop my head, feeling shy.

Okay, this is nice. And unexpected. Though I shouldn't

be surprised, I guess. He confessed that he likes me. That he wants to be with me. That could be interpreted in a multitude of ways, but I like to think that he wants to be with me in a serious relationship. That's how he's acting at least. Both now and during lunch. On the walk home. In the elevator on the way up to the suite.

And while that's what I want too, it's still kind of weird for us to be affectionate with each other on purpose.

Like now, with him sitting so close, I could practically crawl into his lap.

I wouldn't mind crawling into his lap. I wonder what he might do...

"The cogs are turning in your brain." He taps his index finger gently against my temple. "What are you thinking?"

I shake my head, my cheeks growing warm. "You don't want to know."

"Now I definitely want to know." His arm drops so it's around my shoulders, his fingers stroking along my upper arm. "Tell me."

"I was thinking about how much I want to sit your lap."

He's quiet for a moment before he murmurs, "What's stopping you?"

Nothing, I think as I do as exactly what I want. I reach for him, straddling his thighs, settling my butt right on top of them as I rest my hands on his shoulders. We still have some time, but we probably should be getting ready for tonight's engagement party. I wanted to take a shower and wash my hair, and that means I have to dry it, which is a total chore, especially with crappy hotel hair dryers.

But I don't care about any of that right now. I want to test the chemistry Jared and I share. I know we've been playing as a couple for the past twenty-four hours, but I want to see what it's like when we're doing this for real. When there's no one else around.

Just the two of us.

In a hotel suite.

Alone.

He's big. Solid. I squeeze his shoulders. Run my hands down his arms, squeezing his biceps. They're hard as rocks. "Do you work out?" I teasingly ask him.

Jared chuckles, his eyes sparkling. This is the most relaxed I think I've ever seen him. "Is that a pickup line you're using on me?"

I pretend scowl at him. "It is a sincere question, Mr. Gaines. You have very firm muscles."

His mouth kicks up on one side in the cutest smirk ever. "Back to the formalities yet again, Miss Harrison?"

I nod, unable to take my hands off his biceps. "We sure are, Mr. Gaines. As I told you before, I think you like it when we speak to each other like this."

"You think so, hmm?"

Nodding, I lean in, positioning my mouth right at his ear as I whisper, "Truthfully? I think you get off on it. Mr. Gaines."

He turns his head the slightest bit, our mouths level with each other. I can feel his breath feathering across my lips, and now I'm the one who's aroused. "Miss Harrison, you really believe I get off on this type of thing?"

Oh shit. He's making me doubt myself. "Maybe?" I ask.

With the slightest shift, his mouth is on mine. And all I can think is *finally*. Finally, a real kiss from the Mr. Jared Gaines. We start with one kiss. Two. Lips coming together. Pulling apart. Breaths quickening. Bodies shifting. Lips parting. More. More. Until our tongues are touching. Sliding against each other.

His arms come around and pull me in closer, until my body is flush with his. I wind my arms around his neck, my fingers sliding into his thick, soft hair, and he groans against my lips.

That agonized sound sends an electrical current racing through my veins, landing right between my thighs. I readjust my position, pressing my pelvis more firmly against his, and he growls low in his throat. His mouth becomes hungry, the kiss turns deeper, and our hands begin wandering.

Everywhere.

We kiss for minutes. Hours. I'm not sure exactly how much time passes, but when we finally come up for air, I tilt my head to the side, breathing heavily as Jared runs his lips along the length of my neck.

"You smell fucking amazing," he whispers against my throat, just before he nips me with his teeth, making me shiver.

"So do you," I murmur, giggling when he kisses my ear. Bites it. Nuzzles it.

"I haven't done something like this since I don't know when," he confesses.

"What do you mean?"

He grabs my face with both of his hands, forcing me to meet his gaze. "Kiss a woman like this, expecting it to go nowhere else."

"There's nothing better than a good old-fashioned make-out session," I tell him, turning my head so I can press a kiss to his palm.

"I agree, as long as the make-out session involves you." He kisses me again, and I feel like I'm drowning. Drowning in his taste, his tongue, his hands, his body, his sweet, sweet words. I could lose myself with this man so easily, and knowing that he has that much power over me is quite frankly...

Terrifying.

But exhilarating, all at the same time.

After a few minutes of more kissing, and more touching —Jared is this close to approaching first base—I pull away, needing to catch my breath. Calm my racing heart. "I should probably start getting ready," I tell him.

He brushes my hair away from my shoulder, his fingers tangling in the strands. "We don't have to be there for hours."

"It starts at seven?" I don't know why I'm asking. I already know it most definitely starts at seven.

"Yeah, but we don't have to be there on time." He pauses. "Though I do have a thing for punctuality."

"Right." I lightly sock him in the shoulder. "And don't you forget it." Leaning over him, I tap my phone screen to see that it is currently 4:45. "It's almost five. I need to take a shower. Wash my hair. Dry it. Straighten it. It's a process, Jared. And I need to get on it."

"You look beautiful just as you are right now," he says, his voice, the glow in his eyes gentle. Sweet. Like he might be a little over the moon for me.

It's a great feeling.

"You're a sweet talker when you want to be. But I really need to go." I press a kiss to his cheek and then climb off of him, noting the impressive bulge beneath the black joggers he changed into when we got back to the hotel room.

Hmm. I can't dwell on that now. We have plenty of time to explore each other later.

I'm downright giddy at the thought.

TWENTY-SEVEN

JARED

THERE IS nothing like a make-out session on a couch with the woman who drives you crazy with lust. Though she definitely makes me feel other things too, it was definitely all about the lust while we kissed and kissed. I wanted to take it a little further, but I didn't want to push. Not yet.

I'll push tonight. After we get this party over with and all the pressure of having to look like the perfect romantic couple is off of us.

Though it won't be a difficult task for us any longer. I want us to be a romantic couple. I pretty much think we *are* a romantic couple.

And I'm pretty certain Sarah feels the same way.

Once she left the living room to take a shower, I went to take my own shower, where I also jerked off to the mental image of Sarah wearing the panties with the heart-shaped cutout in the butt. Sarah, smiling at me as she slowly turns around to show me her perfect ass on total display.

It doesn't take long once I imagine her on her knees in front of me, wearing nothing but those skimpy panties. Jesus.

Last night when I jerked off before I went to sleep, I used the moment when I saw her curling her hair wearing nothing but that black bra and the matching panties. And like an idiot, I panicked. Plus, she was wielding a hot curling iron in her hand, so I knew I had to be careful.

Seeing her like that turned into perfect fantasy material for later.

This is what she drives me to do. Jerk off in a hotel when it's just the two of us in this suite. Any other woman and I would've dropped all pretenses and finesse. I would've asked her if she wanted to fuck, I can almost guarantee she would've said yes, and we would've done exactly that.

Fucked.

But I'm not going to approach Sarah like that. She wants something romantic. She deserves something romantic. And sweet. She deserves to see me acting like I care. And I *do* care.

That's why I agreed to talk to my family tonight. Deep down I know she's right, no matter how reluctant I am to put her plan into action. I'll do it, though.

I'll do it for Sarah. And for me.

My mind was overrun with all sorts of thoughts once I finished myself off in the shower. I replay the story she told me about losing her parents. How young she was, how overwhelmed she became taking care of her siblings. So much responsibility for such a young age. That didn't give her much time to do something just for herself. She probably didn't have many serious relationships. So does this mean she's a...

Virgin?

Hell, I hope not. I'm not the gentle, sweet type in bed, no matter how gentle and sweet I might've been toward

Sarah on the couch earlier. Virgins aren't my thing. Not that they're a thing, but you know what I mean.

I don't want to hurt her. And considering how I feel about her, and how much I want her, I'm afraid I'll be too rough. Too fucking overcome with my need for her.

The more I think about Sarah's potential virgin status, the more nervous I become. Until I can't think about anything else but the possibility that I could be Sarah's first.

Some guys might get off on that shit, but I am not one of them.

The shower is done and I'm drying myself off when I realize I can't take it any longer. Wrapping the towel around my hips, I head for Sarah's bathroom, where I find her—wearing one of the plush robes the hotel provides, inter-esting—blow-drying her hair.

The blow dryer shuts off the moment she notices me standing in her bathroom doorway wearing nothing but a white towel. Her gaze is locked on my naked chest, and I can admit that feels pretty good, to have her staring at me like she's dying to eat me up.

"Everything okay?" she asks, lifting her gaze to meet mine in the mirror. We've done a lot of communicating in mirrors this weekend.

"I'm fine. But I have a question to ask you."

"Go ahead," she says, sounding unsure.

Taking a deep breath, I decide to just go for it. "Are you a virgin?"

She bursts out laughing, setting the blow dryer on the counter and turning so she's facing me. "Is that what sent you into a panic? Thinking I'm a virgin?"

"I wasn't panicked." She tilts her head, the look on her face saying *really?* This woman knows me far too well. And that's a little scary. "Fine. Uh. Yeah. I was a little."

Sarah steps closer, her hands going to my chest, her finger stroking my still-damp skin. Her lids lower, she parts her lips, and she is the sexiest thing I've ever seen as she says, "No. I'm not a virgin."

"Thank God," I breathe, making her laugh harder.

"I mean, it's been a while, I can't lie," she confesses, her hands still wandering all over my skin.

I grab hold of her wrists, stopping her before she makes me pop a tent in the towel. "How long?"

Her cheeks turn pink and she wrinkles her nose. "A couple of years?"

Damn. That's a long time. "Well."

"I know, right? I think I might've revirginized."

I'm frowning. "What did you just say?"

"Revirginize. Haven't you heard of that before? When someone hasn't had sex in a long time, especially a woman, they say you can...revirginize. Turn into a virgin all over again. Maybe that's happened to me." She says the last sentence brightly, like it's a good thing, and I want to tell her no. No, this is not a good thing, and there's no way I want her to turn into a virgin all over again.

But then I see the look on her face. How her lips are pursed, like she's trying to hold back laughter that wants to spill, and relief fills me.

"You're trying to trick me, aren't you?" I accuse, and she's laughing again.

Women have never tried to trick me. Play jokes on me. Or joke with me. I've been a serious bastard for so long, Jesus. I am absolutely no fucking fun, huh?

So I'm not used to this sort of thing. The teasing. The joking. Sarah's smile makes my chest feel funny, but in a good way. And seeing her in that robe, I can't help but wonder what she's got on beneath it.

"Whatcha wearing under this?" I reach out and trace my fingers along the robe's lapel, stopping at the deep V where they meet.

"Wouldn't you like to know," she says cheekily, turning so her back is to me, our gazes meeting in the mirror once more.

"I want to find out." I told myself I wouldn't move too fast, and look at me. I'm standing directly behind her, my cock is telling me it's about to pop that tent, and I'm reaching for her, toying with the belt that's loosely tied around her waist.

"Then maybe you should take a look," she says breathlessly. "Since you're so curious and all."

Her ass is pressed against the towel and I'm doing everything I can not to thrust against her lush backside. I slip my hand inside the front of her robe, encountering nothing but soft, smooth skin. Bare breasts. Hard nipples.

She arches into my hand when I cup her right breast, my thumb skimming back and forth, making her nipple harder. She closes her eyes but I keep mine open, watching the two of us in the mirror, how open she is with me, how trusting.

With my free hand I undo the belt, and the robe falls open. Not all the way, but just enough for me to catch a glimpse of her flat stomach, the curve of her hips, the shadowy spot between her legs.

Keeping one hand around her breast, I let the other hand wander. Across her stomach, down the slope of her belly, until I encounter pubic hair. She jerks against my touch, a whimper escaping her, and my hand shifts lower. Lower still.

Until I encounter wet, creamy hot skin.

"Jared," she whispers, her head falling back against my

shoulder as I begin to stroke. Her eyes are still closed, her lips parted, and I increase my pace, the towel falling from my hips and leaving me naked.

In the mirror, I'm covered by her body, and her body is covered by the stupid fucking robe. The next thing I know, I'm pulling it off her, until it drops to the floor and she's completely nude. Her back is still to my front, her lush body on full display in the mirror, and I can't stop staring.

She is gorgeous.

"Open your eyes," I whisper in her ear, and she does as I command, her gaze finding mine in our reflection. "See how beautiful you are?"

The breath hitches in her throat and she starts to close her eyes again. I wonder if she's embarrassed to see herself like this. I remove my hand from between her legs, making her gasp in frustration and those pretty baby blues fly open, downright accusing as she glares at me.

"Don't stop," she murmurs.

"Keep your eyes open and I won't ever stop," I promise her.

Slowly she straightens her spine, thrusting her chest out, and I know she's looking at herself. Her skin is flushed, her rosy nipples hard little points, her still-damp hair a wild tangle tumbling past her shoulders. She has a tiny waist and flaring hips and slender thighs and the prettiest patch of dark hair between her legs. She's gorgeous.

And right now, she's all mine.

I didn't mean for us to take it this far. This wasn't my intention when I came to the bathroom to ask her if she was a virgin, yet here we are. Naked. My hands all over her body. My fingers moving between her legs once again. Her thighs parting for my hand. She's wet and hot and so responsive. Little moans and whimpers fall from her lips, and every time her eyes start to slide closed, I still my hand.

Then those eyes fly wide open and I'm able to continue.

"Oh God," she whimpers when I hit a particular spot, and so I stroke her there again. And again. Her full weight is leaning against me, and I tell her I've got her, I'm not going to let her go, and I want to see her come.

I'm desperate to see her come.

It doesn't take much longer until she's falling part in my arms, her entire body shaking. Shuddering. She says my name. Shouts it, really. And I keep up the pace, rubbing her, getting her off, until she collapses against me with a breathless laugh.

"Oh my God, Jared!" She turns and nestles her naked body against mine, my cock jerking against her stomach upon first contact. "That was *amazing.*"

I've never had a woman so enthused after I gave her an orgasm. I know what I'm doing. I've given more than a few women plenty of orgasms, but no one has shouted at me with glee before.

And that's exactly what Sarah just did.

"I can make that happen again," I murmur right after I kiss her softly.

"Promise?" she teases, her blissed-out expression making me smile.

"Definitely." I'll give her as many orgasms as she wants.

"I'm going to take you up on that." She reaches between us, her fingers wrapping around the base of my erection. My cock jerks in her grip, startling her, and she smiles up at me. "Someone's eager."

"You don't have to—"

"Oh, I am so going to." The smile is still there, her eyes

glowing, her entire presence seeming to glow. "Can I admit something to you?"

She likes admitting things to me. I've noticed that about her. "Sure."

"It was hot, watching you touch me in the mirror." She strokes me once, nice and slow, her grip firm. "Maybe it's your turn to watch me?"

Slowly she lowers herself to her knees, and my jaw drops open, a surprised huff of laughter leaving me. My eyes go to the mirror, and I can see myself, her head right there at the perfect level, her fingers still wrapped around my dick. She glances over her shoulder, our gazes meeting in the reflection, and she smiles before she returns to her task and wraps her mouth around just the tip.

Holy hell, this girl is fucking dirty.

And I love it.

TWENTY-EIGHT

SARAH

I AM on a high and nothing can stop me tonight. Seriously, I look damn good in the jumpsuit Candice picked out for me. It fits like a dream, and because I was feeling like a naughty bitch after everything that transpired between me and Jared in the bathroom, I decided not to wear a bra *or* panties underneath it.

Yep, I'm completely naked under this jumpsuit, and I feel like a freaking dirty girl. Something I've never felt before in my entire life. It's hard to feel like that when you're in your early twenties and you have to take care of your teenaged sister. That leaves you with no time to date guys.

This is all thanks to Jared. I almost want to laugh while remembering how scared he'd looked when he came to my bathroom, asking if I was a virgin. He was seriously worried about it, which was cute. And then everything went from cute to hot in a matter of seconds. Feeling him pressed next to me, his erection rubbing against my backside, his hands on my body, in between my legs...God.

I am still trembling just thinking about it.

I'm also pretty much ready. Staring at a mirror yet again, this time in my bedroom, I'm slipping on the drop pearl earrings Candice convinced me to get that night we went shopping, when Jared was purchasing my jumpsuit. He didn't even flinch when I made the addition, and I worried about maybe getting a necklace or bracelet, though Candice advised me understated was best for this outfit.

Couldn't go without a necklace though. I'm wearing the thin gold chain my father gave my mother when they were first together. It's plain, no pendant or charm hanging from it, and I like it that way.

"You almost ready?" Jared calls from the living room as I slip on the other earring.

"Give me another minute," I answer, pulling my favorite red lipstick out of the clutch purse Candice let me borrow. It is absolutely the cutest thing. Completely covered in tiny white beads, some of them in a giant daisy pattern on the top of the clutch, I am absolutely in love with it. I would've never thought to take a white bag with a black outfit, but Candice insisted it would work.

She was freaking right. I need to listen to her more often.

Slicking on a layer of red lipstick on my lips, I rub them together, toss the tube back into the clutch, close it, then make my way out to the living room.

My stomach is jumpy over seeing him. We went our separate ways after the interlude in my bathroom. I still can't believe I did that. Me, giving Jared Gaines a blowjob in a hotel bathroom. So trashy!

Isn't it great?

I enter the living room to find him at the bar, making himself a drink. Ugh, he's so unfairly attractive in a black suit, white button-down shirt, and thin black tie. My heart starts beating extra fast when I realize that this guy is mine.

All mine.

Lucky, lucky me.

He lifts his head, his eyes widening when he sees me. His drink forgotten, he makes his approach, until he's standing directly in front of me. It feels like his hot gaze could gobble me up, and I shift on my feet, dying for him to say something.

"Damn, Sarah."

And that's all he says.

"That's it?" I ask when he remains quiet. "No, 'shit, girl, you are hot like fire'? Or, 'fuck me sideways, I've never seen a sexier woman in my life'? Really?"

He laughs, shaking his head as he settles those big hands on my hips. He leans in for a kiss, murmuring just before his mouth lands on mine, "Shit, woman, you are hot like fire."

I laugh against his lips, grateful that he didn't get offended by my teasing. But I did want a big reaction. And after everything that happened between us only an hour ago, I'm feeling confident enough to ask for what I want.

It is a liberating feeling, let me tell you.

"You ready to go? he asks once he withdraws from my lips.

"Sure." I watch as he goes back to the bar, finishes pouring himself a drink and then knocks it back in one swallow.

"You want one before we leave?" he asks.

"No thanks." I shake my head. "I'm nervous enough."

He's frowning. "You're still nervous?"

"Of course. I want to impress your family, Jared. I want them to like me."

"You impressed them pretty well last night," he reassures me.

"I know, but tonight I get to meet Kevin's fiancée. And more of your family. You said you come from a big one," I remind him. All those cousins and aunts and uncles with names I'll surely never remember.

It'll be overwhelming, but I should be fine with Jared by my side.

"They'll love you. Don't worry," he says with all the confidence of a man without a care in the world.

He should feel that way. Our fake relationship shifted into reality rather quickly. All those dreamy looks we're going to shoot each other from across the room tonight will be one hundred percent authentic.

"What about Kevin's fiancée? What is she like?"

A shadow crosses his face, and he becomes instantly somber. "She's—nice."

And that's all he gives me.

Weird.

"Let's go," he says with brisk efficiency as he closes the door on the bar and then walks over to me, placing his hand at the small of my back and escorting me over to the door. Trademark Jared Gaines, for sure. "We're meeting Candice down in the lobby. She's riding over with us."

"Are you driving?"

"Taking an Uber," he says as he reaches for the suite door. "You got everything you need?"

I hook my arm through his and smile up at him. "Now I do."

Oh Lord. That was cheesy. But he's smiling at me, kissing me, whispering in my ear how much he wishes we didn't have to go to this party. I shove him away from me, not wanting him to ruin my Killer Queen vibe.

I'm owning my look and my confidence tonight. Jared and I can mess around later.

We've got all night for that.

"YOU   TWO   ARE   EXTRA—AFFECTIONATE TONIGHT," Candice points out.

We're in a black Yukon SUV, Candice sitting in one of the captain seats, Jared and I crammed into the backseat together. Hands still restlessly wandering like we can't help ourselves, his mouth occasionally pressed upon my forehead. In my hair. On my neck.

It's when he kisses my neck that I get squirmy, especially with his sister sitting in front of us.

"Did you see her?" Jared asks, referring to me. "How can I resist?"

Candice turns and rolls her eyes at us, though I can tell she is loving this. Probably not used to seeing her brother so carefree, so happy. "I'm guessing this sort of thing, um, turns you on?"

Jared lifts himself away from me completely so he can really look at his sister, confusion clouding his eyes. "What the hell are you talking about?"

"You two fought earlier. And now it looks like you definitely made up." Candice waves a hand at us. "Are you one of those couples who fight so you can make up?"

"Well, the making up was really good. I can't deny that," I say as Candice plugs her ears with her fingers and starts chanting *la-la-la-la-la* to tune me out. "But I'm not that big on fighting."

"Me either," Jared agrees, slinging his arm around my

shoulders, tucking me in close. "Though I will agree the making up after the argument was really, *really* good."

I elbow him in the ribs. "Stop saying that kind of stuff. You're freaking your sister out."

"Yeah you are," she agrees, her back to us once more.

I giggle. Candice giggles. Jared just scowls.

What else is new?

"How much longer until we're there?" I ask him after a few minutes of silence.

"We're pretty close." He strokes my bare shoulder with his fingers. I really like his fingers. "Eager much?"

"I'm excited to go, yes," I admit to him.

"I wish I would've had one more drink."

"Why?"

"I need the liquid courage to get up the nerve to talk to everyone," he says, his voice low, probably so his sister won't hear him.

"You've got this." I rest my hand on his rock-hard thigh, giving it a squeeze. "You'll be fine."

"Should I apologize to Candice now?" I can tell by the expression on his face that he'd like to get it over with.

"Sure," I encourage.

"Hey, Candice?" She turns to look at him. "I just wanted to apologize for being such a jerk to you earlier."

"It's okay," she says sweetly.

I nudge him in the ribs again.

"And I'm sorry for being a complete ass to you over the last few years."

"It's fine." Candice tilts her head. "You don't have to apologize for who you are."

Ha. So basically his baby sister just called him a complete ass.

"I'm turning over a new leaf, thanks to Sarah." I smile

up at him. No more jabs in the ribs for him. "I'm trying to right my wrongs."

"I think that's really great," Candice says. "Can't wait to see who you apologize to next."

I laugh. I can't help it.

We arrive at the venue a few minutes later, just as Jared predicted. It's being held at an exclusive club in the financial district downtown, and as we get out of the car, I can already hear the beat of the music outside. When I glance over at Jared, the look on his face is nothing short of pained.

"Are you all right?" I ask him once we're out of the SUV.

"I hate parties with loud music," he says, glancing up at the tall building before us.

"It's a rooftop party," Candice tells us. "Meaning it's outside. So of course you can hear the music."

"Still." He's grimacing, like he's going to be led to the torture dungeon.

"Oh my God, you are such an old man." Candice takes Jared's hand and leads him up the steps, and I fall in behind them. "Let loose for once in your life and have some fun."

"I know how to have fun," Jared says, sounding like a hurt little boy.

I keep my comments to myself. He does know how to have fun—the bathroom incident was a hell of a lot of fun, not that we can tell Candice about it.

But she's right. He's so serious all the time. Cranky. I'm sure most everyone who knows him believes he's just...unhappy.

That is the saddest thing ever.

The moment we enter the building's lobby, I am in awe. It's so warm and welcoming, with exposed brick walls, rough-hewn wood beams crisscrossing the ceiling and comfortable-looking leather chairs placed closed to one another for intimate seating.

I'm tempted to plop my butt in one of those seats and test it out, but Jared takes my hand with his free one, leading us to the bank of elevators.

"Everyone's already up there," Candice tells us once we're all in the elevator. "They've been texting me for the last twenty minutes, asking when we're going to get here. Especially Kevin. He really wants to talk to you."

"That was my fault," Jared says, his expression dead serious. "I was running a little late. You can blame me."

"Actually it was really my fault," I add. "It takes a long time to blow dry my hair." And blow someone else too, ha ha.

I am on a roll tonight. At least in my head.

Jared sends me a look and I pinch his side, making him jump.

"You two." Candice shakes her head. "Are being ridiculous."

The doors sliding open saves us from saying anything else. We exit the elevator and make our way down a short, dark hall before another set of double doors appears before us. Jared pushes them open first, and it's like opening a portal to a whole other world.

There are people everywhere. Music is playing, wait-staff are walking around with trays laden with appetizers or glasses of what I assume is wine, and in the center of the rooftop, there's a giant square surrounded by brick, with a fire burning in the middle. People—mostly women in short-sleeved dresses—are sitting around it trying to keep warm. There are flowers and balloons and a giant banner that says *Congratulations Rachelle and Kevin!* hanging above the open walkway where we enter the party.

Jared takes my hand once more, his palm sweaty, and I glance up at him to see that his face is impassive, his jaw like stone. A tiny muscle moves there, though, barely noticeable. But I see it.

I notice everything about him.

"Hey?" I tug on his hand and he glances down at me, frowning. "It's going to be all right, you know. Just relax and have fun."

"Okay." He blows out a harsh breath. "You're right. I need to relax."

"Yeah, you do. You've got this." I lean against him, breathing in his delicious scent. Candice has already abandoned us, and I can hear people calling her name in greeting. But everyone loves Candice.

And maybe that's hard for Jared to deal with. He's the least popular of the Gaines siblings. If he'd put himself out there more, he could change that. He'd be just as beloved as Candice and Kevin.

Hopefully tonight he can make a change for the better.

TWENTY-NINE

WITHIN TEN MINUTES of walking into the crowd, Jared and I are separated. I don't know how it happens, and I have no idea where he went in such a short span of time. I try to text him, but he hasn't responded yet, though I'm not worried. He wasn't exaggerating—this party is pretty loud. And packed.

Here's the deal. I expected one of those staid, boring parties you see in movies with a few rich people staring at each other disdainfully while eating weird-looking appetizers and drinking white wine spritzers. Clearly, that's not the case. This party is *happening,* with the majority of attendees appearing around my age into their early thirties, and these people seem to know how to have a good time.

Which is great—I'm ready to have a good time too.

The one person I do find is Candice, surrounded by her cousins who are all waiting their turn to hug her and tell her how much they miss her. She is so adored, it's unreal.

I wonder if that bothers Jared. It has to, if he feels so unlovable.

Once Candice spots me, she pulls me into the cousin

circle and introduces me to all of them. They smile and hug me like they've known me forever, and I return their hugs and greetings with the same enthusiasm. I do get that they were related on Jared's dad side—their father is Marcus's younger brother—but once we leave them, I confess to Candice I don't remember any of their names.

"Don't worry," Candice tells me as we're milling about. "You'll meet them again. Probably at Kevin's wedding."

I hope I'll still be around for Kevin's wedding. Will Jared and I go the distance? Right now, all giddy and hyped from our earlier sexual interlude, I'm full of confidence and thinking we're gonna make it for sure.

Give me a few days. I'm sure something will happen, or he'll say something and my self-doubt will kick in.

"Oh, there's Kevin! Let's go say hi. And you'll get to meet Rachelle," Candice yells, pointing. I see Kevin standing next to one of those tall cocktail tables they always have at parties, looking handsome in a navy blue suit, white shirt and pale blue tie. The woman standing next to him is striking. Tall, willowy, with sleek black hair that hits just above her shoulders, and her long dress with the flirty ruffled hem the same color as Kevin's tie. They're smiling at an older gentleman who's talking rather animatedly to them, and I start to hang back, afraid to interrupt their conversation.

Candice has no qualms whatsoever, barging right in and throwing herself at her brother.

"You look so handsome!" she squeals as she wraps him up in a smothering hug.

I stand behind her, shooting Kevin a sympathetic smile when his gaze meets mine, his eyes going wide as Candice attack-hugs him.

My heart pangs at the way Kevin is looking at me. He

reminds me of Jared. And I hate that they aren't close. They should be.

Once Candice lets go of her brother, she hugs Rachelle, a lot more restrained this time around. Rachelle returns the hug, her expression serene, complimenting Candice on her dress, which is candy apple red and like a beacon amongst all the dark clothing we're surrounded by, including myself.

"Rachelle." Kevin grabs her hand and brings her to where I'm standing. "This is Sarah, Jared's girlfriend."

Rachelle smiles, her expression friendly, her dark eyes glittering. She's even more beautiful up close. Her skin is smooth, and her lips remind me of a pretty pink bow. "It's so nice to meet you. Kevin told me this morning that he thinks you're so good for Jared." She takes my hand, clasping it in between hers for a few seconds before she lets me go.

"Oh." My cheeks are warm. I'm blushing. Flattered. I didn't think Kevin really noticed me last night. I guess maybe he did. "That's so sweet of Kevin to say, thank you. It's nice to meet you."

"Nice to meet you too. Are you having fun?" She glances around, tilting her head back to stare at the tower of balloons we're standing next to. They're white and blush pink, mixed in with silver and gold balloons, and it's downright artistic, how they're arranged. Nothing like the balloon arches in our school colors when I went to prom.

"So much fun. Your party is *amazing*." I smile, instantly afraid I sound and look fake, so I take it down a notch. Jared would be proud. "It's beautiful up here."

"Right? I love how all the buildings surround us." We are indeed surrounded by tall buildings, including the famous Transamerica Pyramid, which is directly in front of us. "It's like decoration we didn't have to pay for."

"It's gorgeous. I love it. I think everyone else is having

fun too." I smile, nodding toward the crowd. I still don't see Jared. Candice has left us too, though she's easy to spot with the red dress.

"Where *is* Jared?" Kevin asks as he approaches us, stopping to stand directly beside Rachelle. He slips his arm around her slender waist, pulling her close to him, and she goes willingly. They're an attractive couple. They look good together.

"Oh, I don't know. I lost him as we made our way through the crowd."

"Probably hiding in a corner somewhere," Rachelle says with a faint smile.

I frown. How would she know that? I mean, that sounds like something Jared would do, but I didn't think they were that close. He told me he rarely talks to Kevin, so how would Rachelle know that Jared is standoffish? I guess Kevin could've told her.

For all I know, Rachelle might not be a big fan of Jared. And I really couldn't blame her. He doesn't spend time with his brother—her fiancé—and that might be upsetting.

"How long have you two been together?" I ask, curious.

"Oh, what's it been, Kev?" She glances up at him with adoring eyes. "Three years?"

"More like three and a half." He drops a kiss on the tip of her nose. Yeesh, they are almost sickeningly sweet together.

"That's a long time," I say.

"We've known each other for longer than that," Rachelle says, turning her focus on me. "Through Jared and—"

"There you are! I've been looking for you everywhere."

I turn at the sound of Jared's voice, relief flooding me at seeing him. I didn't realize until I had him in front of me that I was feeling untethered. Adrift. This is his family's event after all, and I don't really know anyone here.

But I know him. And I am so, so glad to see him.

"Hey," I say softly, smiling at him when he sweeps me into his arms and kisses me right on the mouth, his lips tasting of liquor. Not a quick peck either. More like a lingering, *I can't wait to get you alone later* type of kiss. Nothing like that squeaky-clean nose kiss Kevin delivered to Rachelle.

I mean, nose kisses are cute, but I prefer Jared's greeting for sure.

He pulls away first, his gaze for me only, and it is scorching. I'm blushing again, and I take a step away from him, needing the distance.

"Kevin." Jared goes to his brother and hugs him, the shocked expression on Kevin's face priceless. Bet he wasn't expecting that. "You look good, man. This is quite the party. Congratulations."

"Thanks, man. You're enjoying yourself? This place is awesome," Kevin says. "Rachelle found it. Well, actually it was Evelyn's idea—"

"Rachelle." Jared's already abandoned his conversation with his brother, turning his focus on Rachelle. He offers her a polite hug, not near as enthusiastic as the one he gave Kevin. "You're looking as beautiful as ever."

"Thank you, Jared," she says, taking a big step away from him.

Yep. I knew it. She doesn't like Jared. He's got some major making up to do with his brother and his brother's fiancé.

The brothers resume their conversation, leaving Rachelle and I standing in front of each other and not saying anything. Talk about awkward. I wish I had a drink in my hand. Where's one of those waiters wandering around with the tray full of wine glasses? I need one badly.

Rachelle is the one to break the ice first. "How did you and Jared meet?"

"Oh." I stand a little straighter, remembering what we went over yesterday. "At a work function."

That is so general that no one would question it. At least, that's what Jared thought.

"Do you live in Monterey?"

"Seaside actually." I probably shouldn't have said that. Seaside is the poorer side of the Monterey Peninsula. "I've lived there my entire life."

"Oh. That's nice. Monterey is such a beautiful area to live in." She nods, her lips curling in a faint smile. "How long have you two been together?"

"Not long." I smile in return. "A couple of months. It's been a total whirlwind."

Oops. Maybe I shouldn't have added that last part.

Rachelle's eyes alight with interest. "Really? Such an interesting way to put it. A whirlwind."

Uh. I need to explain myself. "He's just—a total romantic." Sort of. "Always giving me gifts." That part is true. "He's very generous." In all ways, if you get my drift, lady.

"Generous? Jared?" She laughs, but it's forced. As in, not real. I'm frowning. I don't know if I like this. "I've never heard him be described that way before."

How the hell would she know how people describe Jared? I mean, yes she's been a part of the Gaines family for over three years. I'm guessing she's seen Jared at his absolute worst, or at least described that way. Maybe?

I don't know. I don't truly get the family dynamics here.

"He's *extremely* generous," I tell her.

"And so you're happy with him? Truly?" Her delicate brows lift in question as she waits for my answer.

That's a totally weird and invasive question. In fact, this entire conversation has been weird.

"Very happy," I stress. "He's such a wonderful man. And trust me, no one can give me an orgasm like Jared. Now if you'll excuse me, I'm going to go in search of a drink."

I escape before she can say anything in response, but I saw the shocked look on her face when I said the word orgasm.

Blinking wide eyes, mouth formed into a little O. I stunned her silent.

I probably shouldn't have said that, but her questioning made me more than a little upset. Not full-blown mad, but just...why would she ask me if Jared made me happy? What kind of question was that?

"Hey. Sarah, wait up," Jared says from behind me.

Slowing down, I turn, waiting for him to catch up, which only takes a few seconds. "Where are you going? You didn't even tell me you left."

"Sorry." My smile is strained and I give up, letting it fall. Should I tell him the truth? That I didn't like Rachelle's line of questioning? I don't want to fill his head with negativity, so I decide to keep my opinions to myself.

"I'm dying of thirst," I finally say, which is the absolute truth. "Let's go find a bar."

"I know exactly where one is." He places his hand on my elbow and steers me to the right, bending his head so he can whisper, "You are so fucking sexy in that jumpsuit."

My skin goes warm at his words, and I realize quick he's staring down the front of it. I'm giving him a nice view of my boobs, lucky guy. I suddenly feel anxious. "Am I flashing too much skin?" I tug at the front of the jumpsuit, pulling it up, but it doesn't really budge. It feels like I'm showing some major cleavage. Probably *too* much. I'm meeting his family, for God's sake, not going out with the girls for a weekend in Vegas.

"You're fine. You're not flashing too much skin, promise." He slings his arm around my shoulders, keeping pace with me as we head toward the makeshift bar. Of course, there's a long line. I'm not the only one with tremendous thirst. "I wish you were flashing more, to be honest."

We take our place at the end of the line, and I count the people ahead of us—it's eight deep, making us the ninth. I hope those two dudes with the trendy-looking mustaches mix their drinks extra fast.

"Thank God I'm not," I tell him, glancing down at my chest once again. Maybe it's not so bad. A hint of cleavage, nothing too scandalous. He's just excited because he had his hands all over my boobs only a few hours ago. I know I can't get that moment from the bathroom out of my head. I'm guessing he's feeling the same way. "This is a family function, Jared."

"I know, and all I can think about is when can I get you naked next." His arm is now around my waist, his hand resting basically on my ass. He has no shame, I swear.

"In a few hours," I promise, sending him a closed lip smile. "We have to get through this party first."

"You're right." He glances around, nodding and smiling at someone he must know before he resumes his attention on me. "I told Kevin we all need to get together soon. A double date or whatever. He said they'd love to."

Hope lights me up. He wants us to double date with his brother and Rachelle. This means he still believes we can be an "us." I don't know how I feel about spending an entire date with Rachelle as company, but I'd do it for Jared.

"You did? Well, that sounds like progress." I'm still contemplating telling him what Rachelle said to me, but I really don't want to ruin his good mood.

"I think so. And hey, sorry I lost you when we first walked into the party. I saw my dad and Mitzi, and he was waving me over. I thought you were following behind me, but when I turned around, you weren't there."

"It's okay. Candice rescued me. She introduced me to all of your cousins." It dawns on me what he said and excitement fills me. "Wait a minute, did you actually talk to Mitzi?"

His eyes light up. He looks very pleased with himself. "I did. I told her she looked nice."

"That is major progress for you."

"She gave me a funny look. I think she was waiting for a follow-up insult." Jared chuckles. "I didn't say much else to her, though. I was afraid I might ruin it."

"You do have a skill for that," I tell him, my voice full of sarcasm. He keeps running his hand up and down my butt, and I send him a stern look. "You probably shouldn't keep rubbing my butt. What if your father sees you?"

"Like he'd care. He probably wouldn't even notice."

"Jared." I wiggle my butt, trying to shake his hand off, but it doesn't budge. "Come on."

"I'm trying to find panty lines," he says, like that's the most logical thing ever.

Of course he is. "Well, you should give up. You won't find any."

"I won't?" He's frowning.

"Because I'm not wearing any," I tell him, my voice low.

The slow smile that curls his delicious lips makes all my

girly bits tingle. "You are a bad girl," he murmurs, smoothing his hand over my backside one more time before he lets it drop.

"Only bad for you." I tip my head back and he kisses me, another one of those lingering, *I want to get you alone and strip you naked* type kisses. This time even with a hint of tongue.

Seriously, we are acting like horny teenagers right now. I'm feeling like one for sure. I can't really remember the last time I've had sex, and if our earlier interlude is any indication, I'm guessing it's going to be pretty spectacular with Jared.

I'm kind of wishing we could ditch this party too. Maybe we'll only stick around for an hour or so. Not like any of them will miss us, right?

"Can't we leave already?" Jared asks with a ragged sigh after we break apart. "No one gives a shit if we're here or not."

His thoughts echo mine. "An hour. Let's get our drinks, make the rounds, find as many people to talk to as possible, then leave. What do you say?"

"I really like that idea." He kisses me yet again. A quick one this time that leaves me wanting more. "I also really like you."

His simple words make my heart freaking sing.

I am such a cornball.

THIRTY

JARED

THIS PARTY IS TORTURE. Making endless small talk with various relatives and old family friends is not how I usually spend my Saturday nights. In fact, this is the sort of thing I avoid as much as possible.

But I'm here for my family tonight, and for Sarah. I promised her I would do right by my brother, and that's what I'm doing, damn it.

She's part of the torturous experience, though. Sarah. Sexy as hell in that strapless black jumpsuit that shows so much skin, wearing the Louboutins I bought her, her hair perfectly straight and hanging down her back, her lips bright red, tempting me to kiss that lipstick right off of her.

She's brimming with confidence and sassy as hell, and I am dying to get her alone.

Once we get our drinks from the bar, we start wandering around, me introducing her to people I know. My aunt and uncle. My other aunt and uncle. A couple of cousins who demand to come visit my house sometime, and for once in my life, I agree that they should stop by, shocking the shit out of them.

Candice finds us at one point, and I'm pretty sure she's a little buzzed since she's louder than usual. Considering she's pretty loud when she's sober, she's practically yelling at everyone when she sees them.

Every time I see them, Kevin and Rachelle are immersed in conversation with someone, which takes the pressure off me to try to make things right with my brother. I really did tell him I wanted us to get together more often, including going out on a double date with him and Rachelle and me and Sarah. He also mentioned that he wanted to talk to me tomorrow, one on one, and would I mind going to lunch with the family before everyone took off to go home?

I agreed, though the last thing I want to do is share another meal with my family. They're not the ones I want to avoid—it's Rachelle's family I don't want to be stuck at a table with.

Luckily enough, I've dodged them the entire evening. I saw Rachelle's parents and guided Sarah with a gentle nudge, sending us in the opposite direction. I know she spoke to Rachelle for a few minutes while I was chatting with Kevin, but I keep forgetting to ask her what Rachelle said.

If she blew my cover and revealed that we know each other because I used to be engaged to her older sister, I think Sarah would've confronted me about it by now. As it stands, I'm a freaking idiot for not telling her the truth already. I keep telling myself she won't care. She shouldn't. I could give two shits about Evelyn, despite the fact that she was my first heartbreak. The first woman I loved.

I'm over that. I've been over it for a while. At least, that's what I tell myself. And yeah, it's been difficult with Evelyn here this weekend, though I know she wasn't the woman for me. Thank God we didn't get married because I can guarantee we'd be divorced by now. Or maybe we would still be together and completely miserable, I'm not sure.

That would've been terrible. Then I wouldn't have met Sarah.

It may have happened quickly, but there's no one else I'd rather be with than her. And maybe it didn't happen quickly. We've been hate-flirting for the past six months, every time I saw her at Bliss. We just finally got around to actually doing something about it.

"I'm freezing," Sarah says with a little shiver as we stop by one of the outdoor heaters. She steps closer to it, holding her hands out. The wind has picked up more in the last half hour or so, making it colder.

"You didn't bring a jacket." I take mine off and set it over her shoulders, but it just completely envelopes her, making her look like a little girl wearing her daddy's coat. "Is that better?"

"No, because it's hiding my outfit." She shrugs out of my jacket and hands it back to me. "I love this jumpsuit. I need to get as much joy out of this as I can."

"But you're cold," I point out.

"I'll suffer through it," she says with shrug. "Beauty is pain. Haven't you ever heard that before?"

"No," I say carefully, wondering what the hell she's talking about. "What do you mean?"

"Sometimes women have to suffer in order to look good. My mom used to always say that when she kicked off her high heels or was so relieved to take off a dress that was too tight or uncomfortable. She'd tell me beauty is pain. And then she'd get this weird look on her face, kneel down and stare right into my eyes. She'd tell me beauty really shouldn't be painful and I should suffer for beauty only if *I* want to, not because I'm suffering to look beautiful for someone else." Sarah's smile is wistful, her gaze growing distant.

I know that expression well. I'm sure I look the same when I'm thinking about my mother. "She sounds like she was pretty great."

"She was the best mom ever." Her gaze meets mine, her blue eyes turbulent with emotion. "I'll have you know I'm not suffering in the cold wearing a strapless jumpsuit for you, Mister Man. I'm doing this for myself. I swear this jumpsuit gives me confidence."

"Super Sarah?" I tease.

"Yes, Super Sarah, I like that. Do you like superheroes?"

"I got your Spider Man reference that one time, yes," I tell her with the utmost sincerity.

"What are you talking about?" She frowns.

"When you asked who was going to be here at this very party—you mentioned Uncle Ben and Aunt May," I explain to her.

She starts laughing, shaking her head. "Brent loved Spider Man so much when he was a kid. I know all about Uncle Ben and Aunt May." She rolls her eyes. "God, I was such a jerk to you, I swear."

"I drove you to act like a jerk because of my dickish ways," I remind her, and she only laughs harder. The sound of her laughter is infectious and I can't help but join her, and I realize at this moment I've never felt lighter.

Or more content.

And it's all because of this woman standing before me, making me laugh. Making me want her. Making me want to protect her. She brings out all of those feelings I thought I couldn't feel anymore. The ones I stuffed away and forgot about after my engagement ended with Evelyn. That very woman is here at this rooftop party with us, yet I haven't seen her at all. Not once.

As if I'm not meant to see her, which I'm perfectly okay with. I don't need to see my past tonight.

Right now, at this moment, with this woman—Sarah—I get the sense that I'm looking at my future.

Once the laughter dies, I pull her to me, nuzzling her cheek with my nose before I murmur close to her ear, "Let's get the fuck out of here."

"Our hour isn't up yet," she tells me, shivering when I must hit a sensitive spot just below her ear.

"How long have we been mingling and playing nice?"

"I don't know. I didn't check my phone when we started," she admits, giggling when I nip her earlobe.

"Then I say it's been an hour. Let's go." I grab hold of her hand and we start walking, both of us keeping a fast pace, like we're eager to get the hell out of here.

I won't even make eye contact with anyone, too worried they might stop us and want to chat for twenty minutes. I'm over making small talk and asking how everyone is doing. I know how they're all doing—*fine*. I know how their lives are —*busy*.

"You guys are already leaving?" Candice appears out of nowhere, standing right at the rooftop entrance, below the banner congratulating Kevin and Rachelle.

We stop short, both of us sharing a glance before we look at Candice. "Yeah, Jared's not feeling very well," Sarah says, sending me a sympathetic frown.

I nod, my manner solemn. "Had a little too much to drink."

"Aw, that's terrible!" Candice tugs me into her arms, her

perpetual cloud of perfume surrounding me, almost making me cough. "I hope you feel better."

"I'm sure going to bed early will take care of whatever ails him," Sarah says, her tone so serious, even I'm starting to believe her.

"You guys got a car coming to get you?" Candice asks, whipping out her phone. "I can get one for you."

"Do you mind?" I wince, really putting it on. "I want out of here as soon as possible. I'm a little dizzy." Sarah's stern gaze tells me to rein it in.

"No problem." Candice taps at her phone, the light from her screen illuminating her cute face. "Done. They'll be here in less than five minutes."

"Then we better get going," Sarah says, grabbing hold of my hand and dragging me toward the hall that leads to the elevators. "Thank you so much, Candice."

"You two are going to lunch tomorrow, right?" she calls as we're walking away. "I hope you feel well enough to show up!"

"I'll try," I tell her.

"Love you guys," she yells, and the moment she's out of view, we start running down the short hallway toward the elevators. The moment we arrive, Sarah's stabbing the down button with her finger again and again.

"That's not going to make the elevator show up any faster, you know," I say as I stop to stand beside her.

"I just want it to get here before Candice follows us and sees that you're feeling just fine." She turns to face me. "I didn't know I could lie so well."

"You did a stellar job," I say, my voice, my expression serious.

"Hey thanks." She leans into me, her hands on my chest, her face tipped up like she wants me to kiss her.

Nope. Can't do it. If I kiss her, I'll pull her into the elevator and keep kissing her. I'll also touch her. Everywhere. Things might get heated in the Uber. And then I'll end up making an ass of myself.

That means I have to keep my hands off her until we get to the hotel.

THIRTY-ONE

SARAH

I AM DYING. For some reason, Jared thought it would be a good idea to keep his hands to himself until we got to the hotel. He announced those very words to me when we entered the elevator and I tried my best to attack him.

He fended me off, his hands wrapping around my forearms, stopping me from touching me. "Let's wait," he said in that annoyingly calm voice I hadn't heard in a long time.

Like, since the last time we were together at Bliss.

Once I realized that nothing was going to happen in the elevator, or in the backseat of the Uber, I cross my arms in front of my chest, plumping my boobs up as much as I can, and put on a good pout.

He doesn't even look at me, the bastard. He's too busy scrolling on his phone and answering a text from Candice.

And then his father.

And then his brother.

Jared doesn't tell me what they're saying, just lets me know with every notification of his phone who's texting him. Finally, curiosity gets the best of me and I can't stand it anymore.

"Why are they all texting you anyway?" Shouldn't they be having fun at the party?

"Candice told them I didn't feel well. Now they're all worried about me." He chuckles. "Why are they worried? You told Candice that you thought I drank too much. I'm supposedly drunk, not sick."

"Maybe she didn't hear me. She was buzzing too. I'm sure she's made up her own story and is telling everyone you're on your deathbed," I suggest jokingly.

"She's always had a flare for the dramatic. I wouldn't doubt it."

We talk like this for the rest of the drive to the hotel—which is much shorter than when we rode over earlier, thanks to less traffic. By the time Jared's at the suite door using the keycard to open it, I'm an anxious, nervous mess. I'm itchy, the jumpsuit suddenly feels too tight, and I wonder if this is what it feels like right before you explode from extreme sexual frustration.

I've never experienced this before, so I'm at a loss.

The moment the door shuts behind us with a quiet click, I'm in Jared's arms. He presses me against the wall, his mouth finding mine, his hands gripping my hips. I give in to his hungry kiss, my hands going to the lapels of his jacket so I can shove it off him. He helps me get rid of it, shucking it to the floor before he reaches for his tie, fumbling with it like he's as shaky as I am before it too finally disappears.

Reaching for him, I unbutton his shirt with trembling fingers, my breaths coming fast, my head spinning. I am an addict. I want him. So badly, my entire body is burning up. His mouth returns to mine, devouring me, his kiss all-consuming as his lips meld with mine. He removes his hand from my hip to slip it behind my head, his fingers burying in my hair, and holds me still as his tongue explores my mouth.

I kiss him back with the same ferocity, desperation clawing at my insides, making me whimper low in my throat. He takes over me trying to unbutton his shirt, finishing undoing it before he tries to take it off with a single flourish.

It doesn't work. He forgot to undo the buttons on his cuffs and the shirt hangs from his wrists. I know this because I opened my eyes and watched the entire incident go down.

There's no containing my laughter. He looks ridiculous, his hair a mess, his swollen lips and smoldering gaze, that glorious muscular chest on full display, yet his shirt is hanging from his hands, still attached around his wrists. Still laughing, I reach for one hand and undo the button, then the other, and he shakes it the rest of the way off.

"Thanks," he mutters as his mouth hovers above mine. "I tried to be cool and I ended up looking like a dumbass."

"The worst part is that you used the word cool," I whisper, sighing with longing when he dips his head and starts kissing the side of my neck.

"What's wrong with the word cool?" he asks, his murmured words against my sensitive skin making me shiver.

"Everything. It's not cool." I run my hands up and down his hard chest, marveling at his muscles. The smattering of hair between his pecs. I can feel the faint ridges in his abdomen, and I'm impressed. He doesn't quite have a six-pack, but he is close.

My fake/maybe real boyfriend is smokin' hot.

"I think you're just making fun of me for the hell of it," he says, lifting his head so he can look into my eyes. There's a single lamp burning in the living area, and that's it. The suite is mostly dark, but I can see his face, the shadows hiding some of his features and emphasizing others. He is truly so gorgeous, it almost pains me to look at him.

"You're right," I tell him with all the seriousness I can muster. "I enjoy making fun of you. It's my secret hobby."

"I know. You did it all the time at Bliss," he tells me as he's about to kiss me.

I press my hands against his chest, stopping him. "I did not."

"Yes, you did." He tries to kiss me again, but I still hold him off.

"No. I really didn't. I just did what you asked, mostly."

"Uh huh. Some of the things you said were just to antagonize me," he murmurs, running his fingers up my right arm, his touching tickling. "Like always using the word mistress."

"They were your mistresses," I say primly.

He shakes his head, his hand dropping away from my arm. I immediately miss his touch. "I hate that word."

"Mistress?"

"It's the worst," he says with a nod.

"Almost as bad as cool," I say, and he chuckles.

"Right. Both of those words are terrible."

"I totally agree." I smirk. "I will never call them mistresses again."

"Good, because I don't have any mistresses. I haven't had one in at least six months," he confesses, this time his mouth landing on mine.

Wait a minute. Six months?

I break the kiss. "You were buying a lot of lingerie these past six months, Jared."

He shrugs.

"So who was it for?"

"Probably the first set I bought from you was for an

actual someone. After that..." His voice drifts. He shrugs again.

We're quiet for a moment. Him from embarrassment, I'd guess, and me because I can't believe I'm hearing this. "So you just have a bunch of lingerie sitting in Bliss bags at your house?"

"Not quite." He hesitates. "Some of it is at my office."

"So you *are* some kind of weird pervert with a lingerie fetish," I tease.

"Not quite. More like I had a total fetish for you," he admits.

"Ha! No freaking way." I shove at him so he steps away and I start walking into the living room, but Jared follows me. Picks me up, as if I weigh nothing. I shout. He flips me around and slings me over his shoulder.

Like he's some sort of caveman.

"Put me down." I beat on his bare shoulders, pausing when I see he has a tattoo there, just below his shoulder on the right side. "You have a *tattoo?*"

I'm shocked. Seriously, the guy who gets aroused by formality and punctual people has a freaking tattoo? Get the hell out of here.

"I do." He carries me into his bedroom, dropping me onto the bed so I land on the mattress with a bounce. "What's the big deal?"

"You are the last person I thought would have a tattoo." I wave a finger at him, indicating he should turn around. "Show it to me."

He turns, and I rise up on my knees and scoot until I'm on the edge of the mattress so I can see it better. It's a red heart, done in that old sailor style, with a banner across the center of the heart that says:

Mom

Oh shit. I'm touched. More than touched. I'm freaking emotional, on the edge of tears, and I reach out, tracing each letter, pressing my palm against the tattoo when I'm done.

"This is the sweetest thing I've ever seen," I say, my voice extra quiet in the hushed silence of the room.

"I miss her," he says. The words are simple, but the emotion behind them isn't. I feel like he's been walking the edge of being a complete emotional wreck all weekend, and I'm sure spending time with his family and me forcing him to be nice has been pretty stressful.

"I'm sorry if I've been too demanding," I say, meaning it. "I wanted you to work on your relationships with your brother and sister and dad, plus Mitzi, and I probably pushed too hard."

"You didn't." He hangs his head as I skim my fingers across his back. Goose bumps rise and I continue scratching him lightly. "That feels good."

I scoot back to give him room. "Sit down."

He does as I say, settling on the edge of the bed, the mattress sagging beneath his weight. I position myself behind him and start rubbing his shoulders. They're tense, no surprise, and I dig my fingers into his muscles, trying to get him to ease up. Slowly but surely, I rub the tension right out of him, until he feels good and loose. He bends his head forward, giving me total access, and when I lean in and press a kiss at the bottom of his nape, I heard him suck in a breath.

"There is so much more to you than meets the eye," I tell him, hoping he doesn't take it as an insult.

Because it's not. I feel like with every day that passes, he's revealing more of himself to me. And I love it.

"I am a man of mystery," he says, his tone teasing.

"You really are," I agree, shifting away so I can study the tattoo once more. "When did you get it?" The colors are so vibrant, that deep red heart seeming to almost glow.

"Right after I turned thirty."

So not very long ago. "Where were you? Who were you with?"

"An old friend from college, Scott. He'd just moved back to town, and we went out drinking, which turned into a drunken night of going to bar after bar, until we were completely wasted."

Why is that everyone gets a tattoo when they're wasted? I say that's the worst time ever to get a tattoo, but what do I know? I don't have any.

"I was telling him how I always wanted a tattoo to honor my mom, and he said he knew about this one place, and the next thing I knew, I'm at a tattoo parlor, and this old dude who's covered in ink—and I mean *covered,* there was barely any actual skin showing, I swear—and I couldn't stop staring at him." He laughs. "That old guy said I was making him uncomfortable, and I said he should take it as a compliment, and then I asked him if he had any mom tattoo examples he could show me. And he did—showing me this identical tattoo he had on his right bicep."

"So you copied him."

"It was exactly what I wanted. He said he'd just lost his mom, which I found hard to believe because man, was he old, and extra wrinkly too. But he was saying he got the ink to honor her, the best woman he'd ever had the privilege to know, and I knew that's what I wanted to do too, so I told him I wanted his tattoo."

I run my fingers across the tattoo once again. "He did a fabulous job. It looks amazing."

"You really like it?" He sounds surprised.

"Yes," I say firmly. "Especially when I know the reason behind it."

He turns and the next thing I know, I'm flat on my back on the mattress, Jared hovering above me, his hands braced on either side of my head, the muscles in his arms straining. He's watching me closely, his gaze roaming over my face, down my throat, across my chest. I'm still wearing the jumpsuit—seriously, I'm reluctant to take it off—and my breasts are threatening to fall out.

And he's looking at me with this dreamy expression on his handsome face, like I'm the best thing he's ever seen in his life, and all I want to say is...

Same.

I feel exactly the same way.

How did we get so lucky to find each other? I am probably totally overthinking this, with all my mushy-gushy emotions overwhelming me at the moment. Right now, we are in the throes of a fresh relationship. Crap, we're not even in a *real* relationship, but we like each other. We're discovering each other.

And I am becoming a complete sucker for this man.

"We need to get you out of this thing," he tells me, tugging on the front of my jumpsuit. "Maybe you should roll over so I can unzip you."

My entire body goes hot, imagining all of the things he could do to me after he unzips this thing. I have no panties on, and no bra. It's just me beneath the fabric.

"You'll need to get out of my way first," I tell him, and he immediately does, shifting so he's lying on his side, right next to me. I roll over onto my stomach, moving my arms so I can prop myself up on my elbows. "Okay. Unzip me."

He reaches for the back of my jumpsuit, his fingers

skimming along my skin, making goose bumps rise. I bend my head, my hair falling in front of my face, waiting in breathless anticipation as to what he might do next. Slowly, he pulls the zipper down, the fabric falling open, revealing my bare back. Once he's done, he spreads the fabric aside even further, running his fingers down my spine.

"You don't have a bra on."

"Nope." I press my lips together when his fingers move lower, right above my butt.

"You don't have panties on either."

"I told you I had nothing on beneath the jumpsuit earlier," I remind him.

He's quiet for a moment, as if absorbing this information. "I just find it funny that I bought you lingerie. More than you can imagine. I've given you bra and panty sets twice. And every time we start to—mess around..." I hear him move and then the next thing I know, warm, soft lips are pressing against the base of my spine. "You're already naked. Not a scrap of lace or silk in sight."

"Hmm." I inhale sharply when I feel his tongue swipe across my skin. "You're right. That is rather odd."

"Yes." Another kiss. Another lick. "It is. Lift your hips for me."

I do as he asks, a huff of surprise escaping me when he tugs the jumpsuit down. It catches on my hips, my backside, and then he's tugging again, pulling it down the length of my legs, my shoes dropping to the floor before the jumpsuit joins them.

I stay in position as I hear him climb off the bed. The sound of his belt being undone, the clank of metal, the familiar whirring noise of a zipper. I can tell he's kicking off his shoes, getting rid of his trousers, and then he's back on the bed, his hands on my ankles, pulling my legs apart ever so slightly.

Oh God, I am so turned on. He could probably breathe on my toes and I'd come. This is pure torture, his hands on my legs, joined by his lips. He's kissing his way up my calves, the back of my knees, my thighs. I spread my legs a little farther, prop up on my knees to give myself some leverage.

"Don't move." The commanding tone of his voice is another turn on. Oh, I knew he would be like this in bed. Just from the way he behaved every time he shopped at Bliss, I had a feeling he would be demanding. Maybe even a little...rough?

I don't have any experience in that sort of thing, but with Jared, I'd be willing to try just about anything.

Because he asked me to, I remain in place, still propped on my knees, my legs quaking, my breathing heavy. He shifts, the mattresses squeaks, and I think he's on his knees, looming above me. The position is confirmed when he grabs hold of my hips and readjusts me, pulling my butt close to his front, and I realize that he kept his underwear on. I feel cotton—and his erection straining against the fabric.

"You are so fucking beautiful," he whispers, his hands stroking my hips. I squirm against him, trying to drive him as crazy as he's driving me, and his grip becomes firmer, keeping me in place. "I won't let you take control of this."

Oh, is he one of those *submit to me* kind of guys? I don't know if I can do that. I might laugh, and he might get mad, or worse, I hurt his feelings, and then I'd worry it might not work between us—

"You are thinking way too hard." He leans over me, his chest against my back as he grips my hips, pulling me up so

I'm on my hands and knees. "I don't want you thinking at all," he whispers close to my ear.

I don't want to think either. I want to lose myself in this. As long as he doesn't do anything too cheesy, I'll be fine. I'll be fine, fine, fine...

"*Oh.*" I jolt against him when I feel him leave an open-mouthed kiss on one butt cheek, then the other. He's getting terribly close to a spot I'd really like to have his mouth on, and I think he knows this and that's why he's purposely avoiding that particular spot.

The man knows exactly what he's doing. He's driving me out of my mind with all the teasing. More kisses on the back of my thighs. Murmurs of appreciation buzzing against my skin. He disappears for the quickest moment and then he's back, and—oh my God—he's lying on his back, face to vagina, people. Clinical terms and all that, but it's the truth. His arms curve around my hips, his hands are firmly planted on my ass cheeks, and then he's pulling me down, until his mouth makes contact, and that is *it*.

I can't think anymore. Nope, all I can do is savor the sensation of his tongue on my sensitive skin. I am basically sitting on his face and he is licking me to oblivion, and I am loving every second of it. My hips are moving. My thighs are straining. He's sucking on one particular spot that is totally working for me, and it doesn't take long. I'm close. So close to coming all over his chin and I don't even think he cares.

He's saying encouraging words, like he wants me to come and so I let go. I just let it all go, closing my eyes, reaching. Reaching. Reaching...

"Oh God." The words fall from my lips as that first wave hits me, teetering on the precipice before I completely fall over. I'm coming. I'm moaning his name and I'm coming. My entire body is convulsing like I have no control over it because I don't. I flat out don't, and I don't know how I'm ever going to recover from this. Muscles are involved that I never use and when the tremors finally, *finally* calm down and I'm feeling like myself again, I aim for the mattress and fall on my side, lying right next to him in a boneless heap.

He doesn't say anything for a few minutes. I watch as he repositions himself so he's lying on his side facing me. He's still got his underwear on—black boxer briefs—and his erection looks ready to pop through the fabric.

"You are really good with your tongue," I finally tell him, making him laugh.

"I have never been with a woman who's made me laugh while having sex," he says, pulling me into his arms.

I snuggle close to him, though it proves difficult, what with his erection poking me in the belly. "I'm here to entertain you."

"I thought I was the one who just entertained you."

Now I'm laughing. "Oh, you did. That was the best entertainment I've ever had in my life. In fact, if you want to keep entertaining me like this, let me know. I'll give you a full-time job."

The moment the words leave me, I realize they sound kind of serious. As in, I want him to be in my life all the time, giving me delicious orgasms and whatnot. And that's not what I meant. Not really. I'm just so overcome. My body is still tingling, little aftershocks running through my body, making me shiver.

But then he says the best thing ever, easing my worry with a few choice words.

"Where do I apply for this position?" He raises his brows.

"Right here," I murmur. "You have to kiss me first. That's the first step. I want to see if you have potential."

He kisses me. I can taste myself on his lips, but it doesn't bother me. If anything, I think it makes everything that much hotter, and turns me into a greedy little animal who wants more.

And he is just the man to give it to me.

THIRTY-TWO

JARED

I'M DESPERATE FOR HER. She comes so easily. She must be just as aroused by me as I am by her, and she's driving me crazy.

Crazy.

In the middle of our lazy kissing, I start taking off my boxer briefs, and she helps me, her fingers tugging impatiently around the waistband, those same fingers curling around my dick once it's exposed, giving it a squeeze. Her soft hand wrapped tightly sends a bolt of lust straight through me, and I'm almost afraid if she keeps this up, I'll come all over her fingers and embarrass the shit out of myself.

So I gently push away her hand, preventing her from touching me as I finish removing my boxer briefs. Then I'm as naked as she is, and soon we're a tangle of limbs, mouths fused, tongues twisting, her hand still around my cock, my hand between her legs. She's soaking wet, ready for me, and I can hardly wait any longer.

I need to be inside her.

Pulling myself away from her, I climb off the bed,

thankful the drapes are open, letting light from outside into the room so I can see. Sarah immediately sits up, watching me walk across the room. "Where are you going? What are you doing?"

Her desperate sounding questions are a reassurance that she wants this to happen as badly as I do. But I have to grab something first before we can actually make this happen.

I go to the giant dresser that's opposite the bed, opening the door that reveals the small fridge within. There's a mini bar in there, and I find exactly what I'm looking for.

A box of condoms.

Yep, I'm that idiot who didn't plan ahead. Luckily enough, we're staying in a sex positive hotel.

Turning, I wave the small box at her. She raises her brows. She's smiling. Completely naked. Beautiful. "How many are in there?"

I shake the box. "How many times do you think this is going to happen?"

"As many times as possible?" Her hopeful tone makes me chuckle.

"There are three condoms."

She pouts. "That's it?"

"I think we can manage. We *are* leaving tomorrow." I tear open the box and pull a condom out, then toss the box onto the bedside table. I leave the single wrapped condom on the table as well, and rejoin Sarah on the bed, pulling her into my arms. She comes willingly, kissing me like she's starved and I'm the only one who'll satisfy her.

I like that. Her eagerness. Her enthusiasm. The women I've been with recently—if you can call six-plus months ago recently—never seemed that into sex. They said the right things, moaned at the right moments, but it always felt...

Fake.

Not so far with Sarah. Is it because she's younger? A tad —sex-starved? I know it's been a while for her. And it's been a while for me.

Maybe that's it.

Within minutes I'm reaching for the condom, rolling away from her so I can put it on. She moves so she's lying in the center of the bed, her head propped up by a mountain of pillows, a big, expectant smile on her face. She watches my every move, her gaze tracking my hands as I roll on the condom, and her lips part.

"You're kind of—big," she observes.

"Only kind of?" Her words do great things for my ego.

"Well, I didn't have a difficult time managing it in the bathroom, but I don't know. My shop's been closed for a few years," she explains.

"Your shop?" This girl is just...

Unbelievable. In the best possible way.

"Well, yeah. I haven't had sex in a long time. Remember?" I move so I'm lying on top of her, her legs parting so I'm in between them, and I brace my hands on the pillow on either side of her head. She shifts beneath me, her stomach brushing against my dick, and I close my eyes, hissing in a breath at the contact. If she keeps that up I might not be responsible for what happens.

Like me coming too early. Wasting a precious condom.

She'd probably be pissed.

"How long has it been again?" I stroke the hair away from her forehead, drinking in her features. She's so pretty. Beautiful. Young. But smart. Confident. She's been through a lot, and losing her parents has formed her into the woman she is today. She's pretty fucking great.

I don't know what I did to deserve her.

"A couple of years?" She shrugs one bare shoulder and I bend down, kissing it. "And it was with a guy I wasn't serious about at all. We went on maybe seven dates."

Seven dates. Interesting. "What's your limit?"

"What do you mean?"

"Two dates and you let him kiss you. Four dates and you let him feel you up. Six dates and you have sex with him. Is that about right?"

"I never thought about it like that before." She purses her lips, her brows lowering like she's concentrating hard. "I had sex with that guy on date six. After the seventh date, I knew he wasn't for me. He didn't even try to kiss me." Now she's rolling her eyes. "Men should know that kissing is the best part."

"You think so?" I kiss her. With hungry lips and a searching tongue. By the time I break the kiss, she's panting.

"Yes." She nods. "It's the best. He was okay. I can't believe we're talking about this right before we do it."

She's right. But I'm enjoying this. "Interesting that it took that poor guy six dates." I'm smiling. More like smirking. "Only took me one to get you naked."

"You're awful." She shoves at my shoulder, but she's smiling. Her eyes are glowing, and she's staring at me like I'm her favorite person. "And since you brought me here for the entire weekend, that's like six dates in one."

"Whatever you say." I dip my head, kissing her softly. This is the most unusual sexual experience I've ever had. It usually doesn't play out like this. Where we can talk so easily. Tease each other. We're lying here naked and we're chatting about the last guy she had sex with like it's no big deal.

Before, I would've never wanted to know any of that information. I always kept plenty of distance between myself and the woman I was involved with. I never told her too much, never wanted her in my business. Deep down, I know this is why they never worked out.

I never wanted them to work out.

I'm starting to feel differently about Sarah. I can actually see us together. I can see her becoming a part of my life.

I want her to.

But I can't think about that, not now. Not when I have a willing woman in my arms, all soft and fragrant. Responsive. Our kissing gets carried away, and within minutes I'm sliding inside of her. Claiming her.

Making her mine.

THIRTY-THREE

SARAH

I WAKE UP DELICIOUSLY SORE. And alone. Can you believe it? Jared woke up early and went for a run.

I suppose he's totally into keeping himself in shape. How hot is that?

Stretching, I sit up, pushing my hair out of my face before I grab my phone. It's almost ten-thirty, and he's only been gone for about thirty minutes, so I guess he didn't get up *that* early. It just felt that way, considering we didn't fall asleep until around four in the morning.

We used up every one of those condoms too. Ha.

I have a text from Andie—she's been staying at a friend's house all weekend and checking in with me every few hours, just like I requested. She's asking when I'm coming home, and that makes me happy because maybe it means she misses me.

Or maybe she's just sick of being at her friend's house. Who knows.

Snuggling under the covers once more, I keep checking my phone. No messages from my friends, which surprises me. But since I shared that photo of the room Friday night to my private IG story, I haven't sent them anything else. I've gone completely incommunicado for the most part, and not one of those bitches reached out to see if I'm alive.

My friends are jerks!

I could be dead in a gutter, you know.

I fire that text off to our group chat, then scroll through Instagram. They might not even be awake yet. It *is* Sunday.

Caroline: **Didn't want to interrupt you. I figured you were getting continuously banged by your fake boyfriend.**

Stella: **Remember when you had me add you to my Find a Phone app? I know where you're at. At all times.**

Then she sends a screenshot that shows I'm smack dab in the middle of downtown San Francisco.

Kind of freaky.

Me: **Oh. Right. I forgot about that.**

So they *did* know where I was the entire time. I'm glad Stella still has me on her app. That's actually pretty reassuring.

Another text comes through.

Eleanor: **Are you having a good time?**

Kelsey: **You never answered my question about the pervy lingerie guy.**

Me: **I'm with the lingerie guy. And he's not pervy.**

There. Hopefully she'll stop calling him that.

Caroline: **Did you bang him or not?**

Her impatience is showing. And my lips are twitching. I can't contain the smile.

Me: **Eleanor, I'm having a GREAT time.**

I'm purposely ignoring Caroline.

Caroline: **Don't ignore me, Sarah!**

Ha ha. She knows me too well.

Me: **I don't like to kiss and tell.**

Stella: **THIS MEANS SHE TOTALLY HAD SEX WITH HIM!!**

All sorts of emojis start flying. Kissing lips. Heart eyes. Eggplants.

The quietest one of our friend group, the one who's always working or with her stupid jerk of a boyfriend who no one likes, actually responds.

Amelia: **You have a new boyfriend? Maybe we could double date sometime!**

Um, no. I love Amelia. She's fun. But her boyfriend? Is a Class A douchebag.

Me: **Oooh yeah. Maybe.**

Caroline sends me a text apart from the group.

That guy is an asshole. Do not encourage her.

I shake my head. I wish Amelia would get her head out of her butt and dump the guy, but who am I to tell her what to do?

I know, I know, I respond.

We chat a little more in the group, me offering up a few tidbits about the weekend, but I keep pretty mum overall. I don't feel right, exposing Jared's secrets. He confessed a lot to me, and I told him a lot too. They don't need to know all of that.

But I can tell them how he makes me feel (awesome), and how we've had a great time, and that he's a most excellent kisser (understatement).

The door opens and I send a quick goodbye text, set my phone on the bedside table and pull the covers up to my chin.

Seconds later, Jared's entering the bedroom, wearing a black T-shirt and black athletic shorts, looking a little sweaty.

A lot hot. Literally and figuratively.

"You're awake," he says when he spots me clutching the covers like I'm a scared virgin on her wedding night.

"I am. How was your run?" Wow. This actually doesn't feel awkward. I was scared of the morning after conversation. Jared can be a hard man to figure out sometimes, and I was worried he might make it weird.

He has a way of making things weird a lot of the time.

"It was great. I feel invigorated." He rubs a hand through his hair before letting his arm drop. "You all right? You sleep good?"

I'm thinking what we've been doing in this very bed is actually why he feels invigorated, but whatever.

"I slept great. But I am a little sore," I admit.

Concern etches his features. "Did I—hurt you?"

"No, no. Just, you know. From having sex for the first time in a while."

He smiles. "We had sex more than one time."

"You know what I mean." I'm smiling too. We're grinning at each other like lunatics, and I don't want to stop. We watch each other for a moment, before he shakes his head once and starts to speak.

"Lunch is at noon at a restaurant down the street. Kevin already texted me with the details," he says. "Have you taken a shower yet?"

"No." I wince. I probably smell. He's probably grossed out by my lack of hygiene.

But then I remember how I basically sat on his mouth last night and I realize there's no way he can be grossed out by me.

Jared studies me, his head tilted to the right. "Tell me why are you hiding behind the covers?"

Modesty got the best of me at first, but screw it. "Oh, I don't know." I sit up, toss the covers aside and climb out of bed. I stop right in front of him, completely naked, and his gaze is eating me *up*. "Guess I decided to come out of hiding."

"I like it when you don't hide." He sneaks an arm around my waist and tugs me close to him, his hand splayed across my butt like he owns it. "Let's take a shower together."

"We don't have any more condoms," I remind him, slipping my hands beneath his T-shirt. Oh, his skin is still damp with sweat. I know that shouldn't arouse me but it does.

It so does.

"We can do lots of things without condoms," he says suggestively, wagging his eyebrows.

Laughing, I take his hand and we practically run to the bathroom.

WE SHOW up at the restaurant at ten minutes after

twelve, hand in hand as the wind seems to push us through the door. We are grinning. Glowing. Our eyes sparkle and our cheeks are pink and every time we look at each other, the air seems to crackle. It's heady stuff.

When we check in with the hostess, she lets us know that our party is already seated and are in a private room in the back.

"How many people are here anyway?" I ask, curious.

"Don't know. I didn't ask." Jared smiles down at me warmly. I can only describe his current expression with one word: satisfied. "Hope you like Chinese food."

"I love it." The smells coming from the kitchen are making my stomach growl. I never did eat breakfast, and I don't think Jared did either. "I'm starving."

"Me too."

We enter the private room where Jared's family is to find one giant round table with every seat occupied, save for two that are together. One empty seat is next to Kevin. The other is next to Candice.

Oh thank God. I'm grateful to be able to sit by Candice.

"There you guys are," she calls, rising to her feet to embrace us both at the same time. Her head swivels from me to Jared. "We were afraid you wouldn't show."

"We're only ten minutes late," Jared says, his voice low. Uh oh. I can tell he's already irritated. Has he ditched his family before, with events like this? I'm guessing yes.

"We slept in," I tell Candice with a gentle smile. "But Jared is feeling much better today, after what happened last night."

Ha. Yes, he is most definitely feeling better after what happened last night.

"Oh thank goodness." The relief on his sister's face is

clear. "Well, come sit! We already ordered a bunch of food. We're just going to eat it family style."

Candice settles into her chair and I'm about to do the same, when I notice Jared hasn't moved. He's looking at an older couple sitting on the opposite side of the round table, and I assume they must be Rachelle's parents. There's a stunningly beautiful woman who's sitting next to them. She reminds me of Rachelle too. Maybe her sister?

"Jared?" My voice seems to penetrate his brain and he looks at me, offering a tense smile. "Let's sit down."

He does exactly that, not saying a word to me. He turns his focus on Kevin, and they launch into a deep conversation that I am not about to interrupt.

"Candice." I tug on her sweater sleeve and she turns her head. "Who is the older couple sitting across from us?"

"Oh, that's Rachelle's parents, Vera and Ang. They're really nice. And that's Rachelle's older sister sitting with them. Evelyn." Candice makes a funny face, one I can't immediately interpret. "But I'm sure you've heard all about her."

I blink at her, feeling dumb. "No, I've never heard about her."

"Really? Not ever?" The surprise on her expressive face is obvious.

"No," I repeat. "Who's Evelyn?"

"I was trying to tell you about her before Jared found us at breakfast yesterday," Candice explains. "She was uh...she and Jared used to, um. Be together."

I glance over at Evelyn and see she's talking rather animatedly to Marcus, Jared's dad. Like they're old, close friends.

My heart pangs at the easy familiarity between them

and I look away. Is she the one? The girl who broke Jared's heart?

"How long ago?" I ask Candice.

"It was a while ago now. Years. Like, ten years. I was barely in high school." She glances around to make sure no one is paying attention to us before she whispers, "They were engaged."

My blood runs cold. Like, I'm frozen in shock. Oh God, Evelyn is the *one*. Why am I finding this out from Jared's little sister and not him? "*What?*"

Candice nods, her brown eyes wide and full of fear. I bet she regrets opening her mouth. "Yeah, oh my God, he didn't tell you? I figured he would, since Kevin is marrying Evelyn's sister and all. We're basically going to be related to Evelyn, which is you know, hella awkward, especially for Jared."

"No." I sit up straighter, my head spinning with this new information. "He didn't tell me about her. At all."

Well, he sort of did. Without mentioning any names or telling me that the woman who broke his heart and ruined him for years was going to be here this weekend. A normal person would consider that an important factoid to tell someone, don't you think? That motherfucker. Seriously, why didn't he tell me? Does this guy have zero balls or what? Did he really think he'd get away with this? He knew I'd have to find out eventually.

I just wish I could've been told versus finding out from his sister, who's watching me like she'd rather be anywhere but here.

Yes. This is hella awkward, as Candice put it.

"I suppose you two are going to really enjoy making up after this, right?" Candice asks nervously. "Since your favorite part of a fight is the making up?"

Yeah, I don't know about that. Does this constitute a deal breaker? He didn't outright lie, he just withheld information.

Which is basically lying.

I sit there, quietly steaming while everyone else is chatting, having a great time. I eavesdrop on Kevin and Jared's conversation. He doesn't even realize I'm not talking to anyone, he's so focused on what Kevin is telling him. And he's asking his big brother to be his best man. This is a big deal, especially for these two.

"Is Evelyn going to be Rachelle's maid of honor?" Jared asks, apprehension in his tone. "If that's the case, it'll be— weird. And you know it."

I clench my hands into fists. Ooh, he is such an ass.

"She just got married," Kevin tells him.

"Really?" Jared practically scoffs. "I had no idea."

"If you answered my calls once in a while, you'd know. I'd keep you in the loop," Kevin jabs, irritation in his voice.

Yeah, Kev. Stick it to your jerk brother. He deserves to feel like shit.

"You know I feel bad about that," Jared admits. "Work keeps me busy—"

"Work is just an excuse," Kevin interrupts. "Ever since Mom died, you've shut yourself off from everyone."

My heart cracks a little at hearing that. It's not easy to deal with losing a parent.

"Okay." Jared's voice is extra deep, and I wonder if he's mad at Kevin. "You want me to be honest? At first it was— difficult for me that you're with Evelyn's sister. After everything that happened, I preferred to think none of them even existed."

"Nice way to deal with your messed-up emotions, bro."

Kevin has zero sympathy for his brother, and I kind of like it.

"Hey, tell me how you'd feel if Rachelle decided to dump you four months before your wedding day," Jared says viciously. "It would fuck you up too. I know it would."

Four months before their wedding date? Is that what happened to Jared? How awful. No wonder he's so cautious when it comes to opening up his heart to women. Obviously, he's still harboring some resentment towards Evelyn dumping him like that.

I can't blame him, but still. He should've told me.

"We've been together a long time. I didn't rush into this relationship, not like you did with Evelyn," Kevin accuses.

This is starting to make me uncomfortable. Jared is going to catch me listening in on this conversation, and while I know I shouldn't feel bad, I sort of do.

Luckily enough, four servers enter the room, all of them bringing trays of food. The smell makes my stomach growl, and I rise to my feet, needing to get away for a quick second and wash my hands.

"Hey." Jared turns and smiles up at me, like nothing's wrong. He has no clue what I know. "Where you going? The food just got here."

"I'm going to use the restroom." My voice is so cool, and I try to smile at him, but it doesn't work.

His smile fades. "You all right?"

"Just want to wash my hands." I pat his shoulder and take off before I say something stupid and he figures out I'm pissed at him.

Because I am. Pissed at him. Now I look like an idiot in front of Candice. And she'll probably tell Kevin and their dad and Mitzi and oh God, Rachelle. And Evelyn.

Why not tell everyone I didn't know that Jared almost

married Evelyn? Let's make an announcement to the entire family and then laugh over how dumb Sarah is.

Tears threatening to spill from my eyes, I go in search of the bathroom, grateful when I finally spot the door. I push my way inside, even more grateful to find it empty. I go to one of the sinks and prop my hands on the edge, staring at my reflection.

This weekend has been all about mirrors, and I really don't get why. But I'm sure there's symbolism here somewhere.

Taking a deep breath, I give myself a pep talk. I'll be all right. Jared and I can discuss this on the drive home. And while I'll tell him I'm angry and I think it was a huge mistake that he didn't let me know about his previous engagement with Evelyn, I truly believe I'll be able to forgive him.

Maybe.

I'm still staring at myself in the mirror when the bathroom door opens and in walks...

Oh shit.

Evelyn.

THIRTY-FOUR

CLOSE UP, she's even more beautiful, and I immediately hate her for it. She's definitely prettier than Rachelle, if that's possible. And Rachelle is a stunner.

So is her older sister. With elegant features, sharp cheekbones, the darkest brown eyes, and those same pink bow lips as her sister. Her thick black hair is longer, falling well past her shoulders, and I wonder if she's ever modeled. She's very tall. Slender, with a great rack.

Ugh. Jared is a boob man. I hate him.

I turn on the water and add what feels like twenty-five pumps of soap in the palms of my hands before I start scrubbing vigorously. "Hi," I say, though I'm not really looking at her. "Um, I'm sorry I didn't get a chance to introduce myself. My name is—"

"Sarah. I know." She smiles, and it's oddly reassuring. Her expression is open. Kind. I remember how Rachelle was toward me last night, but knowing what I know now, I sort of get it. She was feeling defensive of her sister. "I've heard a lot about you."

Wait. *What?*

"From who?" I glance down at my hands, realizing they're still covered in sudsy soap and I rinse them some more, then turn off the water. Evelyn is standing right next to the paper towel dispenser, and like a chicken shit, I'm afraid to approach it, approach *her* and grab a towel.

So I stand there and drip-dry my hands like a fool.

"I spoke with Kevin last night. He seems quite taken with you. Same with Candice. She could not stop telling me how great you are." Her smile grows, and I wonder if she adores Candice like everyone else. I'd guess yes. "Mr. Gaines had nice things to say about you, as well as Mitzi."

I'm thrown for a moment with her use of the words *Mr. Gaines*, but I figure out quick that she's talking about Marcus. Their father.

The only Mr. Gaines I know is Jared. And that's become my special name for him, as weird as that sounds.

"They said that about me?"

Evelyn nods. Great. She knows every freaking member of the Gaines family, and they all went and told her how awesome I am, yet I had no idea who she was to Jared.

I didn't even know she existed. Not in the context of being Jared's freaking former fiancée. That's major.

Huge.

"He didn't tell you about me, did he," she says, and I wonder if she's some mystical witch who knows how to read minds.

"No," I confess, and I go ahead and approach her, waving my hand in front of the paper towel dispenser and tearing off a piece. "Candice just told me only a few minutes ago."

"I'm sorry," Evelyn says with a sigh. "I hate that you found out that way."

On first impression, I would've pegged her for being a

petty bitch who'd come to find me in the bathroom so she could rub it in my face that she had Jared first. But that first assumption was just me being the petty one, and that's really not what she's about.

I get the sense that she's being one hundred percent genuine right now. And I appreciate that.

A lot.

"I suppose that's just—Jared's way." I sound like I'm making excuses for him.

"Don't make excuses for him," she chastises, confirming my mystical witch feelings. "He can be so cold sometimes. Standoffish. Rude. It's almost like he can't help it."

Despite my anger towards Jared, Evelyn's words anger me more. To the point that I have to say something.

"Don't forget that's my boyfriend you're talking about," I tell her, lifting my chin. I sound possessive as hell. "I know you were engaged to him, but that was a long time ago. And he's changed."

Well, he's *trying* to change. I don't know if it's possible.

"You're right. I was out of line for saying those things, and I'm sorry." She reaches out and lightly touches my arm. "His family has said that too. That they hope he's a changed man, and some of them told me they believe it's thanks to you. I'm so glad to hear that. I only want him to be happy."

I glance down at her left hand, which still rests on my arm, momentarily dazzled by the giant diamond on her finger. It's so big, it looks fake. "You're married." I lift my gaze to hers. "I heard Kevin say that."

"Yes, and I'm so happy." Her hand drops away and she smiles. "And that's all I want, for Jared to be happy too. I have no ill will toward him. Not anymore. We were young, and we rushed into the relationship, so giddy and in love.

But it was all smoke and mirrors, and once real life intruded, it became, I don't know. Boring? He was never around. Always working, never wanting to spend time with me, and I believed it was my fault. That something was wrong with me."

I blink at her, wishing she'd tell me more, yet not wanting to hear any of it. I'm intruding on his past relationship. Only hearing it from the other side, and that's dangerous.

I also don't like hearing about Jared being in love with someone else. A gorgeous woman who actually seems really nice. Someone I could possibly like as a friend, which is kind of weird.

This entire situation is weird.

"Then he asked me to marry him, and I believed he must've loved me after all. A man must love you if he's asked you to marry him, right?"

I nod, but don't say a word. I'm guessing she doesn't expect me to.

"After the newness of our engagement wore off, and I stopped staring at my ring all day long, I realized we'd fallen back into the same pattern. He never told me his feelings. He was very...closed off. I believed it was because he lost his mother, and he never fully dealt with it. I don't know if that's true, but it's what I thought."

My heart is heavy with all of the information she's giving me.

"I was talking with my friends one day, and they all told me, 'Ev, if you're so miserable with this guy, then why are you marrying him?' And I realized they were right. Do you have friends who are always real with you, no matter how much it might hurt?" Evelyn asks.

"Yes." I inhale a shuddery breath. "I have some of the best friends in the world."

"That's good." She smiles.

"Was it—was it difficult for you, when you broke it off with Jared?"

"So difficult, but he responded in that typical Jared way." Her lips twist. "He really didn't say much at all. Oh, something along the lines of, 'I'm sorry you feel that way,' like I was ending a business merger, but otherwise, that was it. He didn't fight for me. He didn't shout his undying love. He took back the ring and slipped it in his pocket. Told me that he would miss me, and at that point, his voice broke a little. I suppose he was trying to show some emotion, but by then, it was much too late. His immediate reaction confirmed I did the right thing."

I remain quiet, absorbing everything she said. If I tried to end it with him right now and he reacted that way toward me, I'd be furious.

Yet I can't imagine him behaving that way. I don't think he would. I may have only known him for a few months, and known him intimately for only a few days, but I just can't see it. I believe he'd fight for me.

If that makes me an idiot, then so be it.

"We should probably get back," I tell Evelyn, my stomach choosing this exact moment to growl loudly. "Obviously, I'm hungry."

Her expression turns serious. "I'm glad you let me talk to you."

"Why wouldn't I?" I ask incredulously.

"Most women wouldn't want to hear what their current boyfriend's ex-fiancée has to say about him. I appreciate your openness."

"You were the one who was so open with me, Evelyn," I say. "And you've given me a lot to think about."

"All good, I hope?" She lifts a delicate brow in question.

"We'll see," I answer ominously.

We exit the bathroom together, making small talk, and by the time we're entering the private room where everyone is eating and talking, Jared is sitting there, looking like he wants to die. Evelyn and I are laughing about a stupid meme we both saw recently on Instagram.

Jared's gaze finds me, and it's almost comical, how wide his eyes get. I keep my expression neutral, touching Evelyn's arm and letting her know how glad I am to meet her, before we split apart and I settle in my seat in between Candice and Jared while she goes and sits with her parents.

"You were just talking to Evelyn?" he asks, his voice sharp.

Nodding, I turn to meet his gaze. "I was."

And then I help myself to a giant spoonful of chow mein, dumping it on my empty plate.

He's speechless. I'm able to add a small helping of sweet and sour chicken and Mongolian beef before he finally says something. "You know who she is, don't you?"

Ah. He is so smart.

"I do," I say, keeping my voice even. "And we definitely need to talk, but not now. Not in front of your family, Jared. Let's eat and you enjoy your time with Kevin and everyone else."

Ooh, I am such a mature adult. But I mean every word I say. I don't want to argue with him at the table. I don't want to drag him outside and scream at him. They'd all think I'm insane, and I'm not the insane one here.

That would be Jared.

But we'll talk about it later, on the car ride home. He's not going to get away with this. I'm calling him out on his bad behavior, and he's going to have to answer to me, since we're trapped in a car together for two hours.

That should be fun.

THIRTY-FIVE

JARED

SARAH'S calm behavior is freaking me out. Seeing her enter the room with Evelyn, both of them laughing like they were old friends? Maybe even laughing about me? I thought my head was going to explode.

Seeing the two of them together made me realize that maybe I wasn't completely over what happened between Evelyn and me. Not that I'm still in love with her—I'm not—but because of the way our relationship ended, that's why I put up the walls. I haven't let anyone in for years, including my own family. I keep everyone at a distance, say shitty things on purpose to drive them away so they can't hurt me.

And Evelyn's rejection of me, and our future together, hurt me. It's only taken me this long to realize the full extent of the damage. Damage I've also done to myself.

Once Sarah returned to her seat next to mine, I tried talking to her, but she wasn't having it. She hasn't been rude to me, but she's definitely ignoring me, focusing on everyone else, and all I can keep thinking is that finally, a woman comes along that I can see a future with, and I've ruined it.

I've ruined us.

My appetite gone, I shove my plate away from me, exhaling loudly as I cross my arms and slump in my seat.

"You okay?" Kevin asks.

"Not really," I answer truthfully, earning a shocked look from my baby brother. "But I'll be all right. Eventually."

I hope what I'm saying is true.

"Does it have to do with Evelyn and Sarah walking into the room together?" Kevin asks, his voice cautious.

"You saw that too?" Great. The whole family probably saw it. God knows what they're all thinking. Or saying.

"I did, though you shouldn't worry. Evelyn never says anything bad about you."

"I find that hard to believe," I mutter.

"It's true." He shrugs. "She's moved on, Jared. I would've thought you had too."

"I have, trust me. I'm totally over her." I sound like I'm protesting too much, so I clamp my lips shut. Though it is true. I *have* moved on from Evelyn. I can't say it's thanks to her that I don't have long-term relationships with women.

That's on me.

The rest of lunch goes mostly the same. Me not eating, trying to talk to Kevin but having a hell of a time focusing. I've agreed to be his best man, and I know he's happy about it. I should be too. But all I can think is that I'll have to walk with Evelyn, and Sarah probably won't like it.

Hell, Sarah probably won't be with me by the time Kevin and Rachelle get married, so I'm getting ahead of myself.

By the time everyone's finished eating, we've all moved around, switched seats, or are standing in a corner talking. Some people—Rachelle's parents—have already left. My father and Mitzi are the next to leave. I find myself near the door of our private room after telling them goodbye when I turn to see Evelyn standing directly in front of me.

Everything inside of me wilts. I've avoided talking to her for so long—years—that I'm half tempted to run out the door and never look back.

But that would make me a coward. So I stand my ground and smile at her.

"You planned on avoiding me the entire weekend, didn't you." She didn't even say it as a question.

"I guess that didn't work." I'm joking, but her expression doesn't change, so I assume it fell flat. "It's been a long time, Evelyn. What am I supposed to say to you?"

"We're going to be in-laws. We should be civil to each other at the very least. But you won't even give me a chance." Her words are vaguely accusing, but not her tone.

"You have to admit we're entering strange territory," I say.

She's slowly shaking her head. Evelyn is a beautiful woman. I'm a sucker for a pretty face, and I fell hard for her in those early months. But once the newness faded, I realized quick that maybe she wasn't the woman for me.

Not that I ever wanted to admit that. Not then.

"We entered that strange territory years ago when Kevin and Rachelle first got together," Evelyn points out. "You were never around to deal with me—with us—in the first place. Now that it's gone on so long, it's become awkward."

"I'm trying my best here. I don't want it to be awkward." And that's the damn truth. "But what were you saying to Sarah earlier?"

Evelyn rolls her eyes. "Is that all you're worried about? That I spilled all of your secrets to your new girlfriend?"

Hell yes. "No. I just never thought I'd see the two of you so—chummy."

"She's a nice woman. Very sweet. Very real." Evelyn points. "Don't mess it up. You've got a good one."

Her words settle in my gut, making it twist and turn. It's the words don't mess it up that freak me out. I might've already done that.

"What about you? I hear you're married."

Her expression goes from shrewd to serene in the blink of an eye. "Gregory is a wonderful man. He's a doctor. That's why he's not here this afternoon. He had to work. Though I'm sure he would love to meet you."

I'm slightly taken aback by the enthusiasm in her voice. "Why would he love to meet me?"

"So he can thank you for not being married to me. Greg and I found each other instead." She laughs, and it hits me.

Evelyn is completely over me. And I'm completely over her. We weren't for each other, we never were, and that's all right. It's more than all right—we dodged a bullet, thanks to Evelyn's foresight. Our lives could've taken a completely different path if we got married, and we would've never met the people we were meant to be with.

Gregory for Evelyn.

And...maybe...

Sarah for me.

Now I just have to convince her that I'm not a complete asshole.

THIRTY-SIX

SARAH

JUST AS I FIGURED, the ride home is all kinds of weird. Traffic sucks. Jared's mood is hard to read. I'm a fidgety mess. Oh, I planned on acting like a badass bitch and was going to call him out on his lies, but once reality hits and I'm trapped in the car with him, my inner badass bitch takes off and replaces her with Chicken-shit Sarah instead.

So I'm quiet. Pouting, even. Not a good look for me. Not a good look for any woman who wants to have a serious talk with her man to clear the air.

That's why I'm surprised when Jared says something first. "You spoke with Evelyn."

That's all he says.

The jerk.

Clutching my hands into fists, I take a deep breath before I say, "Your ex-fiancée? Yes, we talked."

That tiny muscle in his jaw flexes, the way it does when he's irritated. I'm already learning his tells. "You're mad at me for not telling you sooner."

"So mad!" The words explode out of me and oh my God, I feel better already. "Why didn't you tell me before we came to San Francisco? We had a two-hour car ride Friday. You could've dropped that interesting little fact then, you know."

He's clutching the steering wheel so tightly, his knuckles are white. And I know it's not the crappy traffic that's bothering him either. It's me. And this difficult conversation. "I didn't know how to bring it up."

"It's real easy, Jared. You should've said, 'Oh hey, Kevin's fiancée? Her older sister used to be my fiancée. Strange, right?' And then explained the entire situation to me." He says nothing, so I barge on. "Instead I find out from Candice, and then when I went to the bathroom, freaking Evelyn followed me in there and proceeded to explain your entire relationship history."

Jared looks positively horrified. "Our *entire* relationship history?"

Why is it so satisfying to see him squirm? Oh, I know why, he made me look like a complete fool to both his sister and his ex. "Maybe not your entire relationship, but a good chunk of it. And you know what's the most surprising thing of all?" I think he's afraid to ask, so I keep talking. "Evelyn is so damn nice. She was *kind* to me. Reminded me of one of my friends, if I'm being truthful, and Jared, I am nothing but one-hundred percent truthful with you all the time. I can't say that about you."

He's quiet. I cross my arms and look straight ahead at the heavy traffic on the freeway. God, if this ride home takes longer than two hours, I might lose it. Especially if he's not going to talk to me. I need him to respond, to say something, to do something.

Finally, he speaks. "I wanted to be truthful with you. I did. But I just—I didn't know how to tell you that Rachelle's older sister is my ex." That's all he says. And I guess he's right, it's as simple as that, but...

"You should've figured it out so I didn't look so stupid. She *knew* you hadn't told me, and I felt really dumb when she asked me and I had to admit the truth. She knows you that well, Jared. She has you all figured out still. Ten years after the fact. I guess that shows you haven't really changed."

He says nothing. Neither do I. I can't help but be stuck on that one fact. That he hasn't changed. That he will mostly likely never change. He's thirty-four years old. Does that mean he's set in his ways? I'm thinking yes.

And that makes me realize we will probably never work. Ever.

Traffic finally clears and it's a smooth ride straight through to Monterey. Jared never really says anything else and I decide I have nothing else to say either. I'm too tired, too overwhelmed, too frustrated by everything that happened this weekend. I thought we were having a break-through. I thought we'd connected. And maybe we did.

Maybe it wasn't enough.

I take a nap but sleep fitfully. I dream of Jared showing up at my house, meeting my brother and sister, and Andie hating him on sight. The moment he walks in, she starts yelling at him. How he treats me badly, how he's a complete jerk to his family—as if she would know, but it's a dream. They don't have to make sense.

They're arguing in the kitchen when Andie reaches into the cabinet and flings a can of green beans at his head, knocking Jared out cold. I run to him, pull his head into my lap and brush the hair away from his forehead while I cry, but he never wakes up.

Andie killed him with a can of green beans.

The car slowing down causes me to wake up. I startle out of sleep, realizing that I drooled on his Tesla's passenger side window again, but this time I feel no guilt. Exhaling loudly, I sit up straight, pushing my hair out of eyes and figuring out quickly that we're almost to my house.

Shit. And everyone should actually be there too.

"You can just drop me off down the way from my house," I mumble when he turns onto my street.

He sends me an incredulous look. "Are you that embarrassed you don't want your neighbors to see me?"

"No, of course not. It's just—" I pause, not sure how I want to say this. The truth is more hurtful sometimes, and this is one of those situations. "My brother and sister are home, and I don't know how to explain to them that I went with you this weekend."

He's frowning. Hard. "Who do they think you're with?"

"My friends." I shrug. "I told them it was a girls' weekend."

"So you lied too." He says the words casually, but I know what he's trying to do. He's trying to make me feel bad for supposedly doing the same thing he did to me.

It's not going to work.

"That's different. I didn't know how to explain to them I was going away for the weekend with a man I don't know very well." Just saying it out loud makes our entire situation sound shady. Why did I agree to do this again? "I didn't want them to worry."

"How is that different? You lied to your family, I lied to mine. We're both a pack of liars, Sarah. Just at varying degrees." He pulls the car over two houses before mine and puts it in park. "But I'll do as you ask. I'll even help you with your suitcase. Go ahead and take your walk of shame home by yourself."

He gets out of the car before I can say anything else.

My jaw is hanging open as my brain plays over every-thing he just said. My mother would've told me to shut my mouth before a fly swooped in, but I can't help it. He's tired of this shit? Well, I'm tired of his shit, too. I'm so over what-ever the hell this thing is between us. Sick of lying to him, to myself, to my family, to his family.

I'm sick of all of it.

I climb out of the car, slamming the door with all the force I can muster. He's already opened the trunk and pulled out the blush colored suitcase I borrowed from Stella, setting it onto the sidewalk with a loud thump.

Not even seven hours ago we were in the shower together. Naked. Wet and soapy, hands everywhere, mouths fused. He found another small box of condoms in the mini bar—he told me this just before we stepped into that amazing shower—so we had sex. Of course. He picked me up in his strong arms and held me against the tile, thrusting deep. We stayed in that shower so long, the water grew luke-warm and I was shivering. Probably not from the cold, though. More like because he gave me two orgasms in a very short span of time.

The man really knows what he's doing when it comes to my body.

Now I'm considering taking Stella's suitcase and swinging it at his knees just so I can watch him fall to the ground. God, he's so frustrating. Of course, inflicting violence on Jared is not the answer. Look at my weird dream, for instance. Not sure what it meant, but I probably need to calm down.

"Thank you for coming with me," he says solemnly as he hands over the suitcase. "I know you're mad right now, but hopefully we can get together in a few days and talk."

Talk. Is he for real? "Are you willing to talk to me, Jared? Really?"

He blinks at me, and I'm guessing I've offended him. "Of course I am. Why wouldn't I be?"

"I think you have a hard time facing the truth."

"No one wants to face the truth, Sarah—" he starts, but I cut him off.

"Adults who want their relationships to work face the truth every single day. Unlike you. When Evelyn told me how she called off your wedding, she said you didn't even bother fighting for her. I was so smug in that moment. I truly believed—even though we've barely spent time together—that you would never do that to me. I knew you'd fight for me."

"I would." He says those two words quietly. "But I can't force you to change your mind, Sarah. If this isn't working for you, well..." He hesitates and then says, "I'm sorry you feel that way."

My brain implodes. Seriously, that is *exactly* what Evelyn told me he said to her when she ended their engagement. He doesn't give a crap about me.

He doesn't give a crap about anyone.

"I'm such an idiot. You wouldn't fight for me. You won't fight for anyone, not even yourself." I yank on the suitcase handle and start walking along the sidewalk toward my house. "I can't do this anymore, Jared," I toss over my shoulder. "I don't want to be with a man who just lets everything happen to him without actually doing anything about it."

I walk away. My head held high, my chin trembling, the tears filling my eyes and already spilling down my face. I sniff, press my lips together, and speed up my pace, making my way into the house and slamming the door behind me. I collapse against the door and let the sobs come, thankful no one is in the living room to see me fall apart.

I never did check to see if Jared tried to follow me to my house. I suppose it really doesn't matter.

Not like he would've done anything to make it better between us.

THIRTY-SEVEN

TONIGHT IS SUPPOSED to be fun. I'm with my friends. We have a huge table at Tuscany, Stella's brothers' restaurant, and we are having fun. Loads of fun. There's lots of wine. Baskets full of warm bread. The appetizers were just dropped off and we still have our entrees to look forward to, and I should be happy. Hungry. Thankful for my friends' support, for them being there for me during my darkest hours.

If that sounds like major drama, then I'm feeling majorly dramatic. I'm also tired. Sad. All cried out. A little angry.

Okay, fine. I'm a lot angry.

Reaching out, I grab the wine bottle closest to me and refill my glass. It's a red when I was drinking a white. Whoops. It doesn't really matter.

"Sarah." A hand settles on my forearm and I turn to see Eleanor sitting next to me, concern filling her cornflower-blue eyes. "Maybe you should ease up on the wine."

"It makes me feel better." I take a sip. Then a gulp. Then I down half the glass. This is how I've been drinking since we arrived at Tuscany, and we've only been here an hour.

Meaning, I've probably consumed a lot of alcohol in a short amount of time.

"Stel, can I stay the night at your place?" I ask my friend.

Stella, who is sitting across from me, nods. "Absolutely." She shoots Eleanor a knowing look, and I realize these two have been talking about me.

They've all been talking about me. It's why they're here, rallying around me during my time of need. We did it for Caroline when things were going south for her and Alex, but now they're going so well, we're all secretly a little jealous. Maybe even Amelia is jealous, though she always claims she's happy with her asshole of a boyfriend. But I see she's sitting at the head of the table, sucking down the wine about as fast as I am.

Huh.

"What about Andie?" Eleanor asks. "Where is she?"

"At school right now helping out with end of school year stuff." She's on the student council in a leadership role, and that always keeps her busy. She likes being involved. I like it because it seems to keep her out of trouble. "She's staying the night at a friend's house."

"Okay." Eleanor pats my arm. "Just making sure."

They're worried about me, and I get it. I'd be worried about me too, if I were them. I haven't heard from Jared in over a week. Over a *week,* people. He hasn't tried to call me, or text me, nothing. No fun little gifts either. It's like he was never a part of my life.

Ever.

When I'm working at Bliss, I half expect him to come walking through those doors in one of his sexy suits and demand I help him. I'd make a snappy remark, he'd snap right back, and then we'd fall into each other's arms, Jared telling me repeatedly that he's sorry, that he cares about me, that he'd fight for me no matter what happened, and I'd hug him close. Kiss him. Tell him all is forgiven.

Would I let him get away with it that easily? I shouldn't. He is the type who needs to be called out for his bad behavior, and no one has ever done that to him. Not his family, not his ex-fiancée. Not any of them. The only one who seems to tell him he's being a complete jerk is...

Me.

Still didn't work, though.

The appetizers arrive and my friends switch into their actual seats, and I find Kelsey sitting next to me.

She's the newest friend to our group. She's Caroline's boyfriend's assistant, and Caroline brought her into the fold one night after some jackass dumped her. It happened right here at Tuscany. Next thing we knew, Caroline walked Kelsey over to our table, and she fit right in, like she belonged with us.

I really like her a lot. She can be quiet, yet sarcastic, and I have such mad love for sarcasm. Makes me think of Jared and how sarcastic he can be...

A loud sigh escapes me, and I shake my head when Kelsey tries to offer me a stuffed mushroom. "I hear you haven't been eating," Kelsey says just before she takes a huge bite out of that mushroom.

"I eat." It's a lie. I'm living on coffee mostly. Oh, and tonight's wine. Maybe the occasional bagel.

"No, you really don't." Kelsey scrunches her nose just before she adds another stuffed mushroom to the plate in front of me, along with a slice of bread. My stomach growls at first smell of the fresh, warm bread, and without thought,

I reach for it, tearing off a piece and stuffing it into my mouth.

Carbs are my weakness.

Carbs and sickeningly handsome men who don't know how to be in a relationship.

"You ordered something for dinner, right?" Kelsey asks.

I nod. "I did, so stop trying to mother me."

Oh Lord. Saying those words does me in. I'm crying, the tears streaking down my cheeks, my lungs aching from holding in the sobs. Kelsey notices and the shocked expression would almost be comical if I wasn't so damn upset.

Rising to my feet, I run into the bathroom, Kelsey on my heels. I lock myself into a stall and perch on the edge of the toilet, gathering a wad of toilet paper so I can wipe the tears from my face and blow my nose.

"Sarah, I am so sorry." Kelsey sounds upset and I feel bad for falling apart on her. It's not her fault I'm currently in a fragile state. "I'm not sure what I said, but I feel like an asshole."

Leaning over, I unlock the door and it swings inward, revealing Kelsey standing in front of my stall, and she looks miserable. "You're not an asshole."

She slides into the stall and locks the door, then leans against it, facing me. "I didn't mean to bring up your mom."

"You didn't. I did." I jab my thumb at my chest, trying to smile, but it's weak. Doesn't help that my face is splotchy—I don't need to look in a mirror to know this—and my eyes are red from too much crying. I wish I could handle eye drops but I always blink right before I do it, so they never work.

"Yeah, well, I didn't mean to upset you. I know this breakup has been hard."

"See, that's the funny thing." I laugh. It's the most pitiful sound I've ever heard and I stop. "Jared and I didn't break up. It just sort of...ended before it ever began. Does that make sense?"

Kelsey nods. I wonder if she's humoring me. Lately, I feel like I make no sense. "He doesn't know what he's missing."

"I suppose." I grab more toilet paper and blow my nose again. "What's worse is I miss him. So much. It's stupid. I guess he doesn't miss me at all. That's why he's moving on with his life and not bothering to reach out, you know? He already forgot about me."

"You haven't reached out to him either, you know," Kelsey says. She makes this weird face, like what she said just pained her. "I'm not trying to upset you. I just want to keep this real."

"I appreciate that," I say wearily. "And you're right. I haven't reached out to him either. I suppose I could."

Just the idea of sending him a text or—oh God—going to his office makes my heart race so fast I'm afraid I'll have a heart attack.

No thanks.

"Or maybe you say fuck that guy and never contact him again." Kelsey's lips thin into a firm line and she crosses her arms. What with that fitted black leather jacket she's wearing along with the tight black jeans, I have to admit Kelsey looks like a badass bitch, and I have aspirations to be just like that. "He's an asshole."

"He is," I agree. "Fuck that guy."

"Yeah, fuck that guy!" Kelsey repeats enthusiastically.

We're walking out of the stall together, both of us still yelling *fuck that guy* when the bathroom door opens and in walks...

Candice Gaines.

Of course, sweet, friendly Candice would catch me screaming obscenities about her brother.

And by the expression on her face, I'm guessing she knows exactly who I'm referring to.

"Candice." I stand up straight, though I still feel a little wobbly. Too much wine maybe? "How are you?"

"I'm okay," she says carefully, taking me and Kelsey in. She's not smiling, which is so un-Candice of her. "How are you?"

"I'm all right." I nod. Try to keep everything casual and light. "Oh Candice, this is my friend, Kelsey."

They shake hands, nodding and murmuring all the right noises. I stand there at a loss, wishing I could hightail it out of there.

"Hey, so good to see you, Candice, but I have to go." I turn toward the door, almost free, when I feel her tug on my hand, stopping me.

"Can I talk to you?" She glances over at Kelsey. "In private?"

"I'll leave you two alone so you can catch up. I'll be at the table." Kelsey smiles at Candice. "Nice meeting you, Candice."

"You too, Kelsey." She barely smiles at my friend, so I know something's wrong. The moment Kelsey exits the bathroom, Candice places her hands on my shoulders, her expression dead serious. "I *desperately* need your help, Sarah."

If this has anything to do with Jared, I'm going to scream.

"It's about Jared."

I take a deep breath and hold it. I can't scream in Candice's face. That would be a terrible thing to do.

"He's been so awful since the weekend in San Francisco. He won't talk to anyone. I slipped into his office, but he kicked me out. *Me.*" She rests both hands on her chest, and the shock on her face is obvious. No one dares kick out sweet Candice. She's too damn nice. "I asked him what was going on with you two, but he refused to talk about it. I could tell my question upset him, though."

My lips are pressed together tightly. I don't want to talk about it either.

"You two ended it, huh? I knew it." Candice's face falls. I swear, she looks like she's going to cry. "When I realized he never told you about Evelyn, I had a feeling something like this would happen."

"He should've been honest with me," I say, unable to hold back any longer. "I can't be with a man who withholds information like that. I looked like a total fool in front of Evelyn when she talked to me."

Candice is slowly shaking her head, her eyes sparkling... with unshed tears? Oh boy. "So you broke up with him?"

"Oh, come on. How can I break up with him when we were never in a real relationship in the first place?" I slap my hand over my mouth the second I realize my slip.

Whoops.

Candice's eyes are so wide I think they might bug out of her head. "What in the world are you talking about?"

Guess I have some explaining to do.

THIRTY-EIGHT

JARED

THURSDAY MORNING. Exactly ten days since I last saw Sarah. Talked to her. Smelled her hair. Kissed her perfect lips.

Fuck.

I enter my office and shut the door, glancing around the cavernous room with mild disgust. When I have a free moment, I'm calling the interior designer I used when I redid the office. I want it redone again immediately. It's boring and lifeless. And if I have to stare at those *A Study in Beige* paintings one more time, I think I might rip them off the wall and throw them through the window.

Great. I sound like a lunatic even in my own mind.

Without hesitation I go to the walls and pull one of the paintings down, then the other, leaning them against the wall face first. There. Now I don't have to look at them any longer. Maybe I shouldn't use the same designer. I should find someone new. Someone who *doesn't* think beige on beige is a good idea.

This is what my life has become. I can't control the bigger things—like losing Sarah—but I can at least take control of the smaller things. Like the hideous art on my wall.

These last ten days haven't been easy, not that I want to admit it. I went out of town for work for four days in Los Angeles, which was the distraction I needed. Not enough to stop me from thinking about Sarah completely, but decent enough.

Usually after ending it with a woman, I move on quickly. I have this amazing ability to compartmentalize my feelings. That might make me sound like a secret serial killer, but it's true. Evelyn ended our engagement and once it was all said and done, I tucked her away into a mental box and sealed that lid tight.

The women in my life over the years—most of them didn't even earn a mental box. They were forgotten. All it took was a good night's sleep to clear my head.

So why can't I get Sarah out of my mind? What makes her so damn special?

You know what makes her special. You just don't want to admit it.

Sighing, I collapse into my chair, leaning over to tap at the space bar on my keyboard to fire up my iMac. The login screen appears and I enter my password, opening my inbox so I can check my mail.

I always hope to see something from Sarah. I don't know why. She has my email from the customer records at Bliss, but we've never communicated via email before. Why would she start now? Wishful thinking.

My entire existence has turned into wishful thinking.

I'm about to check my voicemail for messages when my office door swings open and in walks my sister.

Great.

Blowing out a harsh breath, I stand. I don't bother with niceties, I'm beyond that. "I can't talk right now."

"Oh, you are definitely talking right now." She strides toward my desk, her pale blue skirt swishing with the movement. She's adorable as usual, but there's fire blazing in her eyes and I realize it's all aimed at me.

"Candice, I don't have time for this." I sound weary. I feel weary. "I have a nine o'clock conference call I need to prepare for."

"Good thing it's not even eight yet. We have plenty of time to talk before you need to prepare for your stupid call." She props her hands on the edge of my desk and leans in. "I found out your dirty little secret."

I fall back into my chair, my gaze locking with hers. "What the hell are you talking about?"

"That you and Sarah weren't in a real relationship?" She raises her brows and I open my mouth, ready to protest, when she cuts me off. "Don't bother denying it. Sarah told me the entire sordid story."

Holy shit. The *entire* story? To my *sister?*

"She'll say anything to make me look bad, won't she?" The words don't sound right once they leave me, and I feel like an absolute asshole.

"Don't even try to pin this on Sarah. She's so upset, Jared." This revelation gives me the slightest bit of hope. "And she's so freaking mad at you, it's not even funny. You need to make this right."

My hope goes straight down the drain.

"She doesn't want to be with me, so there's nothing I can do to make this right." I send her a look. "Besides, we weren't in a real relationship, so why should I bother?"

"You are seriously the most frustrating man I've ever

met," Candice says, her hands bunching into fists. Like maybe she wants to hit me. "I was with you that night she tried on a thousand hideous dresses. I saw the way you looked at her, and the way she looked at you. How you were with each other. The chemistry was off the charts between you two."

"So? Chemistry means nothing." I scoff. Like a pretentious dick.

"Chemistry is *everything*. And you two had it. In San Francisco, I thought you two were going to attack each other in the back of the SUV on Saturday night. Don't try to tell me nothing happened between you two, either. Sarah told me you hooked up multiple times." Candice settles into the chair across from my desk, blowing out a harsh breath, like she's annoyed.

Great. Sarah told Candice we had sex. Multiple times. This is awkward as hell. "It was just...a weekend affair."

"Then why is she so upset over this? And why are you?"

I have no answer for her. And she knows it too, the brat.

"That's what I thought," she says when I remain quiet. "You *like* Sarah."

"Do not." I sound like a little kid and I press my lips together before I say something else that sounds ridiculous.

"You do too. Oh my gosh, you can *fix* this, Jared. I know you can! She still cares about you."

"I thought you just said she's mad at me."

"No one is that mad and drunk if she doesn't care about you," Candice says. "And she *was* mad. And drunk."

"She was actually drunk?" My curiosity gets the best of me. "Where did you see her anyway?"

"At Tuscany last night. She was with some friends. I even joined them. It was a lot of fun. She has a very supportive group of women who love her. They all want to string you up by the balls, too." Candice frowns. "Well, only one of them said that. Stella, I think? Or Caroline? It doesn't matter. They all kind of hate you."

"Yet you're hanging out with them." I rub my forehead, already exhausted. And my day's only just started.

"They were nice! They don't hold it against me that my brother is an idiot who has no idea what he's doing." She smiles serenely. "But like I said, I can help you fix this."

"Fix what?"

"Holy crap, Jared, are you dense? Fix your relationship with Sarah. She cares about you a lot. She doesn't want to admit it, but I know it's true. And I know just how you can win her back." Candice settles in deeper in her chair. "I'm not leaving until you hear me out."

"Fine." I wave a hand at her. "Tell me how you think I can fix this."

My sister rubs her hands together, and I know I'm in for it.

Time to work on my groveling skills.

THIRTY-NINE

SARAH

IT'S FRIDAY. I arrive at Bliss at precisely eight o'clock, a full two hours before we open. Marlo and I are working on a new window display for our summer collection, and she asked that I come in early. We love getting creative with the window displays, and this is the perfect project for me to focus on so I don't dwell on my problems.

Plus, working on the window display will help time pass, and since I have the weekend off—lucky me—I'm eager for my day to end and it's only just begun.

Don't know why I'm so ready for the weekend, considering I'll end up doing nothing. Maybe Andie and I can go shopping. Or to the movies. Or maybe we could watch movies on Netflix. Binge a series. I know she needs to study and work on projects for her upcoming finals, so maybe she can do schoolwork and I can read.

I don't know. It'll be a lowkey weekend, just like all my other weekends for the last, oh what...three years? With the exception of my one weekend in San Francisco with Jared and his family.

Crazy, right? I barely know him, yet that weekend

almost changed my life. I add the word almost because we're not together, so my life isn't really changed. That weekend with Jared just altered things for a little bit.

Oh, who am I kidding? That weekend totally changed my life. Those few days with Jared, the past six months with Mr. Gaines, has ruined me. Ugh, I hate him.

I miss him.

The moment I walk into the back room, I see Marlo is already there, dressed casually in jeans and a black T-shirt. I'm wearing pretty much the same thing—my T-shirt is black with thin white stripes—and she smiles when she sees me. "You ready to work on the window?"

Neither of us will work the floor today. That'll be up to Bethany, who'll be in at nine-thirty, and another one of the part-time associates who's scheduled later this afternoon.

"You know it," I tell Marlo as I clock in. "We're working on other displays too, right?"

"Yep. I have a feeling we'll get a lot done, which we need. I think this weekend will be a busy one."

"Too bad I'm not working," I tease as I walk over to the stack of boxes that are full of new product. "When did this show up?"

"Last night, right before we closed. Maybe you could help out and open all those boxes for me? I guarantee there will be stuff in there we'll want to use for our displays."

I spend almost an hour opening boxes and sorting everything. Once I finish that, I spend at least a half hour steaming the more wrinkled pieces. There are more bras and panties with tiny stars strewn across them—black this time—and I think of Jared. I never did get to wear that teddy for him.

I should return it. The tags are still on it. The tags are still on the original bra and panty set he sent me too. I could use that cash. Heck, I could put it toward Andie's college fund. Donated by Jared Gaines. Would he be pleased to know he's helping my little sister further her education?

Probably not.

Hours later and we're just about finished with the window display when Marlo gets a call. She's on the phone for almost ten minutes, and I finish up our project, then go outside so I can see it in its full glory.

The window turned out great. There's a dark blue background with tiny white dots that look like stars, and we hung silver glittery stars from the ceiling so they string across the length of the backdrop. We dressed the two mannequins we have on display in some of our more modest nightgowns so we don't shock the tourists who pass by. One mannequin wears a black silk-and-lace negligee with thin straps made of silver stars. The other is clad in a silvery, shimmering nightgown with matching panties dotted with iridescent sparkles.

"How did it turn out?" Marlo asks as she exits the store.

"Really awesome," I tell her. She stops to stand right next to me, the look of delight on her face telling me she's pleased.

"You're right. It's gorgeous." Marlo claps, bringing her clasped hands to just below her chin. "I love it."

"I do too."

"You should help other stores in the plaza with their displays sometime," Marlo says, her voice casual.

I turn to look at her. "Why would I work with the competition?"

"They're not necessarily our competition," she points out. "No one else sells lingerie around here. And everyone admires my windows. The other managers and owners are always telling me how great they are."

"That's all thanks to you."

"No, the windows are all thanks to *you*," she says, nodding in my direction. "The last year or so, we've always gone with your vision."

"Really?" People have actually complimented my window display concepts? That's pretty cool.

Ugh. I thought the word cool. And it is the un-coolest word on the planet. That's what I told Jared, at least. I really hate how he always pops up in my mind. Like, it's the worst.

"Yes, really. Something to consider, don't you think?" Marlo smiles.

"Won't you have a problem with me working for other businesses here in the shopping center?" I ask.

"No, of course not. I don't expect you to be at Bliss for the rest of your life, Sarah. Let's be real. You're a huge asset, but someday you're going to grow your wings and fly right out of here." Marlo squeezes my shoulder. "And that's okay."

I don't know what to say. I'm flattered that other people have noticed my work. Maybe I should talk to other businesses around town. Oooh, maybe Lorenzo, Stella's dad, will let me create a display for them. Though they already have such cute window displays most of the time, they get so much traffic that it would be a great place to start to show off my skills...

"Also, you have an appointment in an hour." Marlo adds this little detail nonchalantly, like it's no big deal.

"Marlo, really? Look at me." I wave a hand at my dusty jeans and the smudge across my shirt. "I look terrible."

"You are adorable." She taps the tip of my nose with her index finger. "Don't you have some extra clothes lying around in the stock room?"

The stock room is this cramped little space where we

keep all the extra inventory. It's more like a glorified closet. I usually do keep a cardigan hanging back there. I'm thinking I left my black blazer there too.

But I'm not in the mood to deal with people. Especially potentially picky new clients who might waste my time for an hour and then not purchase anything. It's happened before.

"Can't Bethany take the client?" I'm whining, but I can't help it.

"She specifically requested you." Marlo hooks her arm through mine and escorts me back to the front doors. "Let's go inside so you can clean yourself up a little bit and get ready. You should take a lunch break."

I don't bother protesting. Arguing with Marlo gets a person nowhere.

Once we're in the store, I lock myself in the employee bathroom and wash my hands, take one of the dry washcloths we keep in the supply cabinet and run it under water so I can wipe at the dust and dirt smudges on my jeans. We keep all sorts of extras in the supply closet, including deodorant and various scented body sprays, so I deodorize and spray on my favorite scent of the bunch, then grab my makeup bag from my purse so I can add a smidge of eyeshadow and slick on fresh mascara.

After I primp, I eat a quick lunch, help Marlo pick out a few things for the display table at the front of the store, and go to the stock room to find I do have a black blazer hanging in there. Slipping it on, I walk out into the store to see Marlo emerging from the dressing room area, where our private showing rooms are.

"Your appointment is here," Marlo says with a pleasant smile. "Waiting in the first room for you."

"Did she want to see anything in particular?" I don't

like going into these appointments without at least a little something to show them.

"She didn't say." Marlo walks past me, heading for the cash desk.

I look around in confusion. "Where's Bethany?"

"At lunch. Don't worry about her. I've got the store covered. Teresa will be in soon too," Marlo says cheerily.

I guess there's no getting out of this. I head for the front table and grab one of the new Celestial black bras off the table, along with a pair of sheer panties. I have no idea if the woman is looking for something like this. For all I know, it's a bride-to-be looking for virginal white lingerie for her wedding night. I handle a lot of future brides as clients. Caroline sends plenty of them our way, since she is a wedding invitation consultant at a stationery store. That's probably why this particular customer requested me. I'll have to ask Caroline about it later.

I head for the dressing rooms, surprised there are no customers in the store. Though it is a beautiful day, the sun is shining, and I bet people are enjoying the weather. I know I'd rather be outside, enjoying the sun, walking by the ocean.

Maybe that's what Andie and I can do this weekend. Take a walk. Or a hike. That could be fun.

Knocking first, I push open the door to find...

"Candice! What are you doing here?" I'm clutching the bra and panties in my hand, knowing full well I don't plan on showing her the set. There's something so...innocent about Candice. I know she's a grown woman, right around my age, but still.

"Um, all I have to say is I hope you'll forgive me." She's wringing her hands, her expression full of worry.

"What are you talking about?" I'm totally confused.

"She's talking about me."

That familiar, deep male voice sends a shiver down my spine.

I whirl around to find Jared standing in the doorway. Wearing one of his sexy suits. His hair is a bit of a mess, he has five o'clock shadow on his jaw and it's nowhere near five, and he's a little bleary-eyed.

He is the best thing I think I've ever seen.

My heart threatens to leap from my chest, but I tell it to chill the hell out. I need to hold on to my anger for just a little bit longer.

"What are you doing here?" I ask Jared.

"I brought him here," Candice answers for him. She starts to exit the room, pausing to give me a quick hug and a kiss on the cheek. "Please listen to him. I'm tired of seeing how miserable you two are without each other."

She makes her way out of the room, Jared turning to his side to let her pass. She pats his chest and murmurs something to him before she leaves.

"What did she say to you?" I ask him once she's gone.

"She told me not to screw this up." He enters the room, pulling the door behind him, and I jump at the sound of the door clicking shut. "She was afraid you wouldn't see me if I put my name down as your client. She called and made the appointment with Marlo."

I might have seen him, but I won't let him know that. "So you two tricked me." Wait, the three of them tricked me, including Marlo.

"I tricked you because I wanted to talk to you, and I didn't see any other way of doing it." He leans his shoulder against the wall, keeping his distance, and I appreciate that. His presence already seems to overwhelm me. If he stands closer to me, I might do something stupid.

Like throw myself at him and beg him to kiss me.

"Jared, we've turned into that couple that could've had a simple conversation to clear up the issues we're having," I tell him. "And I hate that."

He frowns. "What are you talking about?"

"In movies, romance books, TV shows, there's always that couple who has an issue that could've been solved with one conversation." I pause, letting my words sink in. "We are that couple."

"You really think so?"

I nod, swallowing hard. The sandwich I ate only a few minutes ago is tumbling around in my stomach like wet clothes in a dryer. I feel a little sick.

"I don't think what happened between us could be considered—simple. We faked a relationship," he says, his voice low, his eyes skimming over me, eating me up, as if he's so, *so* grateful to see me once again. "That felt real."

That's true.

"And you got mad at me because I didn't tell you about my ex. Evelyn. The girl I loved. The girl who broke my heart."

His words hurt more than I want to admit. All I can do is answer him with a jerky nod.

"I was embarrassed. I didn't want to make a big deal out of Evelyn, because I didn't want you to think I still have feelings for her. So I avoided talking about her. I almost got away with it too," he continues as he pushes away from the wall.

"The truth always comes out, Jared," I remind him.

"No shit," he mutters, and I almost want to laugh.

But I don't.

"I'm sorry I didn't tell you about Evelyn." He takes one step toward me. "I'm sorry I put you on the spot that day, and that Evelyn and Candice had to be the ones to tell you." He takes another step. "It was wrong of me to keep it from you."

I appreciate his apology, but I don't even think that's his biggest offense.

"And I'm sorry I just...let you go that afternoon. I didn't fight for you."

Ah, there it is.

"I should've." He takes yet another step. Then another. Until he's practically standing in front of me. "I care about you, Sarah. I know we've really only spent a weekend together, but it feels like so much more than that. I've been flirting with you for a long time. The only reason I came to Bliss the last six months is because of you. I wanted to see you. Talk to you. Aggravate you." He cracks a smile at that and I can't help it, I do too. "I knew from the moment I first saw you that you were special. That I wanted more from you than a stolen hour every few weeks in a room at a lingerie store." He shifts, and somehow he's even closer to me. I can smell him. Feel his body heat. "I don't want to lose you."

A gasp escapes me when he reaches for my hands and takes them into his. I lift my head and meet his gaze, and the sincerity, the emotion I see flickering in his eyes, leaves me breathless. "I want to fight for you," he says, his voice soft. "I will always fight for you."

"Are you here because your sister forced you to come?" I ask, my voice, my heart trembling.

"She helped me see what I needed to do," he admits, dipping his head for a moment before he lifts it, his gaze returning to mine. "I always give up on myself. She made me realize I don't have to do that every time something good comes into my life and I'm scared I'll lose it."

"Am I the something good?" I ask tentatively.

Nodding, he pulls me into his arms and my face is buried in his chest. "Definitely," he murmurs.

We hold each other, absorbing each other's warmth. Strength. I relax into him, so thankful to be in his arms, his heart racing beneath my ear. He smooths his hands up and down my back, and finally I tilt my head back so I can look at him.

I school my expression, going for Serious Sarah. "I'm still not quite happy with you, Mr. Gaines."

"Really?" He raises a brow, his gaze filled with trepidation. "What do I have to do to earn your forgiveness, Miss Harrison?"

"Kiss me."

The trepidation disappears, replaced by longing, and then his mouth is on mine.

Finally.

FORTY

JARED

THREE MONTHS LATER...

I ENTER my house from the garage, calling out a greeting, but I don't receive one in response.

That's odd.

Sarah texted me earlier to let me know she would be waiting for me when I got home from work. It's summertime, her sister is working at Sweet Dreams Café along with Sarah's friend Stella, and since Sarah doesn't have to worry about her sister, this means we're able to sneak away for a few hours when we can. Sarah had the day off, I left work early, and now here we are.

It's been good, these last few months together. In addition to working at Bliss, she's been designing window displays at various in downtown Carmel. I'm encouraging her to create her own business and she's hesitant, only because her sister is still in high school.

But I see that spark in Sarah's eye. The excitement she

gets when she's got a new project. I know she can do it. The woman can do just about anything.

Including forcing me to be more open. I can't get away with shit, and I swear because of her I've become a better man. Some might say she forgave me too quickly, and maybe they're right, but I'm not going to argue. I need her in my life.

I've fallen in love with her.

After shrugging out of my jacket—the Monterey Peninsula summers aren't that warm—I hang it on the coat rack near the front door and start up the stairs, worry filling me. I don't think she's here yet. Usually she'd make herself known by now. I pull my phone out of my pocket and check the time for when she last texted me.

Thirty minutes ago. She should definitely be at the house by now.

I walk down the hall, heading toward my bedroom, and I swear I can smell her perfume. Though that might be because she stays here a lot. She says my view is worth nothing if I don't enjoy it, and she demands we hang out outside on the deck that overlooks the ocean. She's always staring at the water, but I'm usually staring at her.

I've even had her sister and brother over a few times, and I've hung out with her family at their house. Brent is wary around me—I don't think he full trusts me one hundred percent, and I can appreciate his protective brother vibe—but Andie loves me. And I love her. She reminds me of Candice. They also happen to adore each other too.

Tugging my tie loose, I enter my bedroom and stop when I spot who's lying in the middle of my bed.

Sarah. Wearing that sheer pink teddy with the little pink stars stitched all over the fabric.

And nothing else.

"Hi." She's lying on her side, her legs crossed. "I've been waiting for you."

"I see that." I'd wondered what happened to this particular piece of lingerie. I've never had the chance to see her wear it.

Until today.

She rises so she's sitting up, her nipples hard beneath the fabric, and I can't stop looking. Sighing, she shakes her head. "You are so predictable. Staring at my chest."

"I'm a tit man. You know this." I approach the bed, eager to see her more clearly. "Are you going to greet me like this every day when you move in?"

Her eyes go wide and she scoots off the bed, heading right for me. "You want me to move in?"

"Eventually." I shrug, surprised I would make such a suggestion.

This is what the woman does to me. Has me thinking about making things permanent versus keeping it temporary.

"My sister still needs me," she points out.

"She can move in too."

"And what about Brent?"

"He's twenty-one. He can live in the house on his own." Reaching out, I settle my hands on her slender shoulders, playing with the thin straps that lay there. Her skin is so soft and smooth, and this piece she's wearing doesn't hide a damn thing. I can see *everything*.

Every little bit of her.

"Andie still has school." She's frowning. I have a feeling I freaked her out.

"I'll get her a car so she can drive to school every day. It won't be so bad." Leaning down, I press a kiss to the side of her neck. "We don't have to rush things. I just wanted you to know where my head's at."

I think I've also shocked her. I'm not one to rush things, but with Sarah...she makes me greedy. I want all of her, all the time.

"And I—I appreciate that." She releases a shaky breath when I kiss her throat, my hand pressing gently against her right breast just before I cup it. I could tear the lingerie right off her body, but where's the fun in that?

Besides, that thing cost like four hundred bucks. I'm keeping it intact.

"Don't worry. I'm not moving you all in here tomorrow," I whisper against her ear.

She runs her hands up my chest just as I reach around her and grab hold of her ass, slipping my fingers beneath the sheer fabric. "Why are you so good to me?"

"I could ask the same thing of you." I kiss her, getting lost in her taste, the swirl of her tongue, the whimpering sounds she makes in the back of her throat.

It's only afterward, when the teddy is long gone and my clothes are crumpled on the floor, when we're both sweaty and breathing hard and she's had two orgasms when I've only had one, that I tell her that I love her.

She jerks her head up from where it was lying on my shoulder and stares at me. Hard. "What did you just say?"

"I said I'm in love with you." I reach out and touch her hair, pushing it away from her face. "Is that so hard to believe?"

"No." She shakes her head, her eyes filling with tears. Aw, damn it. "I love you too, Jared."

"Then why are you crying?" My heart breaks when she cries. Thank God she doesn't do it that often.

"I'm just so—so happy." She's sobbing. Seriously, this

isn't good. I didn't think my declaration of love would make her act like this. "I didn't think you'd tell me you loved me for at least another year."

"Another year?" No way could I wait that long. "You're crazy."

Sarah wipes at her face. Sniffs. "So you really love me?"

"So much." I kiss her. "You really love me?"

"I do." She's smiling, the tears still spilling down her cheeks. "Does this mean I'll be your date at Kevin's wedding?"

Laughing, I pull her into me and kiss the top of her head. "If I have any say in it, I want you to be my date for life."

"That sounds like a good idea," she says, her voice muffled against my chest.

"I mean it." I kiss her forehead. Her temple. "No one gets me like you, Miss Harrison."

"You say the sweetest things, Mr. Gaines," she teases.

"Don't get carried away. I'm not that sweet." I smack her butt, making her squeal.

Making her laugh.

Making me happy.

CHECK OUT THE FOLLOWING SNEAK PEEK OF HOLIDATE!

COMING OCTOBER 15TH!

HOLIDATE SNEAK PEEK!

CHAPTER ONE

HOLIDAY!

I push open the door, Madonna blasting from the speakers as I enter the building. It's early November. I'm at Starbucks, and this song always makes me think of Christmas, even though it's not what I would consider a Christmas song.

Celebrate!

Be-bopping to the beat on my way to the counter, I place my order—a grande pumpkin spice latte of course, though a gingerbread latte is my true favorite, it's not available yet—and then head over to the pick-up counter, checking my phone as I wait for my drink.

If I'm being real right now, I have to confess I'm not a big Starbucks drinker. I prefer to support local business versus a giant corporation that's slowly but surely taken over the world, but I'm in Monterey this afternoon and this is where we're meeting.

Who's *we* you ask? My little sub-committee of two—me and another woman who are part of the decorating committee for the annual holiday party hosted by the

Monterey Peninsula Arts Council. Actually, I'm on a variety of fundraising committees, and the holiday season is when everything goes full throttle. Meaning I'm extra busy right now. Like, through most of November and all of December, I don't know whether I'm coming or going.

Don't worry about me, though. I love this sort of thing. Fundraising is my jam, which is a strange jam to have at my age (early twenties), I'm sure you're thinking, but I don't have to work and I need something to fill my time.

My mother—rest in peace mama—took care of my financial security when she died. She ensured my future and left me a lot of money, which left me feeling adrift after high school. I didn't go to college because I didn't know what I wanted to be. I traveled a little bit. Spent a month trying to hit up every country in Europe that I could, but doing it alone...sucked.

I can't believe my father let me go alone. I'm a daddy's girl through and through. I bet you're gagging a little right now, huh. But it's true! I love my father so much, even if he can be kind of a bossy jerk sometimes. He loves me, he's very overprotective, and I think it was my stepmother's influence that had him agreeing to me traveling the world on my own.

Once I returned home and after a few months of doing absolutely nothing, I decided to throw myself into charity work. Why not use the money my mother left me—and only me, not my brothers—and help out those in need? Plus, it keeps me busy.

And I like to be kept busy.

"Hello Candice."

I turn to see one of my fellow committee members—Joyce Rothschild—smiling kindly at me. She's probably old enough to be my grandma, and I know when I first started showing up at the meetings for the arts council, I don't think she believed I was sincere. None of them did. The rich society ladies humored me during their get-togethers and meetings, figuring I'd never appear again.

Well, I showed them. And now I'm their holiday party chair. Nothing makes me happier than planning a party. Make it a Christmas party and I'm in absolute heaven.

Heaven, I tell you.

"Joyce! It's so good to see you." I give her a brief hug right as the barista calls my name. I grab my drink, wishing her a good day before I follow Joyce over to a table where there's one other woman already sitting. I don't recognize her at all. In fact, this meeting was just supposed to be Joyce and me. Having too many people discuss the logistics of holiday decorating always turns into chaos, trust me.

So who is this woman I don't know?

Hmmm.

She's definitely older than me, and doesn't look like the usual high society women I associate with fundraising. Not that I'm a judgey person, but I think you know what I mean. For instance, Joyce is dressed in designer clothing from head to toe, completely put together like she's on her way to work at her corporate job.

I happen to know for a fact that Joyce hasn't worked in thirty years, and she definitely never worked a corporate job.

This unfamiliar woman is wearing jeans and a dark blue and white flannel shirt. It's a really nice flannel shirt, I can tell it's high quality, and she has on expensive boots. But she doesn't have a lick of makeup on her pretty face and her long brown hair is pulled back in a single braid, a few wisps of dark hair framing her oval face. Her full lips naturally curve up, like she's perpetually smiling and I can't help but smile back.

I immediately like her. For some reason, I peg her as a nature type. And I love nature.

Who am I kidding? I love everything.

Except snakes. Oh, and grasshoppers. They freak me out.

"Candice, this is Isabel Sullivan." Joyce nods toward the friendly looking woman. "Isabel, this is Candice Gaines. She's the decorating chairperson for this year's event."

"Nice to meet you." Isabel rises to her feet and extends her hand, that warm smile still on her face. "And please, call me Bel."

"Nice to meet you, Bel." I smile up at her—she's super tall—feeling stumped. Huh. I think I recognize her name, but can't quite place her.

"I know it's last minute, but when Bel offered to help us with the party by providing live trees for the event, I absolutely couldn't say no," Joyce says after we sit down, her voice, her entire body practically trembling with excitement.

A-ha. That's why I recognize her name. The Sullivan Family Christmas Tree Farm has been around since I can remember. They pretty much have a complete lock on all the Christmas tree lots in the Monterey Peninsula. As in, every tree lot you see around here during the holiday season usually has that familiar red and green Sullivan sign in front of it. And if you want to have the experience of cutting a live Christmas tree for your house, you can do that too, with their farm they have in the Carmel Valley, which isn't too terribly far. Most families I know who've done it, usually turned the journey to the tree farm into an afternoon trip.

We didn't do that sort of thing when I was growing up,

especially after my mother died. Fake trees reigned in our house. Real ones were dubbed too messy. I always missed the scent, and no candle can replicate it. I've spent big money over the years trying to make it happen.

"That sounds amazing," I say, excitement bubbling inside of me. I could already envision a row of tall, thick trees flanking either side of the entrance to the building we've rented for the event, every tree lit with tiny white fairy lights. The fragrant scent of pine would greet everyone as they entered, plus the lights? They'll all be enchanted from the moment they walk in. "We could make the entrance look like a forest."

"A fairy forest," Joyce adds. "With twinkling lights everywhere."

"That's exactly what I saw in my mind too!" This is why Joyce and I work so well together. We think alike.

My excitement immediately withers and I grow solemn. Is that a good thing, that I share similar thoughts with a woman who's well into her sixties? I'm not sure.

And right now, I don't have the time to look too deeply into it either.

"Whatever you ladies want, I'm sure we can provide," Isabel says with a soft laugh.

It's like this for the next half hour, the three of us with our heads bent together, plotting and planning last minute decorating details. Joyce writing everything down in her spiral notebook with that elegant handwriting of hers while I'm tapping away in the notes section of my phone. I'd come into this meeting with a clear, planned vision in mind, but the addition of the Sullivan Tree Farm donation changed it up a bit.

Not enough to throw me off, though. I live for this kind of last minute stuff.

By the time I'm finished with my PSL, our meeting is through, and Joyce is packing up her notebook into her large Louis Vuitton tote.

I chance a glance at Isabel, who's slinging her nondescript black purse over her shoulder as she stands. I bet she doesn't care about brand name stuff. I already like that about her, though I have no clue if my assumption is correct.

You see, that's a problem of mine. I assume a lot of things. My brother Kevin tells me it's a bad habit. My oldest brother Jared calls it honing my instincts.

I'm siding with Jared on this one.

Isabel aims those curved lips right at me, and I glance up at her, noting just how tall she really is. She towers over me, but I'm kind of a shrimp, so it feels like *everyone* towers over me.

"I have a dinner date with my husband that I need to go home and get ready for, so I have to go. Goodbye ladies! Thank you for your help!" Joyce says with an enthusiastic wave as she heads for the doors. "I'll be in touch!"

Isabel and I watch Joyce go, turning to look at each other when the door closes behind her. Seems that Starbucks is on an 80s kick, because currently Cyndi Lauper is blasting from the speakers. *Girls Just Wanna Have Fun* is a personal anthem of mine, for sure.

"Thank you again for offering to help us out," I tell Isabel as I push in the chair I was just using. "Your trees will look beautiful at our party."

"It's not a problem. My family is trying to become more involved with community activities anyway, especially with the holidays drawing near."

"Doesn't your farm already provide the trees for just about every lighting event in the area?" There are *five* tree lighting ceremonies I can think of that start happening the day after Thanksgiving into early December. And I'm fairly certain every one of those trees comes from Sullivan's.

"Yes, we do." She smiles. "But we want to do so much more. Have an even bigger, more personal presence in the community during the holiday season." She hesitates for the slightest moment before she continues. "I was wondering Candice, if I could ask you a—personal question."

Tilting my head to the side, I contemplate her. This is a confident, self-assured woman, and right now she appears terribly uneasy. Which makes *me* feel terribly uneasy. "Please. Go ahead," I say, unable to hide the caution in my tone.

Curiosity overrides caution for me every single time.

"Well, this is kind of a strange request but...I know how well connected and beloved you are in the local social circles."

I can feel my cheeks heat at her compliment. "Aw, thank you."

Her smile is friendly. As in, her eyes are smiling too, so I know she's being genuine. Kevin would say I'm assuming again, but really, it's just my natural instincts. I'm really good at reading people.

"And I know how much you love the holidays," Isabel continues. "For the past few years, I've seen endless photos of you at every holiday-themed event in the area, always wearing something festive."

This is one hundred percent true. I have so many sparkly dresses in my closet that gathered all together, they might blind a person. I am a huge and unashamed fan of sequins and glitter. "I do love Christmas."

"I know. I can tell." She laughs. Shakes her head. Bites her bottom lip as if she's reluctant to say the next thing. I wait in anticipation, my curiosity growing stronger the longer she takes to continue.

"I feel silly asking you this," she finally says on a burst of breath. "But my son...he's the oldest of my four children, and he'll be taking over the family business one day. While he knows exactly what he's doing, business-wise, I'm afraid he doesn't have the best, um, social skills."

Weird... "What's his name?"

"Charles Sullivan. But we all call him Charlie."

I mull over the name, racking my mind to see if I can come up with a mental image of a certain Charles "Charlie" Sullivan. But no image appears. I've met a lot of men over the years at various social functions, but I don't think I've ever met—

"Oh, I'm sure you haven't encountered Charlie." Isabel's laughter turns nervous. "You would've remembered him, I'm sure. He always seems to make a lasting impression."

I don't know if this is a good thing or a bad thing.

"How exactly do you want me to help your son?" I ask her, remaining polite. And how old is this guy anyway? Why doesn't he have strong social skills? Is he a complete heathen who never ventures out of the forest?

Hmm, that might be kind of fun. Taking a Neanderthal and converting him into a polished, sophisticated gentleman. Sort of a reverse *My Fair Lady*. I love that movie!

"It's not that I want you to be his date per say, but maybe you could possibly...accompany him to some of the bigger holiday events? We're trying our best to get the Sullivan name out. Our goal for the next five years is to take on more philanthropic endeavors, and my husband wants Charlie to become the face of the Sullivan Family Tree Farm, if you will." A horrified expression suddenly crosses

Isabel's face and she reaches for me, resting her hand on my arm. "But if you're already involved with someone, please disregard my request. Goodness, I didn't even think you might have a boyfriend. Not that you aren't perfectly delightful and lovely, but I've seen so many photos of you and you never seem to be attached to any—"

I cut off her babbling mid-sentence, a little embarrassed for her. I know what it's like, to make a *faux pas* and feel like you're insulting someone when that's the last thing you want to do. "I'm currently unattached," I say breezily.

"Then perhaps you wouldn't mind helping my family— Charlie—out?" The hopeful expression on her face makes me feel bad for even considering telling her no.

But I might need to tell her no. I don't know this Charles Sullivan from a hole in the wall (and where does that phrase come from anyway? My father used to always say it), and if he's as, ahem, *memorable* as she makes him out to be, then he might not be a guy I want to associate with?

Crap, I don't know.

"Can I think on it?" I wince, hating that I'm not giving her a yes, but wow. The more I think about it, the more I'm starting to wonder if she came here to meet with Joyce and I so she could specifically meet *me* and drop her outrageous plan on me. Weird, right?

I should run.

Run far, far away.

But I'm a nice person. My niceness has been ingrained in me since I was a baby. My mother was known as one of the nicest women on the peninsula. I have an image to uphold. People who knew my mother see me and always say I remind them of her. I want to be her when I grow up, and most of the time, I feel like I'm *never* going to grow up, I swear.

The only thing I don't want to emulate is my mother's breast cancer diagnosis.

"Of course you can think on it!" Isabel's hand drops from my arm and she shakes her head, seemingly laughing at herself. "You must believe me crazy with my request."

Yes. Yes, I do. "No, not at all," I say laughingly.

"Whew. I was afraid you might." The relief on Isabel Sullivan's face is clear. "Well, I'll let you think on it. You have my business card." She gave one to both me and Joyce earlier and mine is safely tucked into my bag. "So reach out to me as soon as you've made up your mind. Thank you for not telling me to shove my request up my you-know-what."

I burst out laughing at that, and she joins in. "I would never say that to anyone," I reassure her.

Her smile is mysterious. "You haven't met my Charlie yet."

WANT TO READ MORE? PREORDER HOLIDATE!

COMING OCTOBER 15TH!

ACKNOWLEDGMENTS

Hey you,

Thank you for reading **FAKE DATE**! I pray that none of you think Jared is a complete and utter asshole. The original version, oh my. He was...pretty bad. And guess who loved him? My critique partner, Katy Evans! Katy, you are always so supportive and positive. I'm so glad you're my friend, and I'm always thrilled when you read my stuff and tell me where I go right or wrong. But I have bad news: I had to soften Jared up BIG TIME. It's okay though, he's still a total grouch.

My cover designer Hang Le is just hitting it out of the park with these covers. They are so cute (wait until you see the next one!), and our plan is someday, you can line up all the covers, and it'll look like a city street. How fun is that? Hang, you're the best!

I need to thank Nina for being a wonderful friend and a wonderful publicist. For reading this book and pointing out where Jared acted kind of cheap. I kept those cheap moments in though - whoops.

And finally, to the readers: You guys are amazing. The response to **SAVE THE DATE** has been so positive. Thank you for loving Alex and Sarah and all of her friends. If my plans go right, every single one of them will get their own story. I hope you enjoyed Jared and Sarah's book - these two were so argumentative! I adore them.

ABOUT THE AUTHOR

Monica Murphy is a New York Times, USA Today and international bestselling author. Her books have been translated in almost a dozen languages and has sold over two million copies worldwide. Both a traditionally published and independently published author, she writes young adult and new adult romance, as well as contemporary romance and women's fiction. She's also known as USA Today bestselling author Karen Erickson.

facebook.com/MonicaMurphyAuthor

twitter.com/msmonicamurphy

instagram.com/monicamurphyauthor

bookbub.com/profile/monica-murphy

goodreads.com/monicamurphyauthor

SIGN UP!

Dear Readers,

I hope you've enjoyed reading FAKE DATE! If you haven't already, please sign up for my newsletter so you can stay up to date on my latest book news.

Monica Murphy's Newsletter

https://www.monicamurphyauthor.com/newsletter